MW00620833

SAME DIFFERENCE

SAME DIFFERENCE

E.J. Copperman

SEVERN HOUSE

First world edition published in Great Britain and the USA in 2024
by Severn House, an imprint of Canongate Books Ltd,
14 High Street, Edinburgh EH1 1TE.

severnhouse.com

British Library Cataloguing-in-Publication Data
A CIP catalogue record for this title is available from the British Library.

ISBN-13: 978-1-4483-1203-0 (cased)
ISBN-13: 978-1-4483-1204-7 (e-book)

All Severn House titles are printed on acid-free paper.

Typeset by Palimpsest Book Production Ltd., Falkirk,
Stirlingshire, Scotland.
Printed and bound in Great Britain by TJ Books,
Padstow, Cornwall.

Praise for the Fran & Ken Stein mystery novels

About the author

E.J. Copperman is the nom de plume for Jeff Cohen, writer of intentionally funny murder mysteries. As E.J., he writes the Haunted Guesthouse and Agent to the Paws series, as well as the Jersey Girl Legal mysteries and the brand-new Fran & Ken Stein mysteries; as Jeff, he writes the Double Feature and Aaron Tucker series; and he collaborates with himself on the Samuel Hoenig Asperger's mysteries.

A New Jersey native, E.J. worked as a newspaper reporter, teacher, magazine editor and screenwriter, before his first book was published to critical acclaim in 2002. In his spare time, Jeff is an extremely amateur guitar player, a fan of Major League Baseball, a couch potato and a crossword addict.

www.ejcopperman.com

Special thanks to Luci Zahray as ever.
This book is for anyone who knows who they are
when others want them to be something else.

ONE

'Ms Stein, my daughter is missing. And I'm just now getting used to her being my daughter. I need your help.'

Brian Hennessy sat across the desk from me and looked, if I may belabor the cliché, distraught. In my line of work that's not terribly unusual. But Brian's eyes showed pain that went beyond what I was used to and so far I wasn't really registering the source. It looked, from my point of view, like guilt. And that's never good when dealing with a missing person.

I had an idea of what he meant but I needed for Brian to say it, for his own good more than mine. 'Is your daughter that young?' I asked, despite knowing she was not.

Brian, whose face had dropped down to his hands, which held it up adequately but not visibly, straightened up to look at me. I had my desk chair on one of its lowest settings but he still had to crane his neck. I'm tall. We'll get to that.

'I'm sorry,' he said, although I didn't see anything for which he needed to apologize. 'I haven't been clear. I'm just getting used to it, is all.' That didn't really help, but I gave him time to go on. 'Apparently the child I always thought was my son was actually my daughter Eliza. Of course she would say she's always been Eliza and is now just living her true life. And okay, if she says so, but that's what I'm getting used to.'

Transgender people are not rare, particularly in New York City, where I live and work, but I didn't know many myself. 'So your daughter Eliza is missing. How long ago did she come out to you as trans?'

I could see that Brian was trying to understand his daughter, and not succeeding especially well. He was a former trade magazine editor (retail pharmacies, then home improvement stores and funeral homes before going freelance) in his fifties, a man who had just missed being in the generation that would find a person like Eliza absolutely usual, and he wanted to adjust. But old habits die hard and you could see Brian's living in his tight jaw.

'In January,' he answered. 'January eleventh, to be exact. She said it was something she'd decided to tell me as a new year's resolution, can you believe that?' I could, but said nothing. 'And I could kick myself, but I never saw it coming. You have a son when you're in your thirties and you think about throwing a football around or having the talk about women. You don't expect your son to *be* a woman.'

I looked over at my brother Ken, who was sitting as his desk trying to pretend he was engrossed in some research on his laptop, which was resting on his knees and not on the perfectly functional and expensive desk we'd gotten for him when we opened the office. But I knew that Ken was listening to every word being said and would no doubt have some choice comments to make once Brian had left the office. Ken is not insensitive but he will never – *ever* – pass up a chance for a cheap joke. So maybe he is insensitive after all, but in a different way.

'How did you react?' I asked. I was hoping not to get the answer I expected.

'I . . .' Brian didn't seem to know how to respond. Again, the best course of action was to let the moment play out. And never let it be said I didn't follow the best course of action. Because it's rare that I do, but that's not my fault. Meanwhile Brian gathered himself again, took in a larger-than-usual breath and let it out slowly. 'I told her I didn't know how to accept it, that I thought it was just a phase she was going through and that she should see a psychiatrist. I mean, I didn't throw her out of the house or anything, but that must have been how it sounded to her.'

'How old is Eliza?' I asked. I hadn't given Brian the usual client intake form because it wasn't yet clear whether he'd be a client or if I'd tell him K&F Stein Investigations couldn't help him and send him – and our fee – out the door. So yeah, there was little danger of that happening.

'She's nineteen.' Brian was doing his best not to screw up the pronouns he used to identify his daughter. I gave him credit for the effort he was clearly making. But he had a long way to go.

'She's an adult in the eyes of the law,' I told him. 'If she doesn't want to be found, or if we find her and she's unwilling to come back, I can't compel her to return. You know that.' I could tell because Brian was nodding his head in recognition.

'I know. My late wife was an attorney. I understand the concept. But she vanished. Eliza. And I'm not certain she left voluntarily.'

Ken's head rose from the gaze he was using probably to play a game on his laptop.

'You think she was taken?' I asked.

'It's been four months since she came out to me, and I've been trying to understand her better,' Brian answered. 'I don't see any reason she'd feel the need to leave now. There have been some loud arguments, but we don't hate each other.' Parents often think all their children's actions are about them, the parents. They're so often not at all.

'You want us to find Eliza,' I said, because the words hadn't been spoken yet and this was the time in the transaction when they should be.

'Yes.' Brian looked perfectly earnest. He nodded.

'How long has she been missing?' That was Ken. Unable to resist, he had walked over and sat on the edge of my desk, which are two things I have asked him not to do when I'm talking to a prospective client. I gave him a glance only a sibling would recognize and he, being Ken, ignored it. Brian, however, did not seem surprised that the man had walked over to help out the little lady. For the record, I am *not* a little lady. But some sexist attitudes die hard. (In fact, they all die hard.)

'Five days,' he said. To Ken. 'She was home on Thursday and gone that night. I haven't seen her since then. Her phone doesn't answer. She's not responding to texts or emails. She hasn't posted on Instagram. This flat out isn't like her. And that's why I think she didn't mean to vanish like this.'

Brian kept running his right hand over the fingernails on his left as if deciding whether they needed to be clipped. People show anxiety in ways that are specific to themselves. I tend to pace or push my hair back.

'Have you filed a missing-person report with the police?' Ken has learned enough in the two years we've been running the agency to ask that. I again sent him facial indications that he should, if I'm being polite, shut up.

'Yeah, I told the cops. I filled out the forms and they filed them in their computers. He's a trans woman. They could care less if they put in the effort, but they probably won't even do that.'

That might or might not be the truth, but it's certainly the way families of transgender people often believe, and they can quote statistics that might very well indicate a pattern. Whether or not it varied from precinct to precinct, I did not know. My contact at the local cop shop wasn't currently able to look me in the eye. I promise you, all these things will be explained. The fact that Brian was still sometimes referring to his daughter as 'he' was another issue.

Feeling like I needed to shift the conversation back in my direction and let my brother know I hadn't actually needed assistance, I asked, 'Are there people she'd contact? Friends? Other relatives? Does she have aunts or uncles?'

Brian's hands stopped assessing the length of his nails and fluttered a bit to indicate he found the question a bit irritating, of all things. 'If I knew about people she'd contact, I'd have contacted them myself,' he said, his voice rising in pitch a little. Ken looked over at me with an expression that told me he'd detected something. Ken can sense people's respiration and heart rates when he tries. 'She has friends, but I only know first names. Gerry. Rainbow. Michaela. I'm an only child, so there are no aunts or uncles on my side. Her mother has a sister. Had a sister, but . . .' His speech trailed off and although I didn't know what should have come after 'but,' I decided not to press the issue. The information would be on the client intake form anyway.

'Is she involved with anyone at the moment, or has she been recently?' I asked. I knew Brian wasn't going to want to talk about that, but it was necessary information.

His lips tightened so that his mouth was little more than a slit. 'Not that I know about.'

Ken, having read my face, remained silent, which was intelligent on his part. 'All right,' I told Brian. 'If you want us to proceed from here, I'll give you our intake form and urge you to please be as detailed as you can in your answers. You never know what little piece of information leads to a big breakthrough.

But I'll ask you one last question: How is your relationship with Eliza right now? Have you made your peace with her identity?'

Brian made a point of not making eye contact with me. 'I'm a work in progress,' he said. 'That's what she keeps saying, that we're both works in progress. I'm trying, Ms Stein. Believe me. I'm doing my best not to use what she calls her "dead name." I'm calling her *she* and I'm really starting to think of her that way. I've taken her for hormone treatments and my insurance pays for her transition therapy.' And that's when he looked me right in the eye again. 'But more than anything else, I want to get my daughter back safe.'

'We'll do our best to find her,' I told him, 'but I'll remind you, she's an adult in the eyes of the law. If she wants to stay wherever she is, I can't make her return.'

Brian reached out his hand. 'Where's that form?' he asked.

After he'd filled out the form and I'd all but shooed Ken back to his own desk, from which he could more efficiently watch our receptionist Igavda (his favorite hobby, but he knows better than to do anything but look), Brian left the check for our retainer and left, looking approximately one percent less anguished than when he'd arrived. I sat down at my desk and tried to determine exactly how I'd find Eliza Hennessey (she'd kept the last name but didn't use it much) given the almost complete lack of information I had to work with. But then, I was a professional investigator (it said so on our website and would soon be duplicated on the K&F Stein Investigations app Ken was promising to develop) so I had to have *some* ideas.

But not much was coming.

Our main clientele consists of people who were adopted and want to have some contact with their birth parents. On occasion we'll do the opposite and help a person who gave a child up for adoption to find that person, always as an adult, so they can find out what kind of life the baby might have had.

It wasn't completely out of our wheelhouse to look for a missing person, then. Finding someone who does or doesn't want to be found is roughly the same process, but in this case I'd have to assume Eliza was not interested in being located, or that she was being held against her will. She wasn't answering any attempts to communicate with her, and those are the two possibilities.

Actually, there's a third. She could have lost her phone. But that didn't seem the likeliest.

I skimmed the intake form again. There wasn't much. There was a recent picture of Eliza, which was more than I probably would have expected from Brian (I had anticipated a photograph of Eliza before transition), and the same list of her friends' first names. There were no obvious places she might have headed for if she was trying to break free.

She was a student at New Amsterdam University in Manhattan and that was definitely a place to start. I decided that instead of calling the registrar's office, I'd head over to New Amsterdam personally. The face-to-face thing helps, especially when you're a big enough person to seem intimidating no matter how sweet you're acting.

I got up, grabbed my trusty canvas bag and started toward the door, but Ken reached up with one hand to indicate I should stop. Against my better judgment, I did as his hand requested.

'What?' I said. Brevity is the soul of wit.

He gestured in the direction that Brian had left a few minutes before. 'What did you think of him?' It wasn't unusual for us to consult on a client after the first meeting, but it wasn't a strict rule, either.

'He wasn't lying,' I said. 'He meant everything he said as far as I could tell.'

Ken nodded slowly. 'Yeah. His respiration and body temperature stayed normal and steady. He didn't fidget. He didn't look away except when you asked him a question he was embarrassed about answering. He gave the impression of a man who was absolutely calm and in control.'

He was building toward something and the offices of New Amsterdam University weren't open all night, I guessed. 'Is that a problem?' I asked.

'Not if you're having a conversation about a golf date next week or a business meeting that's entirely routine. That guy was supposed to be all kinds of upset over his daughter transitioning and then vanishing before he could find it in himself to respond properly. But he was absolutely calm and in control.'

I would have suggested that Brian was masking his anguish but Ken would have been able to read that in almost every case.

'So you think he's hiding something?'

'Who isn't?' And he gave me a significant look.

Maybe it's time I told you a little about Ken and me.

TWO

I pondered what Ken had raised as I walked to New Amsterdam. Yeah, it was forty-five blocks but I'm a New Yorker and my stamina is better than most. It's part of being who I am. What I am.

I'll give you the short version.

About thirty-five years ago, two brilliant married scientists named (at least then) Olivia Grey and Brandon Wilder experimented with some techniques to greatly accelerate healing and, in one of those crazy flights of fancy scientists have, also solved their fertility problem by creating two children for themselves. Ken and I were *not* stitched together from the corpses of madmen and criminals, so let's get that out of your head. We were, as far as my non-scientific mind can determine, more grown than fashioned. Maybe we're organic. I've never asked.

I know; it's a lot to absorb. But wait, there's more.

Olivia and Brandon, whom Ken and I consider our parents, were being pursued by . . . someone. A government agency? A foreign government? SMERSH? We have no idea. But they became convinced that their presence was now dangerous to their children and they arranged to leave New York City, where we live, for places extremely unknown. We were just toddlers then, so I have virtually no memory of my mother and father, but I do know about my Aunt Margie, who is not my aunt.

Aunt Margie was a radio news reporter in New York and got wind of some incredibly promising results from two scientists then working in the New Brunswick, New Jersey area (guess who). They became close friends over a few years. Aunt Margie never reported on us at all out of affection for Brad and Livvie (as she called Mom and Dad) and was glad to watch us for a while until the heat blew over.

It's been roughly thirty years, and the heat is still as hot as ever, so Aunt Margie is the only parental figure we've ever actually known.

The one thing I haven't mentioned is that Ken and I have to plug ourselves into a wall socket every few days to maintain our energy. No, I'm not kidding. We have USB ports under our left arms and simple charging cords can keep us at top strength. Until I was thirteen I thought everybody had one of those, so that's how clued in I was.

So you're not running for the door or refusing to speak to me now, are you? Because you're a reasonable person. But Detective Richard Mankiewicz of the New York Police Department isn't as nice a person as you are, clearly. Mank and I had been dating briefly before I foolishly decided I could trust him and unloaded my whole admittedly bizarre story on him during a diner breakfast. Let's say it had not worked out as well as I'd hoped.

I got done with the saga (a considerably more detailed version than the one I've given you) and Mank, whose fork had stopped midway to his mouth around the time I'd said I'd never actually been born, stared at me for an uncomfortably long moment. I had actually come to care for him and was concerned that I'd said too much or burdened him with a much more heavy load than I'd intended – after all, I've been this way all my life so I'm used to it – but Mank simply stood up, turned and walked out of the diner.

Carrying the fork.

Since then I'd only seen him twice because I don't frequent police precincts unless I have to, and both times he'd avoided my eyes and mumbled a hello as he passed me. So far he hadn't ratted me out to the authorities, as far as I knew so that was something.

It was among the things I was trying not to think about.

The topic I *was* trying to think about was Eliza Hennessey and her current whereabouts. I had, let's face it, a grand total of nothing to go on, which was just a little less than the usual. Brian had been willing to talk but hadn't known much of anything. I hadn't asked about his daughter's habits from when she'd been publicly living under her deadname and could kick myself for that now, but it probably wouldn't have been a shining beam of light indicating where Eliza might be at this moment. I *had* asked about her living arrangements; she'd been mostly living at home with her father but sometimes staying with friends for a few days at a stretch. But she'd tell him when she was, not like now. I decided I'd go to the apartment to examine her room if the college thing didn't yield any good results.

Walking uptown was the usual pageant of New York being New York. Everyone was in a hurry and thought they needed to get where they were going faster than you. In my case, they had a point, since I had no specific deadline. The New Amsterdam University offices would be open for a few hours yet. To tell the truth, I didn't expect to find that shining beam of light there, either, but it was all I had.

I decided to blame Rich Mankiewicz for my not having a clear direction in Eliza's case. He was just as good a scapegoat as any, and since I had no intention of forgiving him for ghosting me after I told him I was essentially a superbeing created by science, he was basically asking for it. Besides, he wasn't talking to me and would never know about my decision.

The New Amsterdam University campus is pretty much what you'd expect it to be: a college campus in Manhattan. It could be mistaken for a series of office buildings. Of course, that's only one of the college's campuses, as there are a few spread out around the city. It's not exactly pastoral, but you can walk to Central Park if you head west for a few blocks.

I took the usual way too much time to find the office of the college registrar and waited semi-patiently in line for a few minutes before I was granted an audience with a fifty-ish woman behind a counter. In another timeline she'd have been smoking a cigarette and wearing harlequin glasses, but this was now so she was sucking from a bottle of flavored water and wearing contact lenses that made her eyes look green. I hoped she didn't think she was fooling anyone.

I didn't show her my investigator's license right away because it intimidates some people and annoys others. It rarely gets one the level of unconditional respect one might consider appropriate, if one took the time to think about it. 'I'd like to get some information on a student here,' I said. 'Her name is Eliza Hennessey.'

'You're not her, right?' the woman said.

'No. I'm just trying to track down some information . . .'

There was no point in continuing, which was just as well because the woman cut me off. 'You her mother?'

That was problematic in any number of ways. For one thing, I'm biologically capable of being the mother of a nineteen-year-old but I'm hardly the age most women would be and I sort of resented the implication. Also, I was stuck for an answer. When in doubt, Aunt Margie always says, tell the truth and you won't have to remember whatever nonsense you made up later. 'No,' I answered.

'Good, because I couldn't tell her mother anything, either. Our students have rights to privacy. So, sorry, but I can't tell you anything.' Another swig of blueberry water.

Time to bring out the license, which I did and showed it to her. Briefly. 'She's missing and I'm looking for her because her family is worried,' I said. 'What can you tell me now?'

'Remember how I couldn't tell you anything before? That.'

I leaned in, which helped because I can loom over most people and this situation certainly called for looming. 'This girl's life could be in danger and I need a direction to look in,' I said, my voice taking on probably more urgency than I was feeling at the moment. For all I knew, Eliza hadn't done anything more dangerous than leaving home to seek the life she wanted. 'And right now the only thing standing in my way is you.'

'Lady, this kid is a legal adult. If she doesn't feel like being found it's none of my business and, frankly, none of yours. Her family can be as worried as they want, and I get that, but I can't tell anybody anything about her without her actual written permission. Now I got people in line behind you, so let's move on, OK?'

Now I felt urgency. 'No, let's *not* move on. I'm looking for a nineteen-year-old girl who's either in over her head or has been taken by someone and I need to find her. So forget your regulations and look up Eliza Hennessey now!'

Truly, could an episode of *Succession* boast such impassioned speech? I'd have taken a moment to pat myself on the back but I felt that would have diluted the moment and I needed the moment.

But my adversary clearly was not a fan of appointment television. 'It's the law, lady,' she said. 'Do I have to call security?'

She did not.

It's not easy for someone my height to slink, but I was in the process of slinking away from the office when the fourth person in line, a young woman who I assumed to be an undergrad at New Amsterdam, held up a hand as I passed, palm out as if she were stopping traffic.

She was a very average-looking woman whom I was sure could have found herself a boyfriend among her classmates if that was her desire. But I had no time to think about that or ask her about her love life, something I would never have done anyway, because she started off with: 'Did you say Eliza Hennessey?'

Sometimes the investigation gods smile on you when you least expect them.

I admitted that I did and said that Eliza had been missing for a few days and her family (I didn't want to be specific about Brian because I wasn't really clear on how his relationship with Eliza might have been characterized . . . by Eliza) had hired me to find her. 'Do you know her?' I asked the young woman.

'I know her from a class in nineteenth-century women writers,' she said. 'We're not close friends or anything but we went to get a coffee a couple of times. Is she OK?' She looked concerned but not frantic, which fit her description of the relationship.

'That's what I'm trying to find out. May I ask your name?'

A sly smile tried not to appear on her lips. 'You may ask,' she said. She waited a moment, didn't get the light chuckle she might have been seeking, and added, 'I'm Laura Rapinoe.'

'Nice to meet you, Laura. Do you have a few minutes to talk?'

Again there was a slight sense of amusement. 'Well, I'm in this line and I have nowhere to go, so how can I help?'

It turned out that Laura knew a little – not a lot – more about Eliza Hennessey than she has initially suggested. They'd met the first day of class, some ten weeks previous, and had a mutual interest in Mary Wollstonecraft Shelley, a name that had been mentioned to me fairly frequently by my closest intimates, namely Ken and Aunt Margie. But Eliza and Laura had gone beyond *Frankenstein* to Shelley's lesser-known works.

'We started to really focus in on this book called *The Last Man*, which some people say is the first post-apocalyptic novel,' Laura said. She still had to wait for two more people to be served in line. 'Eliza really got into it because it was about people dealing with all sorts of impossible issues, and she was going through some stuff, you know?'

The woman at the counter called the next person in line so I figured I'd better step up the pace. 'Was her relationship with her father that bad?' I said. 'I got the impression he was at least trying to understand who she really was.'

Laura looked at me closely for a moment. 'Her dad?' she said. 'It wasn't great but I've seen worse. He didn't like her getting hormone therapy because he said it scared him. He didn't know what kind of presents to give her for her birthday. But he wasn't kicking her out of the house or anything.'

'So what was she unhappy about in particular?' I asked. It's a common mistake for a client to make, assuming that they are the center of whatever issue has caused a rift. I felt foolish that I had assumed Brian Hennessey's assumption had been correct.

'I don't know,' Laura said. 'Like I said, we aren't besties or anything. Did you ask Damien?'

Damien! I believe we have stumbled across a clue, Watson! The stupid thing to do would have been to pretend I had more information than I actually possessed, but I'd already made an Investigator 101 mistake and was determined not to add to it. 'I don't know Damien,' I told Laura. 'Who's that?'

She did seem to think I should have at least known *that*, but she wasn't going to hold it against me. 'Damien's this guy from class – a friend, not a boyfriend, I don't think,' she told me. 'When she came out they just sort of glommed on to each other and she always talks about him, like whatever he told her that day. Damien's the source of all knowledge to Eliza.'

The woman at the counter finished with her charge and gestured to Laura. 'Next!'

I only had a second. 'Damien got a last name?' I asked.

She shrugged. Even without Ken there I could feel her heart rate rise; she was lying. 'Go over to the Benson Hall and wait. He's almost seven feet tall and has red hair. You can't miss him.' Then Laura walked over to the counter and was immediately engrossed in her registrar business. I thanked her quietly and walked out.

THREE

I spent the better part of an hour trying not to look suspicious while hanging around a college campus despite clearly not being a student, professor or administrator, and doing nothing except if a very tall red-haired young (I assumed) man named Damien might show up. He didn't, so eventually I decided to head back to my office because I had more than one case to work on. I could see an oversized man there, assuming my brother hadn't found an excuse to take half a day off.

Igavda had three messages for me when I walked in, and I could understand two of them, which was an Igavda personal best. Her knowledge of English was . . . well, better than my Bulgarian, so I had no basis for complaint. One of the legible messages was from a client who called three times a day for updates, so I could wait for the next call to respond.

The other one was from Mank.

That was annoying. The guy knew my cell number, after all. If he wanted to apologize for his reprehensible behavior he could call or text me there. Calling the office was his bid to be captain of the Olympic passive-aggressive team. I wouldn't answer him at the precinct and would wait to text until my rage had boiled down to a simmer.

Ken was, a little surprisingly, on his phone but sitting at his desk, which might lead some to believe he was working on a case. I couldn't say for certain that he wasn't but was waiting for more concrete evidence to present itself in either direction.

He wasn't speaking loudly but I can hear almost as well as he can (which, no offense, is better than you're able to do) so I heard him say, 'We might be able to help,' which moved the needle toward him actually working. I don't want to be unfair – Ken does pull his weight at the agency, but he does so reluctantly. I think he feels like he's not a real investigator yet, despite his holding a legitimate license in the state of New York. I love him dearly, but not to the point that I'd spend a lot of time trying to heal his ego on that count. I *am* the better, and more experienced, investigator in our firm and that's not subject to interpretation.

Sorry. Occasionally I need to vent.

I sat down at my desk and booted up my desktop computer. A lot of people prefer to work with a laptop and I get that but I'm a big girl and I like a big screen. For one thing it makes me look less like a freak when a client walks in.

I worked for a while on the case of the client who called a lot in the hope that I'd have something to say to her when she next contacted us. She was looking for her birth mother in New Jersey, less than an hour from where I was sitting, and now it was simply a matter of a few emails and a rental car trip through the Lincoln Tunnel to confirm what I already knew, which was that the birth mother was not interested in meeting with the daughter she'd put up for adoption. It's not an uncommon outcome in my business, but it's never a pleasant one, and I'd do my best to convince her to change her mind. I'd probably fail.

The best thing to do after I'd gotten most of that out of the way was to search for Damien, who was my one and only lead. It would have been nice if I'd known his last name, but Laura clearly had not wanted to give that up, something I'd have to follow up on. All I had for semi-certain was that he could have been drafted by the NBA and had red hair. Granted, that ruled out much of the population but wasn't going to be a slam dunk (if you'll pardon the expression) in locating him and asking him about Eliza Hennessey.

There wasn't a chance that New Amsterdam University listed their current student body by height, or any other attribute, including name. As my 'friend' at the registrar's office had been sure to point out on more than one occasion, they had a right to privacy. I agreed with that, but would have preferred the college make exceptions for private investigators. You'd be amazed at how many businesses and institutions do not.

Ken put his phone in his pants pocket and walked over to my desk. 'There's something going on with Mom and Dad,' he said.

That was a pretty dramatic declaration in our family. My parents left when we were children and we'd barely heard from them since. For years packages of cash would show up addressed to Aunt Margie, which we assumed were from our parents but bore no return address. Some months before now my mother and I had emailed back and forth a few times but she'd stopped replying to me about six weeks earlier. She'd also advised me not to tell Ken about our correspondence because she guessed – correctly, I believed – that he would both overreact and find it impossible to keep such a secret. I had followed her advice.

'What's going on?' I asked. Sometimes you just have to move the conversation along.

'I got a phone call on my cell from a guy who says he works for the WHO,' Ken said, referring (I guessed) to the World Health Organization and not the classic rock band. 'He works in Amsterdam and says that two scientists who sound a lot like our parents have been working there for a few months.'

Immediately my stomach tightened up. 'How did he know to call you?' I asked. 'Nobody knows we're connected to Olivia and Brad.' Those were the names by which Aunt Margie always referred to Mom and Dad.

'He said he'd gotten it off cell phone records, which sounds fishy to me,' Ken answered. 'They haven't called us. I'm not sure I believe anything this guy said to me. But if any of it's true, and even if it's not, we need to do better in finding our parents because they could be in trouble.'

Everything, and I mean *everything*, we'd heard about our parents had suggested that someone, possibly from the government but maybe not, had been on their trail for decades. My mother, in our brief email reconnection, had told me that the reason they'd left was out of fear for our safety, not theirs. So what Ken was saying, particularly given his new contact's sketchy explanation, was not out of the question at all.

'Did you get his number?'

Ken looked sheepish. 'It came across as "unknown caller," and he hung up on me when I asked for it. Is there some way you can get your boyfriend in the NYPD to do a search on my phone?'

OK, so now you know: I'm a coward. I hadn't told Ken about my breakup, if that's what it was, with Mank. I hadn't told him I was going to out both of us to the cop either, and now I was regretting virtually everything I had done – and some things I hadn't – that day. Denial isn't a comfortable state in which to live. The taxes are high.

'I haven't heard from Mank for a while,' I said. 'I guess we broke up.'

Ken is no fool. (Most of what I tell you about him is exaggeration and sibling ribbing.) He narrowed his eyes and ran his tongue over his lower lip. 'What happened?' His voice wasn't sympathetic; it was (justifiably, but he didn't know it yet) suspicious.

'I guess he just thought I was too weird,' I said. That was the truth, if not the whole truth. So help me God. 'He sort of ghosted me.'

Ken regarded me for a moment. He might not be a deep thinker but he has unerring instincts. 'Do we need to have a talk?' he asked.

'Not yet.'

He nodded about halfway. 'You let me know as soon as we do,' he said. 'But in the meantime, what do we do about the WHO?'

That was a good question. 'I'll talk to a friend who has contacts in the federal government, but I'm not sure she can help,' I said. 'The WHO isn't part of any country, so even her friends might not have an in.'

'Get on the phone,' Ken said. 'I'm going to try to call back just by clicking on the call in my recents, but I guarantee you whoever it is won't answer.' He turned and walked back to his desk.

I knew that Shelly Kroft was a US Marshal and probably had absolutely no connection to the WHO, but I hadn't spoken with her for a while and she always makes me feel better. But I put my call to her on my priority list right below trying to find Eliza Hennessey for that very reason: Shelly probably couldn't help.

When you have no information about someone except their first name and their academic affiliation, the best solution used to be that you could search for them on Facebook. That is no longer the case unless the person involved is over the age of forty. Now the best places to look are Instagram and TikTok.

I tried Instagram first because TikTok, frankly, annoys the hell out of me. If I needed a sixteen-year-old to explain Kierkegaard to me while making up dance moves, that would be my first stop. For something slightly more substantive, Instagram was the best first stop.

The thing is, not everyone who opens an Instagram account, even the ones who are currently in college, list their academic affiliation. So I could spend the next three days scrolling through everyone on the app named Damien or I could find another way to track down this redheaded giraffe.

I started by weeding out the Damiens who clearly weren't the one I was seeking based on their profile pictures. That eliminated a lot of them in a hurry because very few had red hair. Unfortunately, the profile photos were generally very small and with the right kind of lighting you couldn't tell what color hair the man (they were all men as far as I could tell) had, if any. There was also very rarely a way to gauge the subject's height because selfies – and most of them were clearly selfies – tend to focus on the close-up shot.

Then age became a determining factor. I knew Damien was an undergraduate. Of course anyone of any age can enroll in a college so I couldn't say for a fact that 'my' Damien was a young man in his twenties, but you have to start somewhere. So I started somewhere by deleting from my list anyone with any gray hair or crow's feet. That brought the overall list down to about fifty Damiens.

It would have been awfully accommodating if Damien had chosen to photograph himself in a New Amsterdam University sweatshirt, but no such luck among this crowd. I did my best to enlarge the profile pictures, to find any fragment of personal information ('Lizzo fan!') that might place a Damien as *my* (or more accurately, Eliza's) Damien.

In short, I spent two hours not finding Damien. By the end I had three finalists, only one of whom I could definitively state had red hair, and he looked to be in his thirties. If Damien was on Instagram, he wasn't making himself especially accessible.

TikTok, because it tends to give me a headache, would have to wait at least until tomorrow.

It's not terribly unusual to begin a search for someone with very little to go on. But what I had now would barely qualify as 'very little.' I needed to clear my head.

I sent an email to the last address I had for my mother, making certain that Ken wasn't looking over my shoulder, that just read: '*Is this address still good?*' It probably wouldn't be answered and might have been pointless, but after all, sometimes a girl needs her mother, even if that person participated more in growing material that made up the girl. It's a complex process that I have never understood. But Mom and Dad pulled it off and now every agency and the odd maniac (almost all maniacs are odd) were looking for them.

I had to remind myself they were searching for Ken and me as well. We needed to stay vigilant about our security.

The phone on my desk rang, which virtually never happens. I do the bulk of my business and most of my personal calls on my cell, and any office calls that come through because of the website or business cards go through Igavda, which is not as good a system as you might think. Igavda tends to talk like the Transylvanian woman in werewolf movies, so it's a crapshoot as to whether you get the call that's meant for you or not.

Because it's so rare an event, the ringing desk phone startled me and I stared at it for a moment. Then I saw that the Caller ID was showing the number for the nearest police precinct and realized who the caller must be. And I supposed this was as good a time as any to hear what I could only assume would be a touching apology.

I picked up the receiver but refused to sound the least bit welcoming or familiar. 'K&F Stein Investigations,' I said.

'Hello, Fran,' Mank said. I was torn between my irritation with him for being, you know, a jerk when I had bared my soul to him, and relief that the call wasn't coming from Emil Bendix, the other detective who knew me fairly well at the cop shop. Bendix, while never having dated me and then ghosted me at the very first sign of my not being a standard human, made up for that by being misogynistic, crude and insulting, so even under the current circumstances it was better to have heard from Mank.

'Detective Mankiewicz,' I replied. I saw no point in letting him off easy.

There was something of a pause. 'OK,' he said. 'I called your office before and was hoping you'd get back to me.'

'Yeah. Did you lose my cell number?' Ken was off his phone

and staring at something on his screen, or just using it to get a better reflection of Igavda. I wasn't in a very man-friendly mood at the moment.

'Actually, my old phone got thrown into the East River and I've had trouble putting my contacts back together,' Mankiewicz said. 'It was on a case.'

It was probably the next genetically perfect superbeing he'd dumped, I thought. 'Of course.'

'Seriously, Fran. I was chasing this guy and he pushed me into the river. My phone was in the pocket.'

And his contacts were in the cloud, but why continue the argument about his phone? 'What can I do for you, Detective? And more to the point, why should I do it?'

'I've been talking to some people in the registrar's office at New Amsterdam University,' he said. 'I'm told you're looking for a student named Damien.'

I've been through some stuff so it takes a lot to completely stun me. But the idea that Mank was calling me about Damien when the two of them couldn't possibly have anything to do with each other left me without a response. I didn't stare at the telephone receiver because I wasn't in a movie, but I started to understand why actors thought that might be a believable response.

'Damien,' I managed to squeak through.

'Yeah. I'm looking for him myself and would like to know what you have.'

FOUR

'**D**amien Van Dorn.'

The interior of the 13th Precinct was just as municipal and depressing as I remembered it. Of course, I'd been here only weeks before, but that was in a different time, when I was thinking of Rich Mankiewicz as a sweet guy who might actually have boyfriend potential. Now I was standing at his desk (he'd offered a chair and I'd refused because when I'm standing and he's sitting I'm easily a foot and a half taller than Mank) after he'd insisted we needed to talk in person. About Damien, who, as it turned out, had a last name.

'A redhead named Van Dorn?' I said. I was being professional. I was being so professional it was practically unprofessional. There would be no extracurricular conversation during this consultation, and you can quote me.

'Why not?' Mank said. It was, in retrospect, a good question. Anybody can have red hair. 'What's interesting, last name or not, is that he is six-foot-nine and skinny.'

I didn't find Damien's statistics *that* interesting, but Mank is five-foot-eight and, in my view, has a height fixation.

But hey. I was being professional.

'Does that help us find him?' I asked. This was, at least technically, a strategy session, although as a New York City police detective, I'm sure Mankiewicz thought he was interviewing a witness who might be able to give him information that he, all by himself, could use to solve the . . . wait. Why was this a case for the cops?

'No, but it'll help him stand out in a crowd.' I used to think this guy was amusing.

'Why are you looking for Damien?' You might as well be direct when you don't care if the guy is going to kiss you ever again. Although he *was* a good kisser.

'He's been reported as a missing person by his parents,' Mank said. 'And when we checked with the registrar's office at New

Amsterdam University, they said a very tall woman with a private investigator's license had been in looking for someone else. The clerk working the window said she heard another student suggest to the very tall woman that she look for Damien.'

I felt my lips straighten out into a horizontal line. 'So you think I'm the only tall female investigator in Manhattan?' I said. Professionally.

He did his sardonic face. Even when I liked him, it wasn't one of my favorites. 'You were looking for Damien, weren't you?'

'Well yeah, but . . .'

Mank stood up and looked at me in the neck. It was the best he could do. 'Come on, Fran. I'm looking for this guy and so are you. Did his parents hire you to find him before they filed a report?'

I folded my arms across my chest and, to his credit, Mank didn't look down to see why. He was craning his neck to make eye contact. 'No,' I said. 'Damien's parents didn't hire me, or I probably would have known his last name, don't you think?'

Mankiewicz literally took a step back. For him it was like trying to take in a whole skyscraper in one glance. 'Can we try to be a little more . . . civil to each other?' he said quietly. 'I'd like to have a talk with you about . . . you know. But not here and not now.'

'That ship has sailed,' I told him. 'You had your chance to talk about *you know* with me and you passed. So the subject is closed. Let's keep it businesslike, OK?'

He took a second and nodded with an air of conviction. 'OK. So tell me who hired you to find Damien if it wasn't his parents.'

My feet were starting to hurt so I took the chair. I could be just as intimidating sitting down, I figured. 'Nobody hired me to find Damien Van Dorn,' I said. 'I thought he might be a source of information in a case I'm working, but I haven't found him yet. If you have any ideas, I'd love to hear them.'

Sergeant Emil Bendix, perhaps the last of a dying breed of awful 1990s New York detectives, ambled over and stood between me and Mank, who had resumed his seat behind his desk. Bendix sat on the side of the desk, which was not something anyone in the room, least of all Mank or I, wanted to see.

'So, Gargantua.' Bendix looked at me with what he thought was avuncular humor but was really sexist, misogynistic crap. 'Haven't seen you around for a while. You and your boyfriend here have a fight?' Bendix had the unerring ability to find the thing he shouldn't talk about and dive right in.

'We're talking about work, Meal,' Mankiewicz said. The cops in the precinct call Bendix 'Meal' because he's never skipped one, but he thinks they're being fraternal. 'You wouldn't understand that. How about you go over to your station and do whatever it is you do?'

Bendix scowled a bit, but he has resting scowl face so it was hard to tell if he'd actually heard what Mankiewicz had said. 'I'm working a case,' he said defensively. 'This guy – you'll love this, Gargantua – shot another guy right in the—'

'I'm sure it's hilarious, Sergeant,' I said. 'But my name is Fran and I'm an investigator who's here to talk about a case with the detective here. So could you give us a little space so I can get out of here as soon as possible?'

Bendix stopped leaning on the desk and shook his head. 'You two aren't any fun anymore,' he said as he walked away.

'We never were,' I called after him.

Mank winced a little. 'What case?' he asked.

'What case, what?'

'What case are you working on that you want Damien Van Dorn to help you with?'

Oh yeah, Damien. And Eliza. That was the mission, wasn't it? I wanted to withhold the information from Mankiewicz but realized that was strictly out of spite. If the NYPD could help me find Eliza, I wouldn't turn down the assistance.

So I told him about Eliza, how she was missing and how she seemed in some way to be connected to Damien Van Dorn. But how I'd just barely gotten started on the case and didn't have a strong lead to follow on either of the missing young people. Mank – and I'll say a lot of things about him but he was not coldhearted or inconsiderate (except after you told him you were a science experiment) – listened with no judgment on his face.

'Can you put me in touch with Eliza's father?' he asked.

Some people think that investigators and clients have a non-disclosure arrangement like that between a lawyer and a client.

We don't. But I don't like to give away client information without permission. 'I'll ask him if it's all right,' I said. 'But he told me he filed a report with the police and that you guys weren't doing anything about it because Eliza is a trans woman.'

Mank bristled. It's something to see, if no one has ever bristled in your presence. 'You know that's not the case,' he said.

'I would know that wasn't the case if you were the detective assigned to Eliza,' I said. 'There are plenty of cops who probably wouldn't look as hard for Eliza as another missing woman.' I gave Bendix a quick glance and I thought Mank noticed where I was looking. 'They probably still have uniformed officers on it, not detectives, and I'm not sure the NYPD is as progressive an organization as you'd like to believe.'

I was hoping Mank would bristle again, but he let a little sigh out and reached over for his computer keyboard. 'Let me see what the status of the investigation is,' he said.

He clacked away for a minute or so and then studied what he saw on his screen, which naturally he did not turn in my direction. Cops. 'Well, it's not this precinct so I don't know the officers on the case,' he said. 'But you're right, there's no detective yet. I'll give a call over there and see what I can find out.'

So I sat and watched him but oddly Mank did not reach for his phone, either the one in his pocket or the one sitting on his desk, which the NYPD naively believes is the phone their detectives still use for work. Silly NYPD. Mank just looked over at me.

'Thanks for coming in, Fran,' he said.

Huh? 'What do you mean, "thanks for coming in?"' I thought you were going to call over and talk to the cops who're looking for Eliza.'

'I am. As soon as you leave.' Not a smidgen of smug on his face, either. He looked, if I'm honest, surprised that I was questioning his decision, which of course I was.

'How's that going to help me?' I asked.

'Fran, I'm a cop. You're a private investigator. You know that helping you is not in my job description.' Still an innocent face. I wondered if he practiced it in the mirror every morning.

It's not like I hadn't had this argument with cops before. But I'd rarely had it with Mank, who in addition to being a cop was also a person. Until recently. And he thought *I* wasn't a human being!

There was no point. I stood up and prepared to leave as abruptly as he had left the diner where I'd bared my soul and a good number of family secrets to him. But just as I was pivoting on my heel, I heard him say in a soft voice, 'Remember, whenever you want to talk . . .'

There are times I despair of the entire male sex.

FIVE

'You know he was just being a cop,' Aunt Margie said.
Like many women do with their moms, I tend to seek out Aunt Margie when someone makes me feel angry and frustrated. I'd gone straight to her apartment, which is one floor down from mine and Ken's, when I'd walked into the building. The last thing I needed was to try and complain about men to my brother.

'He was being a cop who treats me differently than he did just a few weeks ago,' I said. 'That's the part that hurts.'

I had, in fact, told Aunt Margie about the conversation I'd had with Mank and his completely unsatisfactory reaction to what I'd told him. I had assiduously avoided telling Ken because he'd be mad at me for breaching security and, I was afraid, would side with Mank.

(He really wouldn't have. The one thing about Ken and me is that we're the only ones who are like us. He'd know what it was like to feel insecure about being the way we are. At least I think he would. Most of the time he seems to enjoy it immensely, especially when women he wants to impress are around. All they see is a big strong guy.)

'I know,' Aunt Margie said. She sat down on the sofa next to me and put an arm around my shoulder. The cookies I knew would be offered were already on the coffee table. Aunt Margie is predictable in the best possible way. 'But now he says he wants to talk. You have to understand that he needed some time after everything you told him.'

I turned so her hand fell off my shoulder and stopped with a cookie midway to my mouth. 'You're taking *his* side?' I wailed.

She shook her head. 'Oh never, Frannie. You know I'm always on your side. I'm just saying he might not be as big a villain as you're thinking right now. I've known a few men. They need more time to absorb things than we do.'

I was thinking of making Mank absorb a right cross to the

solar plexus but I didn't argue the point. 'The worst part is that I went all the way over there and got nothing to help in my case.'

Aunt Margie nodded decisively and put her hands flat on the coffee table. 'OK,' she said. 'Let's think about that.'

When our parents left us as children (because they were trying to protect us from a threat they couldn't yet identify), they didn't abandon us; they gave us Aunt Margie. Our mother had discovered a way to greatly accelerate the healing process, leading to all sorts of medical possibilities, one of which helped to create Ken and me. But Aunt Margie had become friends with 'Livvie and Brad,' and once we were around, she was not inclined to break the story and endanger the lot of us.

Instead, she became our guardian and for all intents and purposes the parent who raised us.

But the reporter's instinct never dies, and there's nothing Aunt Margie likes better than a good question to answer. She still does some fill-in work at the radio station but that's mostly just reading news copy someone else has written or taken off a wire service. She wants the thrill of the hunt and the chance for a big byline. Even if she hasn't actually reported a crime story in more than twenty years. When she was raising us it was best to keep a low profile, and that was still the case to some extent now.

'What do you know?' she asked me, her face nothing but focus.

'Right next to nothing,' I said, because feeling inadequate and sorry for myself was becoming my new hobby. 'Eliza Hennessey left home about six days ago with no indication as to where she was going and hasn't been seen since. Damien Van Dorn, a guy Eliza knew in some capacity, has been missing about two days. Eliza is a trans woman, but there's no indication that Damien is trans. In any event, they're not answering their phones or emails and that's unusual. In both cases, parents are frantic. The cops are investigating, but don't exactly seem to be putting this on the top of the NYPD's to-do list.'

'You said there might have been some friction between Eliza and her father?' Aunt Margie asked. She was gathering information, not testing me.

I made a 'maybe/maybe not' gesture with my right hand. 'Eliza's kind-of friend Laura Rapinoe says Eliza said it wasn't a big deal. Brian Hennessey seemed to me to be carrying around enough guilt that it could have been more than Laura knew. I'm sure he didn't react well to his daughter coming out as trans. He's still having trouble referring to her as his daughter.'

Aunt Margie nodded. 'So she might have been trying to get to a safer place. Not that Brian was necessarily posing a threat, but a place where she'd be more completely understood for who she is, right?'

I shrugged because I honestly didn't know what I thought. 'It's possible. It's also possible she was taken. There's a lot of violence against trans people and New York isn't always as understanding of LGBTQ people as we like to pretend.'

She picked up a cookie and took the smallest bite possible. I realize I'm larger than most people, but Aunt Margie can make one cookie a meal and sometimes have some left over for later. It's sort of awe-inspiring. 'That's true,' she said. 'But you have a few places to start. If I was researching the story, I'd talk to Damien's parents.'

'Mank already did that,' I pointed out.

'Yeah, and he's got nothing. You know, sometimes an understanding woman can find out more than a New York City cop.'

I sat back and closed my eyes. 'Tomorrow,' I said. 'I'll call them tomorrow.'

'Do you need to plug in?' When my energy gets low, Aunt Margie gets nervous and wants me to recharge through my wall socket booster.

'I don't think so, but maybe later. It's only been a couple of days.' Having my eyes closed did feel good, though.

'Then call Damien's parents now,' she said. 'You can make an appointment to talk to them tomorrow.'

Opening those eyelids was not an attractive proposition. 'I don't have their number.'

'There's this new thing called the internet. I'm willing to bet you can find them there. Or call your friend Mankiewicz and ask him.'

'He's *not* my friend,' I said. 'And he's a cop. He won't tell me.'

'I guess you'll just have to be a detective,' Aunt Margie said. She got up and went into the kitchen to put the cookies away.

It was subtle, but effective. I went upstairs to my apartment and got on the laptop. Sure enough, it took about ten minutes to find the mobile number for Helena Van Dorn, mother of Damien. If I was going to be an understanding woman, it would probably be an advantage to talk to the mom.

She took five rings to answer, which I understood. If my son was missing and the Caller ID on my phone read STEIN INVESTIGATIONS, I'd be perplexed. It wasn't the cops, who might have news, and she hadn't hired anyone to look for her son (or, if she had, it definitely had not been me and my brother). But I was guessing curiosity would prevail, and it did.

'Hello?' The voice sounded cautious and tense.

'Is this Mrs Van Dorn?' Even to me it sounded suspicious. I would have probably hung up on me.

'Who's calling?' Good answer. Never say 'Yes,' because that can be recorded and used in any number of unpleasant ways.

'My name is Fran Stein. I'm a private investigator and I'm looking for Eliza Hennessey, who I'm told might be a friend of your son's.'

'My son is missing,' Helena said.

'I know. I'm sorry to bother you right now, but maybe I can help find both of them. May I ask a few questions?'

There was a pause on the other end of the line and when she came back, Helena's voice sounded vaguely confused. 'Are you a police officer?' she asked.

You actually get that question a lot, particularly when you're speaking to people who might be upset about something going on in their lives, which people like me (not that there are any, other than Ken) do a lot. They skip past the 'private' part in the explanation and jump to 'investigator.'

'No, ma'am,' I said. 'I'm a private investigator hired to look for Eliza Hennessey. Do you know her?'

'No, not really. Damien's mentioned her once or twice but I've never met her. I don't think they're dating or anything.'

'They knew each other from New Amsterdam?' I asked. There didn't seem to be any other way Eliza and Damien could have met.

'I think so,' his mother told me. 'I don't remember hearing about her before he started school, and then only a couple of

times since. Do you have some idea where he might be?' She
was trying not to cry; I understood. I wished I could tell her
something that would help.

'I'm trying very hard, but I don't have anything for you right
now,' I said. That was pretty accurate and didn't sound especially
pessimistic. 'Anything you can tell me would be helpful. Was
there somewhere that Damien and Eliza used to go? Maybe after
class or something?' I knew they hadn't gone back to Damien's
parents' place because Helena had never met her. 'Does Damien
have an apartment of his own?'

'Of course.' How foolish of me it had been to think that an
undergraduate student might not have enough money to afford
rents in New York City. 'But we've been there and he's not in
his apartment.' Helena had returned a bit of patronization into
her voice to indicate that I might have thought they hadn't checked
at their son's place.

'Can you give me the address?' I asked.

'Why?'

Why? 'So that I might go over there and see if there's anything
that might point me in a direction toward finding them,' I said.
I mean, what other motivation could I have had?

'I'm not letting you go over there by yourself,' she said with
newfound steel in her voice. 'Not one item in his apartment is
going to be missing when you leave.'

Now, I could have been offended and let her know. I could
have explained exactly who I was and why nothing of the sort
would ever happen on my watch. But I saw a way to get into
Damien Van Dorn's apartment without having to sweet talk the
super, so I did neither of those things.

'Fine,' I said. 'When would you like to meet me there?'

SIX

Not long ago at all, Alphabet City (Avenues named for letters instead of numbers, a radical concept) Manhattan had been a scary, seedy place. Drug deals took place in broad daylight. The suburban visitors from New Jersey didn't habituate the area. It was, frankly, a little like the New York in movies from the 1970s. It still is in spots, but not very much. The same developers who have managed to gentrify Harlem, parts of East Harlem and a huge amount of Brooklyn have made their way to Alphabet City and it is, depending on one's point of view, either admirably or regrettably losing some of its original flavor.

There were still some public projects for people with low incomes, but there were also wine bars and brunch places with avocado toast. Designer cookie shops and the Apple Store wouldn't be far behind.

I walked up to a clearly renovated building with a new front door boasting video cameras and a security desk just inside the lobby from which a uniformed employee could check on everyone who wanted to enter. Helena Van Dorn didn't have that kind of problem, so as soon as I arrived she waved a key card at the sensor and in we walked.

She had barely spoken to me when I identified myself, looking me up and down as if to decide whether she thought I should be torn down and replaced with luxury condominiums. I get that sort of look a lot, to be honest.

Once we were walking up the stairs (it wasn't *that* renovated) to the third floor, Helena found her voice and it had an edge to it. 'I'm only doing this because I'm desperate,' she said.

Always encouraging words, the kind I was more accustomed to hearing in a dating situation. 'I appreciate it,' I said. I don't think I meant that the way Helena heard it, but that was fine with me.

'After all we've done for that boy, to have him up and leave without a word, well . . . it's *infuriating*.' Helena, who had at least twenty-five years on me, was also two steps ahead of me on the stairs. She was working up a head of steam. 'So ungrateful and insensitive, don't you think?'

Luckily there was no need for me to answer because we reached the third floor. I opened the door for Helena and she led me to Damien's apartment entrance. Helena rooted around in her expensive purse to find a single key on a ring by itself, one which she probably did not use often if at all, and inserted it into the lock.

'Shouldn't we knock first?' I asked. If Damien had roommates or if he'd come home under his own steam, a little advance warning wouldn't be an awful thing.

She blew some air out between her lips. 'Of course not,' she said. 'He isn't here.' I guessed Damien didn't have roommates and, after the speech about 'all we'd done' for him, I guessed he wasn't paying the rent on this place, either. Helena turned the key and opened the door.

There wasn't much to the apartment, no matter what the lobby had promised. There was a small living room as we entered, a galley kitchen to the right and a corridor at the end of which appeared to be a bedroom and a bath. I bet the 'bath' was just a shower.

The furnishings, such as they were, looked consistent with the idea of a young man's first apartment, minus the roommates, who in Manhattan should have been *de rigueur*. Helena and the dad, if there was one, clearly had some bucks. There was the mandatory acoustic guitar on a stand in one corner of the living room with an accumulation of dust that indicated it didn't get played often. There was a small pile of laundry, with which Helena was diligently refusing eye contact, in the hallway. There were no cooking utensils out anywhere but there were takeout boxes sticking out of the lone refuse container in the kitchen.

A college student's apartment. You'd think a dorm room would have made more sense.

'I told you he wasn't here,' Helena said. I was starting to understand why Damien might have wanted to vanish.

'I didn't think he was here,' I told her, largely because I'd done the not-answering-at-all thing and it hadn't made me feel any better. 'I'm looking for anything that might indicate where he could have gone.'

In Bendix's day (which I believe was April 27, 1988), there might have been a note scrawled in pencil with an appointment listed on it, or better yet, a full address book or Rolodex of contacts to ask about Damien. But in real world 2024, all that information would be on Damien's phone, and there was no way Damien would have walked through the apartment door without it.

Being a young man in his early twenties, Damien also had not accumulated many photographs of himself with people Helena might have been able to identify and framed them to make them easier to spot. Again, all on the phone. I was a product of the generation just before his and I was just as addicted to my screen as the next girl, but I had to admit technology wasn't making my job any easier.

'Does Damien have a girlfriend you know about?' I asked. I was fairly certain Eliza wasn't included in that category, but in any event Helena had already ruled that possibility out. 'Do you have information about any friends? Places to contact? People he'd go to?'

'No,' she said. I was getting the distinct impression that Helena didn't want to help me despite my work increasing her chances of finding her son. Maybe she didn't *want* to find her son. Maybe she just didn't like tall women, despite (or because of) her son being almost seven feet tall. In either case, there wasn't much I could do about it. 'Of course not. I don't have phone numbers for everyone my son has ever met.' I was leaning heavily now on the theory that Helena had been fed up with Damien and didn't care if he ever came back. 'Especially not the *transgender* woman.' Aha. So Helena knew about Eliza.

'OK, then,' I said. 'So what can you tell me about your son and Eliza?'

She stopped in her assessment (negative) of her son's home, which had included no picking things up off the floor but a lot of nostril flaring, although I had noticed no especially noxious odor in the room. 'There's nothing to tell.'

I had touched a nerve. Sometimes, as dentists will tell you, that's when you get the real truth out of someone. 'Eliza is missing,' I said. 'Any connection she has with friends, family, even acquaintances can be meaningful. Obviously Damien mentioned her to you. What did he say?'

'I don't see how that has anything to do with this,' she said, advancing on me as if I didn't have seven inches of height and approximately twice her upper body strength on my side. I braced with my right foot but Helena stopped five feet away. 'I already told you they weren't dating!'

'I wasn't suggesting they were,' I answered, not yet relaxing my back leg.

'Well, I don't need to stand here and be insulted!' Helena turned on her heel – no, really – and headed for the apartment door. It closed behind her, loudly.

'I don't know if anybody does,' I said aloud.

Having accomplished my first task, which was getting Damien's mother to leave so I could look around on my own, I turned my attention to the second, which was that looking around I just mentioned. Maybe Damien had indeed left something behind that could point me in a direction.

I didn't find much in the living room. Living area, if I'm being accurate. This was an expensive apartment, but it was still a New York apartment and that meant space was at a premium. There was enough room here for two chairs that clearly used to be from someone's dining room, a small coffee table and a wall-mounted flat-screen TV big enough to provide close-up views of all the sports a young man could want. Or was I stereotyping?

Even now I can't imagine what it was I expected to find, but on my first tour of the living area I certainly didn't find it. The kitchen, tiny and clearly underused, was no help either. That left the hallway, the bathroom and the bedroom.

I glanced fleetingly at the bathroom as I passed it. It was surprisingly clean but of no clear interest.

Damien's bedroom was standard-issue college student chic. No posters on the walls, though. No *anything* on the walls. Damien had a few framed articles from a local newspaper or a website he'd printed out, featuring himself in association with some cross-country running event. With legs as long as Damien's, it wasn't a huge surprise that he could run long distances faster than most.

But it appeared that the only person he felt worth immortalizing for a place in his apartment was himself. I certainly hadn't expected to find any pictures of Eliza, but someone other than Damien would have been refreshing in my view. Damien had, clearly, no such inclination.

The bed was rumpled, hardly a huge surprise. Damien hadn't expected people – not even or perhaps especially not his mother – to be rooting around in his belongings when he'd left the place two or three days ago. I couldn't point to a particular piece of evidence, but I had the feeling he hadn't known he'd be gone this long. There was plenty of clothing in the closet and some in a chest of drawers in his bedroom. There was a hamper full of laundry ready for the washer, which was probably on the street below us or in a basement laundry room here in the building.

And then, as I returned to the living area, I came across that pile of clothing that had accumulated between rooms. Maybe there would be something in those.

Believe me, it wasn't my first choice to look through every item of clothing Damien had left, presumably to be washed or at least folded, on the dusty floor of his expensive hallway. But like they tell you in detective school (there is no detective school), you have to follow every possible lead. And in this case, I truly had no other choice.

There were, as you might imagine, some pairs of jeans, crumpled and looking sad. In the pockets (don't judge me; I'm a detective) were, in total, three face masks, one courtesy card for Dunkin' Donuts, a packet of facial tissues, a pair of dice that were clearly for a game other than craps (I would guess Dungeons & Dragons, but that would seem to be contrary to Damien's brand) and thirty-eight cents in change. No wallet, no mobile phone, no apartment key.

But there also were four small plastic packets with zipper seals, filled carefully with equal numbers of pills. I doubted they were to treat Damien's hay fever. If he had hay fever.

SEVEN

'What do you think they are?' I asked Ken.

'The pills?' Sometimes my brother doesn't pay the closest of attention to what I say. In this case, he was painstakingly dissecting an onion because he'd decided to cook dinner tonight. I wasn't sure what he was preparing, but apparently it required a very carefully sliced onion.

'No, the aliens who landed in Times Square. Yes, the pills. Should we assume that they're not exactly legal drugs, and that Damien was, let's say, supplying them for a small cadre of close friends?'

'For a nominal handling fee, no doubt,' Ken said. Green pepper had shown up on the cutting board next to the onion. I didn't know what we were eating but it was certainly going to be precise. Ken can be a very good cook when he wants to be, which is approximately once every six weeks.

'No doubt. What do you think?' I asked. I was sitting in a chair at the kitchen table watching him cook. Things always go better with food preparation when I have as little to do with it as possible.

Ken looked thoughtful, which I could see because he had turned to face in my direction. 'I think I need the lamb chops we bought.' He was looking past me at the refrigerator.

'They're frozen,' I reminded him.

My brother walked to the fridge and opened the freezer door, pulling out the plastic-wrapped package of what once had been a baby sheep. I chose not to think about that part. 'That's why the good lord invented the microwave oven,' he said, heading for that very appliance.

'The pills, Ken.' Our parents had seen to it that our names were Fran and Ken, not Frances and Kenneth. That was, by all accounts, my father's sense of humor at work. 'What do you think the pills are?'

'If we're going to be trendy, they're probably fentanyl,' he answered. 'That's the big drug on the street these days. But for all you know this Damien was everybody's favorite supplier of Tylenol. We need to get the pills analyzed.'

That meant involving the cops, and *that* meant involving Rich Mankiewicz. I moaned just a bit. 'I suppose so,' I said.

'What's the problem?' The microwave beeped and Ken removed the package of meat – which he had *not* opened before defrosting it – and put it on the counter. 'You never had trouble talking to the cops before. You kind of like it, don't you?'

'No. It's fine. I can do it tomorrow.' After all, Mank was the one who called me about Damien in the first place, and if Damien was dealing drugs that might explain a lot about what had happened to him and possibly to Eliza. Not that those possibilities were exactly pleasant.

Ken (finally) removed the lamb chops from the package and got a frying pan heating on the stove. He poured out just enough olive oil to make the pan slick but not to overwhelm the rest of the food. 'You don't want to talk to Mankiewicz, do you?' he said.

'I can do it,' I said with a little more emphasis than I should have. 'It's not a big deal.' I needed to change the subject quickly. 'What did you find out about your pal at the World Health Organization?'

His mouth twitched a little. Ken hates not knowing stuff. 'Not as much as I wanted to. From what I could get online and from public records, his name is Malcolm X. Mitchell and he holds a PhD in biology from, get ready, Rutgers University in New Jersey.' Rutgers was where our mother was working when she married our father. We think.

'Malcolm X?' I said.

'Apparently his parents were fans. And that assumes it's his real name. This guy hung up on me awful quick when I tried to find out who he was and how to contact him.'

He turned the lamb chops, which were sliced thin, over, and applied a generous amount of black pepper to them. They smelled great.

'Maybe now's the time to check with Shelly Kroft. Maybe there's some internal federal employee channels she can look at to find out more about our new pal.' In the abstract, Malcolm X.

Mitchell was an interesting puzzle. When I thought about him practically, I fought off a shiver. 'What do you think we need to do to protect Mom and Dad?' Ken has been the lead investigator in our attempts to locate our parents, which so far had been remarkably unsuccessful. They'd found *us* once, but then we'd barely moved since they took off on us decades earlier.

'If we were in touch with them, we could warn them, but that's not an option,' Ken said. He removed the lamb chops from the pan and put them on a plate he'd taken from the cabinet over his head. 'Is it?'

Ken didn't know about my emails with our mother and even those had dried up over the past couple of months. When they had been active, I still hadn't any idea where our parents were living or what they were doing. We'd heard some time back that they were teetering on the edge of a cure for all cancers and that some people in the pharmaceutical and hospital businesses were not pleased with the prospect. That meant the danger to Olivia and Brad was real and couldn't be ignored.

What it meant for Ken and me was unclear. We'd had a crazy person track us down months ago but that seemed to be an isolated incident. We had opted not to pack up and move out of New York. With the rent we were paying in this rent-controlled apartment, we'd be fools to break the lease.

'No, we don't know where Mom and Dad are,' I agreed. 'Is there anything we can do from here?'

Ken opened the oven and took out two potatoes that had been baking there for about an hour. He put them on the plate with the lamb chops and gave me a look. 'So. What are *you* having for dinner?'

I grabbed the plate out of his hand and put it on the kitchen table. 'Lamb chops and baked potato,' I said. 'Unfortunately, the chef forgot to include a vegetable.'

'Potatoes are vegetables.'

Potatoes are tubers, but there was no point in arguing that. I got forks and knives from the utensil drawer. Then I got butter and shredded cheddar cheese for the baked potatoes and we both sat down. 'What can we do about Mom and Dad?' I asked again.

Ken chewed and spoke at the same time. Considering how disgusting he is to eat with, it's amazing he has ever had a girlfriend. And yet he seems to have one all the time. The current one's name was Juliet and she was – you'll be shocked – an aspiring model. 'The only lead we have is Malcolm,' he said. 'We need to research back through him. I keep track of most of the major medical web resources and there hasn't been anything about people working on a cure for cancer outside the normal areas. So they're not sticking their heads out just yet. Malcolm is the only indication we have that anyone knows they're out there. And how he got my number, especially since he didn't have yours or the office's, is a serious question.'

I waited until I could swallow (and the food was delicious) before speaking, proving that I am a civilized human being. Sort of. 'Do you think you're in danger?' I asked.

'I don't think he'd call me up and alert me if he meant me harm,' Ken said after taking a swig from a beer bottle. If I didn't know for a fact that it wasn't true, I'd have sworn he grew up in a frat house.

'Maybe he was warning you about someone else,' I suggested.

'If he was, it was a lousy warning,' my brother said. 'He didn't tell me to look out for anything, just asked if I knew anything about Brad and Livvie. I didn't tell him anything and he hung up. That's not exactly making me lose sleep about myself.'

I considered all the facts before I said anything else, which separates me from my brother. Don't get me wrong; Ken is an intelligent, caring person. He'd just cringe if he knew I told you that.

'Two things I'm going to do tonight,' I said. 'First, I'm going to call Shelly and ask her to look into our pal Malcolm X. Then I'm going to bite my tongue and get in touch with Mank to see if we can get some information about the pills I found, and why the cops who are supposedly investigating Damien's disappearance didn't find them. Have they been to his apartment? Are they even really looking for him?'

Ken, having devoured his dinner, sat back and out of courtesy to me refrained from belching, which I appreciated. He entwined his hands behind his head. 'Well, I'm going over to Juliet's place to watch a movie and chill,' he said. 'If you know what I mean.'

I knew exactly what he meant, but I prefer not to have certain mental images lurking so I washed the dishes while Ken changed his shoes or something and then I went into my bedroom to call Shelly.

To be honest, I really didn't expect her to know much about Malcolm X. Mitchell, but it was an excuse to check in on my friend. I met Shelly when we were both studying for our master's degrees in criminal justice on the way to what I thought was going to be a career in the NYPD (turned out they were thrilled to have me file reports) and she thought was going to lead to the FBI, something which I believe my friend still aspires to do. But right now she's a US Marshal in Portland, Oregon. It's a place in which Shelly fits perfectly well but won't admit it because she grew up in New Jersey, and you can't ever coax that out of a true native.

She answered on the second ring. 'Fran Stein,' she said. 'How are things being the biggest girl in Manhattan?' Shelly is nothing if not subtle.

'How are things being the toughest girl in Portland?' I countered. 'You kick down the door on a grizzly bear lately?'

'Touché,' she said. 'Tell me all about your life.'

Having already done that once sort of lately, I decided against complying. 'You know how it is,' I said. 'You track down the odd parent or two, and some of them are *very* odd. You?'

'I'm from the gov'ment,' Shelly said. 'I follow m'orders. I'd spit some tobacco juice now but you know I'm not into that.'

I'll spare you the rest of our chitchat and get to the part where I told her that Ken had been contacted by someone who claimed to be from the WHO and was named Malcolm X. Mitchell. I asked Shelly if she'd ever heard that name.

'Is he a US Marshal?' she asked, full well knowing the answer.

'No.' I'll supply it when necessary.

'Then it's unlikely our paths would have crossed. Do you think there's some big database where all federal employees can find out every other federal employee's shoe size or something?'

'Sort of,' I admitted.

'Well, you're right, but not very.' I could hear Shelly tapping away at a keyboard. 'There is a database of federal employees but it's available to the public for the most part.'

'For the most part?'

She paused. 'You want anybody to be able to track down all CIA agents?'

'Point taken. What can you find out about the current version of Malcolm X?'

More tapping. 'Hang on. I'm zeroing in. What do you want to know?'

'First of all, whether he actually works for the World Health Organization would be helpful.'

'You're aware that the WHO is run by the United Nations and not the American government, right?' she asked.

To be fair, I *had* known that. 'Yeah, but you guys are in contact, right?'

Shelly let out a sigh. 'It's a good thing I love you,' she said.

'You're just trying to get on my good side. *Is* there a common ground you can look into? I just really need to know if this guy is what he says he is.'

She didn't sigh but in not sighing she sighed. 'I can ask around a little. Why do you care about this guy looking into these two scientists, anyway?'

I had been hoping Shelly wouldn't ask that question because I hate lying to her, despite the fact that I've done it on countless occasions when anything approaching this subject would arise. 'They appear to have had some connection to my parents,' I said. That wasn't *lying*, lying. I mean, my parents were connected to themselves, weren't they?

'OK, at least that makes sense,' Shelly said, and I wondered how it did, but as long as she thought so I could go with it. 'I don't know if I can find out anything at all for you, but I know a guy who knows a guy who used to work at the UN. Maybe he'll have a connection.'

I grinned. Shelly was still Shelly. 'All you people from Jersey know a guy who knows a guy, don't you?'

'Yeah, but we can't talk about it.'

After that we just caught up on our actual lives and gossiped about people we'd known in school, which in my case was pure speculation. I hadn't kept in touch with anyone but Shelly.

EIGHT

Asking Mankiewicz for help was considerably more complicated.

I decided it was necessary to make this all play as professionally and dispassionately as possible. Whether or not I was up to the task was another question, and it was after nine in the evening, so I gave serious consideration to putting off the call until the next day.

But then I'd lie awake all night thinking about what I was going to say and dreading the whole thing and I thought it was best to get it out of the way now and not spend the next ten hours staring at my bedroom ceiling. I'd seen it before, and frankly it wasn't that interesting.

Even if I had believed Mank's story about losing his phone in the river – which, for the record, I did not – his mobile number would still be the same, and all I had to do was push the proper button on my iPhone to call him. That was easy, right?

So a little after ten I did just that, having had some warm milk and a cookie I'd stolen from Aunt Margie's place. Because there's nothing that says 'professional and dispassionate' like reverting to your own six-year-old behavior.

I didn't text Mank to let him know I'd be calling, like I might have back in the day, which was only a couple of months ago. It was one of the few times in my adult life that I sort of wished I could drink (I probably could, for the record, but I worry about the effect it might have on my body, although it doesn't seem to bother Ken at all), but instead I had the milk and cookie and then hit the 'Mank' button.

And I'm ashamed to say I noticed I was holding my breath. What was I, in seventh grade?

'Fran.' So he remembered my name. Was that good or bad?

'Hello, Mank,' I said. 'I think I have something that can help with the Damien Van Dorn case.' I was talking too fast, but I wanted him to know immediately that this was a business call.

He did seem to be a little taken aback. He took a long moment. 'OK,' he said. 'We can do that. What have you got?'

'Four bags of pills that were in the pocket of a pair of jeans in Damien's apartment.'

Mank cleared his throat. 'Pills? What kind of pills?'

'That's what I'm calling to ask you. For all I know they're aspirin.'

It was getting a little easier. We were talking about a case. We'd done that once or twice before and it had been smooth and in its own way successful. I knew the protocols for this type of conversation. I didn't need to think about him kissing me and then walking out of a diner holding a fork. Had he brought back the fork later? If not, would that be considered shoplifting? Dinerlifting?

Maybe my mind was wandering a bit. The pills, Fran. Think about the pills.

'You took pills out of his jeans? Where were they, in the closet?' Mank was pushing me a little and I couldn't tell if it was real or light teasing like we used to do. I was hoping it was the former. I didn't need to banter. I needed to get information and then get off the phone.

Tonight might be a good time to take up drinking after all.

'No, they were in a pile of laundry in the hallway. I get the impression your guys didn't do a wildly thorough job of looking through Damien's place. Did you go yourself?'

That wasn't banter and I wanted him to know. I stood up and started walking around my bedroom, which (given the length of my legs and the amount of space in the room) didn't take very long. But I pace when I'm not entirely comfortable, and guess what.

'The uniformed officers who took the first assignment went and reported there wasn't anything especially interesting there,' Mank said. 'I didn't see a reason to override their initial judgment.'

'Well, you might want to talk to them because there were four bags of pills in a pair of pants they must have walked by three or four times and they didn't notice. Now. Can you have them analyzed and tell me what they contain?' I looked out my window and got the usual view of the building across the alley. There was only one tenant uninhibited enough to leave his curtains open and I knew for certain that I didn't want to look in that direction.

'Yes and no,' Mank answered.

'What do you mean? Can't the cops figure out what some pills might be? Do I have to go to the nearest CVS and ask the pharmacist?' There weren't more than three apartments with lights on and that was hard to explain; it wasn't *that* late.

'Yes, I can have the pills analyzed and no, I won't tell you what they contain.' A new reason to be mad at Mankiewicz! Who knew such a thing was possible?

'Why not?' It seemed a reasonable question.

'Because I'm a police officer and you, as far as I can remember, are not anymore. It's not my job to provide you with information, especially when you don't have a client looking for Damien Van Dorn and therefore no reason to be interested in those pills.'

Wow. 'Are you kidding me? Is this because of what I' (and yes, here I dropped to a whisper) '*told you?*'

It took so long for him to answer that I actually glanced toward the window of the guy with no curtains. Then I glanced away.

'No, it's not about *that*,' he said. 'If you're willing to have a conversation about *that*, then we can get back to talking about the case as if we don't hate each other. Is that a possibility?'

The only appropriate course of action there was not to answer him at all. 'If you're not going to tell me what's in the pills, I don't see any reason to give them to you for analysis,' I said. 'You didn't find them, I did.'

Mank was no longer interested in having a discussion about my secret; his voiced hardened to the temper of steel. 'If you're interested in being cited as an accessory to distribution of narcotics, that would be the way to go for sure,' he said.

'You wouldn't.'

'Watch me.'

I closed my own curtains, because who knew who was looking out the window on the other side of the alley. 'Detective Mankiewicz,' I said. 'You have absolutely no evidence that I'm in possession of anything illegal.'

'You told me there are pills.'

'I *told* you they could be aspirin. In fact, I think that's what they are.' I walked back to the bed and sat down next to my laptop. A quick search of images showed me what aspirin looked like. These were in no way aspirin.

Mank spoke very slowly and with a very even tone, a man in desperate need to harness his emotions, which were no doubt conflicting. Good. 'If you are going to require me to get a search warrant of your apartment to find those pills, I don't think you'll be pleased with the results of that search,' he said.

Wow, again. 'You really want to go there?' I asked.

'No, I don't. But you know perfectly well that I can't give a civilian information like that.'

'Why not?'

That seemed to stump him. 'Why not?'

'Yeah. Why can't you tell a private investigator about the results of police testing? Is there a regulation against it?' I'd actually heard something on this subject when I was studying criminal justice. I'd forgotten most of the classroom lectures because they had nothing to do with being a cop (which was what I thought I wanted) but I did recall this.

Mank remembered it too, and he wasn't happy about it. 'No,' he said.

'So then this is all about your little macho cop world not wanting to share with someone who isn't on the payroll, right? Or is it because I'm a woman?' Technically, I was a woman. I really didn't want to think about how I'd react if he challenged *that*.

Luckily he did not. 'Bring in the pills, Fran.' He exhaled. 'I'll let you see the test results after they come back.'

I knew that trick. '*Immediately* after they come back,' I corrected. 'Not sometime in the future after the case is solved and Eliza Hennessey is still missing.'

'Within a day,' Mank offered. 'That good enough?'

'I'll bring the pills by the precinct in the morning,' I said, and hung up.

I believe as I was pushing the button to end the call, I heard Mank say, 'Fran, let's . . .' But I could be wrong.

NINE

'd barely been on the Eliza Hennessey case for two days and I was already frustrated. It was hard to sleep that night. So I got up ridiculously early and dropped the pills off (in a manila envelope) for Mank before he would come in so we wouldn't have to play out that scene. Then I looked for Laura Rapinoe.

Granted, that was grasping at straws, but when you don't have much to grasp at and straws are available, you take the straws.

Never mind where I got her course schedule from, except to say that it definitely was *not* from my good pal at the registrar's office. The truth of the matter is Ken, when I rousted him out of bed at 'the crack of freakin' dawn' did the magic on his computer, gave me the information, and then went back to bed before I headed out for the precinct.

Laura had a full schedule, being an undergraduate, and it happened that on this day she had a first-period class, which meant I could find her outside one of the New Amsterdam University buildings at 8:20 a.m., just ten minutes before the session would begin. She noticed me and I could tell it took a second for her to remember where she'd seen me before. Then it seemed like she looked around for a convenient escape route, found plenty of them and decided against that strategy.

'I told you everything I know,' she said as soon as I was within earshot. Of course, my earshot is longer than that of most other people, but Laura didn't know that.

'Did you?' I said. 'Did you tell me Damien's last name was Van Dorn?'

She pulled her sweater a little tighter around her shoulders, and it wasn't even chilly that morning. 'I didn't know it,' she said. 'I told you I didn't know him very well.'

'No? You weren't one of the people he was dealing pills to?'

It was a long shot, I will grant you. In fact, it bordered on being cruel, but Laura was my only hope of finding Damien and Damien was my only hope of finding Eliza. Desperation brings a certain resolve that you don't have under other circumstances. I remembered the look in Brian Hennessey's eyes, the expression that suggested he might have driven his daughter out of his life just for the crime of being herself, and I had to press on.

Laura's face lost some color but her eyes did not betray fear; she was angry. 'I don't know what you're talking about,' she said.

I took a step toward her and she backed away a little. I'm sort of used to that because people aren't ready for a woman my size and they think I'm scary. Me. Imagine.

'I think you do,' I said. 'I think you were buying from Damien and maybe you even introduced him to Eliza and now you're worried but you're even more worried that you've put yourself in a position that could be seen as criminal so you're denying knowing anything. But there's just enough humanity in you, enough compassion for Eliza, who maybe even became a real friend, that you want to help me find her. So come on, Laura, help me find her and our discussion doesn't have to go any farther than us.'

She wasn't an unintelligent girl; she knew I was (more or less) sizing up the situation accurately. 'I don't do drugs,' she said. Maybe she thought I was recording the conversation to play for the cops. For the record, I was not. The cops and I weren't talking that morning.

'Maybe you don't,' I conceded. 'Maybe you just knew about this guy who had a supply and you hooked up a few friends. Maybe Damien gave you a finder's fee.'

'I never—'

'The fact is, I don't care about any of that,' I went on. 'I only care about finding Eliza Hennessey, so if you know *anything* about where she is, or where Damien is right now, the smart thing is to tell me and then the police never hear your name and your parents never get a phone call from you asking for bail money and the name of the family attorney, who probably specializes in real estate transactions or probate.'

Laura walked to some concrete steps that led to the building and sat down. I followed to make sure she couldn't make a break for it. As soon as she was seated, her head went down into her hands and she started to cry. 'I'm sorry,' she said between sobs. 'I'm so sorry.'

That gave me an opening. 'Sorry about what, Laura? What did you do?'

'It's not what I did. It's what I didn't do. I didn't let anyone know about Damien because I was scared.'

I didn't like the sound of that. Any time your name is preceded by 'about,' it's a decent bet something happened to you that would not be classified as wonderful. 'What didn't you tell anyone about Damien?' I asked.

Another minute or so of crying exclusively. I didn't see any point in saying something like, 'Don't cry,' or 'There, there,' because the person is going to cry harder when you say that (and for the record, where? Where?) So I let Laura cry it out and finally she seemed to get a better handle on her emotions, which seemed to be genuine. She really was sorry for something and she still seemed frightened. Very frightened.

'About a guy coming for him,' Laura said. 'These two guys were following him around for days and he was scared. One of them was named Julio, but he wasn't there all the time. Damien said they thought he had a lot of money or something and he didn't. Then he disappeared.'

'And so did Eliza,' I said, mostly to myself.

'Yeah.' The word didn't tell me much, but the tone suggested maybe Laura and Eliza weren't such close friends after all. Laura sounded a little angry.

'What's the matter with Eliza?' I asked.

'Nothing.' That was an avenue to be explored, but not this minute. There were more immediate issues to contend with.

'Who were the guys following Damien?' I asked. 'Did he mention any other names? Did you see them?'

She shook her head and lowered it into her hands again. It would have been hard for a normal person to hear her with all the traffic noise and people walking by, but Laura didn't seem to take notice of that and I, in case you were still wondering, am not a normal person. To be fair, I don't think I've ever met a normal person, either.

'He never said any names,' she answered into the concrete by her feet. 'I don't even know if he knew their names, except Julio, and I'm not even sure about that. It might have been Julie, or Jules, or something.' Laura lifted her head and looked at me. 'But I saw them once.'

It had been so long since I'd had an actual clue that it took me a moment to recognize one. 'What did they look like?' I said.

Laura squinted, as if trying to see the men from far away. 'One of them was maybe thirty, no mustache or beard but he shaved his head. Big, you know, like you.' Laura was thinking too hard to try to be tactful, and it's not like I don't know I'm tall. 'The other guy was a white dude, skinny like Damien, tall. Had a – what do you call it when they only have a beard around their mouth?'

Most people would call that a goatee. They'd be wrong. 'It's a Van Dyke,' I said.

Laura waved a hand idly in dismissal. 'No, it's not that, but anyway that's what he has. And there's a birthmark or a mole or something right next to his eye. Dark.'

The eye or the birthmark? 'Which eye?' I asked.

'Uh . . .' She put her hand to her temple. 'Right eye.'

'OK.' I sat down next to her so she wouldn't keep thinking about how big I was, trying to establish myself as a friendly, unthreatening presence, which in my case isn't as easy as you might think. 'You're doing very well. But is that all you didn't tell anyone about Damien? Do you have an idea of where he might have been going when he vanished?'

Suddenly her shoes seemed to have become considerably more interesting to Laura; she almost dropped her head between her knees to look at them. She sniffled a few times again. The last thing I needed was for my star witness at the moment to dissolve into tears again. I patted her on the shoulder but she didn't look up.

'You don't have to feel bad anymore,' I said. 'You can tell me what you've been holding back and I can help. I'm not the police.'

'OK.' It was almost a whisper. 'OK. Damien said he was going to get rid of those guys. He said they thought they could get to him but he was going to get there first and they couldn't come after him anymore.'

'Where?' I asked. Maybe I sounded a little bit too intense; Laura flinched a little. I softened my voice some. 'Where were they going to meet?'

'They weren't going to meet,' she said, still looking at me a little warily. 'Damien was going for them and he knew where they lived.' OK, *that* sounded ominous.

'Where did they live?' Already I was making arguments in my head to get Ken to accompany me on this trip. I'm big and tough but my brother looks like the Incredible Hulk's less green sidekick.

'This building in the Bronx near the Stadium.' Everybody in New York calls Yankee Stadium 'the Stadium.' And we have two baseball teams in town. 'I don't know the address, but it has pictures of Yankees on it.'

'I don't suppose you have an apartment number.' Because that would be far too helpful to ask for.

'No. Damien said he was going to camp out in the basement so nobody would see him outside and he could look out the basement window until the guys came back. He had it all planned out.' It's a little frightening the people who can actually get into college. Because that was among the stupidest plans I'd ever heard.

I stood up. 'Thanks, Laura. You've done the right thing.'

She stayed right where she was but she looked up at me. 'It's because he didn't come back. I'm really scared because he didn't come back.'

'Are you and Damien a couple?' I asked.

She shrugged. 'What's a couple?'

It was a good question.

TEN

'**A**ll of the buildings around here have pictures of Yankees on them,' Ken said.

That wasn't literally true, but many of the structures near Yankee Stadium in the South Bronx did bear images of past baseball, um, greats, I guess? I don't know a lot about baseball. When I was in high school everyone wanted me to go out for the basketball team. I took up martial arts instead. It has proved considerably more useful as I go about the investigation business.

I could recognize the likeness of Babe Ruth because that's pretty much ingrained in the American psyche from birth. I recognized a couple of the other names, and there were numerous pictures of Aaron Judge, a contemporary player I could relate to because he was taller than pretty much all the others, to the point that I occasionally wondered if Mom and Dad had perhaps plied their trade one more time, something Aunt Margie assured me had not happened.

'Yeah,' I agreed, 'but a lot of them aren't apartment buildings. Most of them are bars and souvenir stores. Let's look over there.' I pointed.

If what Laura Rapinoe had told me was true – and I couldn't be sure but it seemed to check out after a night of internet research on the area – the building where Damien Van Dorn had gone for a showdown with his adversaries would be on this block or another around the corner. I hadn't been able to show Laura pictures of the buildings I'd brought up in the search because I was already back at my apartment by then and doubted Laura would want to talk to me again. Probably ever.

So I was guessing that this building, with its large, seemingly spray-painted images in monotone of various ballplayers (don't ask me who, but none of them was Babe Ruth), might be the one we were looking for. We'd looked in to a few basement windows but had not yet visited a basement. Frankly, everywhere we'd looked we'd gotten odd stares from bystanders – something neither of us saw as unusual – but a basement is essentially a basement. There had been no reason for us to look more closely.

We walked across the street to the apartment building in question. Ken, who is more a basketball fan but knows a little about baseball, noted the players by name and tried very hard to interest me in why each one might be especially memorable. I'm not recreating any of that information for you now because I don't remember any of it.

When we got to the building's entrance, which surprised neither of us by lacking a doorman or a visible security system, there was an older man sitting on the stoop watching people go by. He was drinking something that from the color of it might have been iced tea and from the smell of it might not.

'There's no game today,' he said when we approached. 'They're out of town. Chicago, I think.'

'We're not here for a game,' I said. 'The Stadium is over there.' Not like he could have missed it; the place is enormous. I pointed from where we had come. I was doing a lot of pointing all of a sudden. 'We just want to visit someone in the building.'

He looked Ken up and down. 'You cops?' the man said.

'No, sir. We're private investigators.' I told him that because sometimes, just every once in a while, people can be impressed by that.

'Uh-huh.' This wasn't one of those times. 'Who you want to visit?'

Ken, who had been looking from side to side presumably for potential assailants, looked down at the seated man. 'We're not visiting anybody,' he said. 'We want to look in the basement first and then maybe go upstairs.'

'The basement!' The man looked amused. 'What you want to look in the basement for? You never seen mice before?'

I don't have a problem with mice on principle, but I'm also not their biggest fan. My stomach fluttered just a little. Go ahead, laugh.

'There might be something downstairs that can help us find a guy we're looking for,' Ken told him. He pulled out his phone and showed the man a picture of Damien that we'd gotten (OK, Ken had gotten) from New Amsterdam's files. 'Have you seen this guy around here anywhere lately?'

To his credit, the man looked thoughtfully at the photograph. 'I don't think so,' he said. 'He don't live in this building, I'm sure of that.'

I knew it wasn't a competition, but I didn't like Ken taking over my interview. I stepped forward, a little in front of my brother. Don't worry, he was still visible. 'Do you know two men who live here, or maybe just hang out here?' I asked. 'One is kind of large, with a shaved head, and the other one is slim and has a van dyke.'

'A what?' the man asked.

'A goatee,' my brother, ever helpful, answered.

'The big guy – he a Spanish dude?' the man asked.

Some people say that. They're wrong, but then so was the goatee. 'Latino, yes,' I said. 'And the slimmer one has a mole or a birthmark on this side.' I indicated the side of my head just to the right of my eye.

'I don't know that one,' the man told us. 'But the big dude, I seen him around. Don't want to mess with him.'

Ken looked interested. He likes a physical challenge. Ken, you should know, is crazy. 'Why not?' he asked.

The older man looked at him as if trying to decide if there was some sort of cognitive deficiency present in my brother. There isn't, but I understood his concern. 'Because he's about your size and he carries a gun,' he said.

'So do I,' Ken answered. He did not offer a glimpse of the weapon, and I wasn't sure he had it with him. This was the usual macho nonsense. Probably.

'Can you tell us what apartment that man lives in?' I asked. Preferably before Ken decided to start marking his territory, I thought.

'He's on the fourth floor,' our informant said. 'I don't know which apartment. I live on the second floor and my knees don't go up the stairs that good.'

'Do you know his name?' I said. It hadn't come up but that didn't mean the older man didn't have the information.

'I heard someone call him Julio once,' the guy told us. 'Then he threw that boy down the stairs, so I wouldn't call him Julio if I was you.' Good advice, I thought.

The man had drunk about half of what he had in his plastic

cup. It definitely wasn't tea, but he had been forthright with us. I reached into my pocket and pulled out a twenty-dollar bill. 'Thanks so much for your help,' I said, and extended my hand with the money.

He stared at my hand as if it held a live rat. 'Don't you even think about it,' he said. 'I'm not a beggar.'

'No, sir,' I responded. 'You are an informant.' I held out my hand again.

'Not in this neighborhood,' the older man said with a growl in his voice. 'Around here, "informants" get cut. Put your money away.'

So I did, apologized, and walked up the stoop toward the front door, which someone (probably our friend) had propped open with a small block of wood, clearly not for the first time. Ken followed behind me, obviously amused that I'd been seen as insulting the man drinking rye (the smell was unmistakable) in front of his apartment building.

The aroma inside the building wasn't better. This place of residence for people who were not the poorest in the city smelled of things better left unmentioned. Yes, our senses are stronger than most, but anyone would have found the place, at best, unappealing.

It was not noticeably dirty, though. This building had probably been pretty grand when it was built, most likely in the early part of the twentieth century. The floor of the lobby was marble tile, now faded and cracked in places from a hundred years of wear and neglect. The stairway to the left had probably once had elegant wooden banisters that were now gone. But Ken and I weren't interested in going upstairs. Not yet.

I looked around for a door or stairway to the basement but came up short. Ken was more successful, apparently, because he whistled to me and pointed toward a part of the lobby wall that looked like the rest. I looked at him and shrugged.

My brother pointed to the doorknob that I had missed. This wasn't my best detecting day and it was only a little after noon.

The lobby was empty for the moment and I did not have the impression the man on the stoop was watching to see what we might do. We walked over to the door so Ken could turn the knob. Surprisingly, it turned. Apparently nobody in this building, even the super if they had one, had been too worried about the security of the basement. It was not a huge surprise; the place was a home to some but not on the order of Damien Van Dorn's apartment in Alphabet City. It was being held together, but just barely.

Ken pulled the door open and looked inside. 'Flashlights,' he said, brilliant conversationalist that he is. I guessed it was dark in the stairway to the cellar. I pulled out my phone and turned on the flashlight app.

Once we were inside the stairway, I closed the door behind us. No sense in advertising our presence in the basement to Julio, or whatever he'd decided his name was, or for that matter to anyone else.

I turned the flashlight's beam out and took a look around. Within ten seconds I had located a switch and used it to turn on the lights, which probably annoyed my brother, who had grown up watching *The X-Files* and thought flashlights made everything cooler. He grimaced a bit and turned his off as well.

This was a completely ordinary stairway to what appeared, from one flight up, to be a completely ordinary basement. The stairs did creak, of course, but that was to be expected. The walls had last been painted most likely during the Carter administration, before Ken and I were, for lack of a better word, born.

'The staircase can be treacherous,' he said, quoting one of our favorite movies. I did not laugh.

We made our way down the stairs carefully because again there was no banister, which probably violated all sorts of housing code regulations. Or at least the one requiring banisters. I was watching my step especially closely because, if I tripped, my first cushion to land on would be my brother and who needed that? He'd never let me hear the end of it.

The light in the basement was not working, probably due to lack of bulbs in the fixtures, both overhead and in one sorry-looking floor lamp to the left side. I reached for my phone again when we got to the basement floor.

'Wait,' Ken said.

I stopped with some trepidation. 'Are there mice?' I asked. I'd decided by then that I absolutely hated mice.

'No.'

'Thanks for not overwhelming me with information,' I told him. 'I'm going to turn my flashlight on.'

Ken took a few steps forward and illuminated his app. 'You're not gonna like it,' he said.

That was it. I put on my light and aimed it in the same direction as my brother's.

Sure enough, there was a very tall, thin, redheaded man. Damien Van Dorn. I recognized him from the photographs we'd seen.

He was lying on the floor with what appeared to be an electrical cord around his neck. His eyes were open and looked appalled.

Damien was quite dead, and now I had to figure out how I'd tell his mother.

ELEVEN

decided, after considering that Helena Van Dorn was not my client, that she had left our last meeting without a common courtesy, and that I am a coward, to leave the notification of her son's death to the police. I pay taxes.

We had called 911 immediately, and the good officers of the 44th Precinct had arrived . . . pretty soon thereafter. This wasn't exactly the highest priority neighborhood in the city, and Damien wasn't going to stop being dead any time soon. We were advised not to touch anything, and since I didn't want to, that was easy to obey.

'We've done this before,' Ken reminded me after Officers Cantrell and Dominguez had arrived and started taking pictures, debating whether they had to call a detective and deciding that yes, they did. 'This is not the first dead body we've found.'

'That doesn't make me feel better,' I told him. 'I was looking for Damien to lead me to Eliza. Now Damien is dead and I think it unlikely he's going to tell me much about where Eliza might be. In fact' (and here I lowered my voice in case the cops were listening) 'she's probably at the top of the suspect list.'

'What about Julio?' Ken asked. 'I'm thinking he's the most likely candidate.'

'I'm not ruling him out. I'm thinking about what their detective is going to say.' I gestured toward the two uniforms, who were measuring distances from Damien's hand to the cord around his neck. I knew they couldn't, but I wished they would unwind that thing and give the boy a chance to breathe.

You have weird thoughts when there's a dead body in the room.

The door at the top of the stairs creaked open and a man who had to be an NYPD detective (given his absolutely generic wardrobe and fairly old shoes) started down the stairs. He was in his forties, clean shaven and chewing what I sincerely hoped was gum. I had to blink a couple of times to make sure I hadn't seen

him playing this exact role on one of the iterations of *Law &
Order*. They film in New York pretty much all the time, so if
you haven't met someone who's been on those shows, you're
not a New Yorker.

Behind him was a large man (not as large as Ken) dressed a
little more carefully, wearing Nikes. He carried an iPad. Detectives
never go anywhere without an iPad anymore. Except Rich
Mankiewicz, who apparently still works on his phone and lets it
get thrown in the river. But I digress.

The first one down the stairs flashed a badge at me. I chose
not to look at it for fear that he'd think I was impressed. 'Detective
Sergeant Louis Merchant,' he said. I took that for his name
because I thought it was pretty clear *I* wasn't Detective Sergeant
Louis Merchant. 'This is my partner, Neil Brooker.' Brooker
nodded in my direction and I did the same back. I appreciated
his not chewing gum.

'Ken Stein,' said my brother, extending a hand. Merchant
looked at it but made no move. He wouldn't want us to think
we were colleagues or peers or anything. Ken retracted the hand
and gestured in my general direction. 'That's my sister, Fran.'

'We're private investigators,' I said, lest the detectives think
we just liked to hang around in grubby basements. 'We're looking
for someone who knew the victim here and we found the body.'

That seemed to remind Merchant that yes, there was a body
on the floor. Brooker had already walked over there and was
taking in the scene, which was gruesome without being gory.

Damien, dressed in strategically ripped jeans and a blue t-shirt
with no legend on it, was twisted in what appeared to be a very
uncomfortable position. His legs were bent at the knee and stuffed
behind him. His arms were tied. There was a chair six feet from
his prone body that indicated he might have been sitting there
before someone decided to deprive him of oxygen. There was a
dark stain, with no color, on his shirtfront. And there was that
thick electrical cord, maybe an extension cord, wrapped multiple
times around his neck and tightened, then tied. It wasn't a noose
but it might as well have been. His mouth was open but tight.
His eyes were open but not bulging. All in all, I'd had better
days, and certainly Damien had as well.

'You know who he is?' Merchant asked.

Ken had apparently decided he was the point man for our team, so I walked over toward Brooker. I could still hear the conversation behind me.

'We had photographs to help us find him. He's Damien Van Dorn,' Ken said with as much authority as he could muster. I'm sure with his deep voice it sounded to the cops like he knew what he was talking about. 'He's a student at New Amsterdam University.'

I watched Brooker work. He was obviously the less talkative of the two and he was observing the macabre scene in front of us the way a detective should, dispassionately and carefully. If there was something here that was going to help identify or find the killer, Brooker didn't want to miss it. But I could tell he was listening to Merchant question Ken at the same time.

'But he's not the one you were looking for,' Merchant said.

Ken pointed at him as if he were the clever student in the class. 'That's right. We're looking for Eliza Hennessey and we think she was friends with Damien here.'

Brooker reached into his jacket pocket, having already put on a pair of latex gloves, and found a small pair of tweezers. He reached down and pulled something from the floor just next to Damien's left ear. I couldn't see what it was before he got it into an evidence bag and then his pocket.

My job had not been to find Damien Van Dorn, yet I had done so in the worst condition possible. 'Friends?' Merchant asked. I didn't know it was possible for a voice to leer.

'Yeah,' Ken said. 'They met at school.' He glanced at me. Should he go on? I considered that Mank was the detective on the other end of that question, decided not to let the grudge go that far, and nodded. 'And we think Damien was dealing drugs.'

Brooker looked up, first at Ken and then at me. He stood and turned in my direction. 'You think this guy was dealing?' he said.

'Is that a big surprise for a guy that ends up strangled in a tenement basement?' Merchant cut in. I was thinking of introducing him to Emil Bendix and then decided that might cause a hole in the space-time continuum.

Brooker, wisely, decided to ignore his partner. 'What gave you that impression?' he asked me.

'We found some packets of pills in his apartment,' I said. No need to give him the mental image of me going through an empty pair of jeans on the floor in Damien's hallway.

He raised his eyebrows a bit. 'What kind of pills?'

'I don't know yet.' Which was true because Mankiewicz hadn't called me yet. Men. 'I really wasn't looking for Damien except as a way to help find Eliza Hennessey. And, as you can see, he's in no shape to help me do that.'

Probably without realizing it, Brooker looked down at Damien again. I'd had the image imprinted on my cerebral cortex and would never be able to get rid of it. He'd forget it by the time he got home to his wife – or husband – at the end of the day. 'This wasn't a planned killing,' he said, to me and to himself and maybe, if he was really desperate, to Merchant as well. 'Whoever did this found the extension cord down here; they didn't bring it with them. Does this Eliza have a grudge against this guy? Did he sell her something bad, maybe?'

I gave Ken an I-told-you-so look, one he's seen enough times to recognize it in his sleep. 'I don't have any evidence that Eliza was buying from Damien or that she was at all upset with him. In fact, she went missing days before he came down here and this happened.'

Brooker shook his head. 'This guy hasn't been dead more than a day. He's not decomposed enough. I think someone held him here at least one day, maybe longer, and then got mad enough to wrap that cord around his neck and yank.'

Happy as I was to be treated like an equal, I felt that Brooker was missing my point. 'I'm saying, I don't think Eliza is a great suspect for doing this.'

'Because she's a girl and wouldn't be strong enough?' Merchant asked. Ken looked at me and stifled a laugh.

'No,' I told him, and before he could make what I'm sure he would have thought was a hilarious comment, I added, 'She didn't have any motive to want Damien dead and she vanished before him, not after. The timeline doesn't make sense.'

The uniform named Dominguez, having done little more than stand around while we had this scintillating conversation, asked Merchant if he and his partner were still required at the scene. The detective told him they weren't but to make sure they filed the proper paperwork when they got back to the precinct. The medical examiner and a car to remove Damien would be here shortly, he said.

So the two cops left and, sure enough, the ME was there before their presence in the room had completely dissipated. She wasn't wearing a white lab coat but you can identify them a mile away. Part of it was the woman's complete and total indifference to the body on the floor. She just walked over and started taking temperatures and things like that. I don't care to look at such things, more evidence that I do not share the DNA of two brilliant scientists. Probably.

'How long do you think he's dead?' Brooker asked the doctor.

'I've been here a minute and a half. You want to give me a chance?' You had to like her style.

'Sorry.' Brooker did not roll his eyes. I wasn't looking at Merchant, but I'd bet you a dollar he did.

'How do you know about the kid dealing drugs?' Merchant wanted to know.

I didn't have any obligation to Laura Rapinoe. She had not asked me to keep her name out of any investigation or communication with the police. On the other hand, she hadn't known Damien was going to end up dead on a basement floor and I guessed that news wasn't going to land softly on her shoulders. Still, she was the source of the information.

'I met a student at New Amsterdam when I was looking for Eliza and she told me Damien was a friend of Eliza's,' I said. 'That led me to look for Damien in his apartment. He wasn't there but he left those packets of pills behind, and I can add two plus two as well as anybody.'

'What's the student's name?' Brooker asked. 'The one who told you about Damien here.'

I don't know why, but I didn't want to tell these two about Laura. Maybe I'd have told Brooker if he was alone but Merchant really didn't seem like the type who was going to treat women with respect and, besides, I didn't like him. 'I'd have to go back to my office and look through my notes,' I said.

Brooker looked at me as if wondering why my notes weren't on my phone, which, candidly, they were. 'Do that. How did you get into the kid's apartment?' Was he looking to bust me on breaking and entering?

'His mother let me in,' I said. 'You want her name? Because I remember that.' It was in the same contacts section as Laura Rapinoe's, but why would I tell him that?

'Yes, please.' I bet this guy was a lot of fun at parties.

I gave Brooker Helena's phone number and told him I'd look for my mystery source's name and contact info when I got back to my office. He didn't ask why the data wasn't in my phone and I didn't offer an explanation that he could identify as a complete lie at a later time. When Ken and I were about to leave, I looked back at Brooker.

'What was that you picked up next to the body?' I asked.

He blinked. It might have been his eyes were dry and it might have been he didn't have an answer ready that he wanted to give to me. I was wagering it was the latter. 'What do you mean?' Wow, that was worse than my evasion on Laura's name.

'I saw you reach into your pocket, pick out a pair of tweezers, take something from the floor next to Damien's right ear and then put it in your pocket in an evidence bag,' I said. I was trying not to sound like I was challenging him and, to my ear, doing an awful job of it. 'What was it?'

'Oh.' Like he hadn't known what I meant before. 'That was nothing.'

'Nothing?' Ken said, because he hadn't been present at school when tact was discussed. 'You find something next to a murder victim and put it in an evidence bag for later and it's nothing?' If Ken had raised his eyebrows any higher they would have left his head completely and hovered waveringly above it.

'It's nothing you need to worry about.' Brooker was wisely turning his attention to me and away from my brother. 'You're looking for this Eliza Hennessey. It has nothing to do with her.'

That meant it had everything to do with Eliza. 'I'm curious why you're so obviously trying not to tell me what you found,' I said. 'Am I a suspect? Do you think that I came down to this basement in the past day or two, strangled Damien with an extension cord and then called the police to come catch me?'

Brooker walked over to his partner, who was standing next to Ken. 'You're not the only one here,' he said. 'Someone who could do that with an extension cord would have to be really strong.'

Merchant moved behind Ken and I wondered if he was going

to try to put a pair of zip ties on my brother's hands. I was considering this completely as an academic exercise because I'd never seen Ken try to break out of zip ties and wondered if he could. I thought so.

But that turned out not to be the cops' plan. Instead, they seemed to be relying on intimidation, which was hilarious as they craned their necks to look into my brother's face. 'And I'll bet you're *real* strong,' Merchant said from behind Ken. I couldn't actually see him but I was fairly sure Brooker wasn't a ventriloquist and an impressionist at the same time.

'This really is the wrong kind of porno movie for me,' Ken said. That's him being witty.

Merchant hit him hard in the kidney, which would have bothered anyone who wasn't one of us. Ken didn't flinch, but did respond by half-turning and grabbing Merchant's shirt front, then lifting the detective five inches off the floor with one hand.

'Yeah, I'm pretty strong,' he said.

'Ken,' I told him in as even a tone as I could manage without actually having breath. 'Put the detective down.'

Brooker made a quick move toward his gun, which was in a holster under his jacket, but I shook my head. 'No need for that,' I said. 'He's going to be *reasonable*.'

Ken looked at me, then at Brooker, then at Merchant, who looked like he was being dangled off the edge of the Grand Canyon. He smiled and lowered Merchant to the basement floor. 'Sorry,' he said. 'Sometimes I don't know my own strength.'

Merchant took a few seconds – OK, more than a few – to catch his breath, bent over at the waist. Then he looked up and glared at Ken. 'You are under arrest for assaulting a police officer,' he said.

'And we're going to sue the NYPD over assault of a civilian and call for your immediate arrest,' I told Merchant. 'I mean, who hit whom?' Note the correct grammar there. I pride myself.

'You have no proof,' Merchant hissed. They always say that when they're guilty.

'I have video on my phone,' I told him, and held up the instrument in question. 'When you took a walk behind my brother I figured I'd better document the moment. For posterity, and possibly a grand jury.'

Merchant swiveled to look at Brooker. 'Did she take video?' he asked.

Brooker shrugged. 'I was looking at you. But if I'm asked, I'll definitely say you hit him before he picked you up like a five-pound bag of flour.'

Merchant's mouth opened and closed a couple of times as if the words were there but were having an amplification problem. Then he turned and walked back up the basement stairs, went through the door to the lobby, and slammed it behind him.

The medical examiner stood up. 'He's been dead about a day,' she said to Brooker. 'I'll need a complete autopsy to tell you anything else important but, if you're asking, I'm guessing he was strangled and asphyxiated.'

'Thanks,' Brooker said. He picked up his phone and said, 'The body is released for transport.' I assumed two medical technicians would appear shortly, but I didn't plan on being around to watch.

'What did you pick up off the floor?' I asked Brooker again.

'Get going before I decide Merchant didn't hit your brother at all. Didn't look like he felt anything.'

'I work out a lot,' Ken said.

So we left.

TWELVE

As you might imagine, Brian Hennessey was something less than ecstatic over my initial report on the investigation into his daughter's whereabouts.

I told him everything I knew, which unfortunately included the fact that Eliza's friend Damien had been found murdered, and that had clearly (and understandably) triggered a father's anxiety over his missing child.

He had a hundred questions, each one of them appropriate and each one unanswerable: Was Eliza there when Damien died? Had she been with him since she'd gone missing? Where did I think she was now? (He did slip and refer to his daughter by her deadname, but only once and immediately corrected himself.)

'There's not very much I can tell you except negatives,' I told him. 'I don't know where Eliza is, but I can tell you that there was no evidence I saw indicating she'd been there when Damien was killed. I don't know whether they even saw each other after she left. I'm looking into some possibilities but at the moment I don't have a very solid lead. I'm sorry.'

'You said he might have been selling drugs,' Brian said. 'Eliza doesn't do drugs. Never.'

I considered reminding him that a parent never really knows what their child might be doing past the age of four, but felt that remark would have had no positive effect on Brian and, besides, was kind of a mean thing to say. So I didn't. 'Nobody is suggesting she does,' I said, which so far had been mostly true. 'I don't know that there's any connection there at all.'

We were sitting in Brian's 'study,' a small corner of his apartment that crammed bookshelves and desk into a space probably meant for a modest easy chair. New York is like that, and this was Queens. Manhattan is far worse unless you're a billionaire.

'Do you know what drugs he was selling? I know something about pharmaceuticals.' Brian had worked for a trade magazine in that area.

'I'm hoping to find out later today,' I answered. I knew how that sounded.

'It seems to me that most of what you're telling me adds up to you not knowing much of anything,' Brian said, perhaps not meaning to sound the way he did, but summing things up accurately. 'Another day has gone by and I still don't know where my daughter is, Ms Stein.'

Did he want to fire me? It was his prerogative, and I'd been fired before. But I wanted to find Eliza Hennessey, maybe needed to find her to prove to myself that she hadn't ended up like Damien Van Dorn. A dead body attached to a missing person is not a great omen, but the fact that she wasn't lying next to him in that Bronx basement gave me some hope that Eliza was still out there somewhere, maybe hiding from her father, maybe from someone much worse. I had to be the one who kept looking.

'We're putting in our best effort, believe me, Mr Hennessey,' I said. 'If you think another agency can do a better job, I won't suggest that you shouldn't hire them.' A little passive aggressive maybe, but I thought it was fair.

Hennessey looked at me carefully, probably weighing the pros and cons of keeping Ken and me on the case. 'I'm not interested in firing you,' he said after a moment. 'I just want to know what you're doing now to find Eliza.'

It was a good question. 'I'm looking into some angles, including the drug business Damien might have had,' I said. 'Those things tend to work in networks.' Before he could object, I added, 'Eliza wouldn't have had to have been directly involved for someone to have noticed her and maybe seen her in the past few days. You said she has some friends. Rainbow, you said was one name. Michaela. Gerry. Any way you can add last names to those? How they were connected? Was it through high school? At New Amsterdam?' (I already knew that Michaela O'Brien was three thousand miles away at UC Berkley and Gerry Freed was living in London, so I really wanted more names from Brian.)

'I don't know,' he said. 'Gerry I think was from high school, and Michaela was from summer camp a number of years ago. Rainbow was just a name I heard her talking about. Maybe they're from college.'

'Can I see Eliza's room?' I asked. I'd already seen Damien's apartment and was hoping Eliza's bedroom would be more helpful in pointing toward her current whereabouts.

Brian led me down a short hall to a closed door. I waited for him to open it and walked in doing my best not to touch anything but to take it all in.

I hadn't known what to expect, or even what to look for in Eliza's room. I knew that Eliza had always been Eliza, but she hadn't always been keen on sharing that information. She'd come out as a trans woman to her father only a few months ago.

But the room was that of a teenage girl, now a young woman. The linens weren't pink, exactly, but they favored pink accents and there was a stuffed elephant leaning on a pillow on the bed, perhaps meant to be a joke, that was pink. No posters on the walls, but a copy of a young adult book about a trans woman called *If I Was Your Girl* on the nightstand. Another book, titled *My Life in Transition*, was among those on a shelf in the headboard.

'I'm going to wait in the living room,' Brian said. He wasn't crying but the room was clearly more than he could handle at the moment. He didn't wait for me to answer and walked away from the door.

That was better. If I had questions I could ask them when I rejoined him in the other room. Without him looking over my shoulder, I could be more dispassionate and thorough in my search. If there was a journal or a diary I wanted to know about it and I didn't want to have an argument about reading it. Politeness isn't a given in the detective business.

There was no journal. A thorough search – a seven on the scale of ten – didn't turn up anything of interest at all. All pertinent information is kept on one's phone these days, which is probably not as efficient as it seems. Makes it so much more difficult to leave behind clues to your favored getaway location.

But then there were those extra three points on the scale. I didn't want to tear the room apart and 'toss' it the way cops or especially nasty searchers (i.e. criminals) will do, but I did look under the bed, between the mattress and the box spring, under the area rug, inside the 'secret' cubby in the closet (covered over with a dress on a hanger and nice try, Eliza, but I'm a professional) and then in the desk drawers. Those were too obvious, but you never know.

The key, I decided, was to try to get into Eliza's mindset, something that is often a useful tool for an investigator. But I didn't have much – OK, no – experience as a trans woman. Still, I *had* experienced being a teenaged girl. Those days were a while back but not so far that I couldn't tap into the feelings when I wanted to. Assuming she had been under considerable stress, I knew what to do in order to emulate Eliza.

I lay on the bed, flung my left arm across my forehead, and stared at the ceiling. And sure enough, an idea presented itself. There was a light fixture hanging from the ceiling and it had a bowl underneath the light bulbs that would, if girls had some commonalities, be a great place to hide something. It's where I would have secreted anything I didn't want Ken to find.

I didn't need it but I was sure Eliza must have had something she would stand on to reach the fixture if she intended to hide something there. And even if she didn't do so now when she was approaching twenty, it was a decent bet that Eliza had hidden something in the room because teenage girls like nothing better than to have a secret.

Sure enough, there was a little stepstool, just one step, something a very small child might have used to reach the bathroom sink and a teenager would find impossible to abandon. It was sitting right next to the closet door and had not gathered much dust. The room had been cleaned fairly recently, but some surfaces were cleaner than others and the stool was one of them. So Eliza had hidden something away, and the light fixture seemed the most likely place in which to do so.

Hoping I would *not* find plastic bags holding Damien's blue pills, I reached up for the bowl and put my hand inside. The ceiling fan was not running, of course, but still presented an obstacle of sorts. I'm feminine but not dainty, to say the least. Getting my arm between blades of the fan to reach the inside of the light fixture's bowl was not my most graceful move ever.

I managed. I know you were worried.

First contact didn't yield anything, but this wasn't my first light fixture. I walked the perimeter of the bowl, dragging the blades of the fan with me, and on the far side felt something touch my fingertip. Something small and, if my sense of touch wasn't failing me, metal. Like a lapel-size pin maybe. I was surprised I hadn't seen it in the bowl, but the only lamp turned on in the room was the one on the nightstand so the object's presence hadn't been that obvious.

But it would have been in direct sight of someone lying on the bed and staring up, like Eliza. Tapping into my angst-ridden teenage years had paid off after all.

Carefully I raised the little object out of the bowl of the light fixture and, making sure I didn't drop it, brought it down to chest level for examination.

It was indeed a small metal pin, probably meant to be worn on a shirt or a jacket. It bore the symbol of a rainbow. It also bore a thick coating of dust, thick enough to convince me it had been somehow lost there (maybe a young Eliza was throwing it in the air and missed?) and never retrieved. This search was turning out to be a bust. But maybe I needed to know more about Eliza's friend Rainbow.

Having searched the room one and a third times I knew where to find the one indispensable source of information for a recent high school graduate: Eliza's yearbook. I pulled it off the shelf over her desk and started to scan through it thoroughly but as quickly as I could. It's not easy to pull that off, but I'm good at what I do.

A fairly painstaking scan of the graduating class found no student named Rainbow, but Brian had suggested that person might have been someone Eliza met at New Amsterdam. I still had Laura Rapinoe's phone number and I used it, trying not to picture the wince on her face when she saw who was calling.

Give Laura credit – she answered. 'I don't know where Eliza is,' she said. 'Did you find Damien?'

Dammit. She didn't know. 'I'll talk to you about that in a minute,' I promised, hoping that I was going to be called away by . . . something. 'Right now I need to know if you know of somebody there at New Amsterdam named Rainbow.'

Laura wasn't pleased that I hadn't answered the Damien question. She took a moment. 'Tell me about Damien now,' she said.

'In a *minute*. What about Rainbow? I'm taking it from your response that you know who that is.'

Laura exhaled audibly, the universal sign for exasperation. 'Fine. Rainbow Zelensky. I've never met her but I'm told she's popular in a certain crowd; they say she's cute. People used to hang out at her apartment in Queens. I didn't go. Now tell me about Damien.'

'How do I find Rainbow? Dorm? Apartment? Phone number?'

'I *never met* her; I just heard about her. Now tell me about Damien.'

She deserved to have the information, but I didn't want to give it to her because, frankly, I wanted someone else to do it. There didn't appear to be a choice, though. So I took a breath and said, 'OK. I really wish I didn't have to say this.'

And Laura cried.

THIRTEEN

t's a reflection of how much I didn't want to deal with Rich Mankiewicz that when I went to the precinct I made Ken come with me.

This was clearly a risky move. If Mank made any reference to the differences Ken and I have, my cover would be blown, my brother would know I'd told someone else about us and in all probability he'd look harder than ever for our parents so he could tell our mother on me. But I didn't have time to play out that scene with him before I went to pump my previously favorite detective on information about the pills I'd dropped off for analysis, the dead body in the Bronx and the possible whereabouts of Rainbow Zelensky.

While we walked to the precinct, which is only a couple of blocks from our building, I filled Ken in on what Brian Hennessey and Laura Rapinoe had told me. He didn't want to talk about that. He wanted to talk about Malcolm X. Mitchell, allegedly of the World Health Organization.

'I hit call on his call and got a very general voicemail message,' he said, completely without my asking. 'So I pretended I was naïve and said I hoped I hadn't hung up on him by mistake and could he call me back.'

'So how many times has he called you back so far?' I asked.

Ken pouted. Until you've seen a six-foot-eight man pout, you haven't really explored the entire panoply of experiences life can offer. 'He could be at lunch.'

Anyone who's been to lunch in the past twenty years could easily deflate that comment, but I needed my brother to be my backup so I let it go. 'Did the voicemail message say anything about being with the WHO?' I asked.

'No.'

'Bingo.'

'I don't think it was ever a serious consideration that he was,' Ken answered, wanting to get his little sister to respect him again.

Like that was going to happen. 'I want to get him to call me so I can find out more, like where he might have heard about Mom and Dad.'

'You haven't seen anything even remotely like them online?' I asked. Ken knows corners of the internet that Al Gore hasn't thought of yet.

He shook his head. 'I think this was another attempt to shake us loose and get us to make a mistake. Like we could email our parents or something and they could tap in.' Ken shook his head again at the idea that one of us could just choose to get in touch with Mom or Dad.

There was a lot I wasn't saying in this conversation. Luckily we had reached the station so we could begin another conversation in which I wouldn't want to say much. It was turning out to be a theme day.

Mankiewicz was predictably at his desk, his face serious and searching the screen on his computer. I used to think he looked kind of cute that way. Now, I told myself, he was posing. (He wasn't, but you know how it is.) I couldn't see the screen as we approached and Mank pretended not to notice the two oversized people heading in his direction.

Bendix, however, thought Ken and I represented a ripe opportunity for hilarity. Or two. 'Gargantua,' he said by way of greeting. 'You bring your bodyguard with you today?' There are misogynists and then there's Bendix, the beta test for misogyny. They'd worked out the bugs before they'd perfected the app.

'You've met my brother, haven't you, Bendix?' I asked. 'He has burps that are stronger than you.'

Ken obliged, which was not what I'd had in mind. 'Nice work,' I said quietly to him as I passed Bendix and walked to the side of Mankiewicz's desk.

Mank had obviously noticed the rising level of comedy in the room and looked very up to see Ken and me standing in front of him. 'Ken and Fran,' he said. 'To what do I owe the honor?'

'You know what,' I answered. 'What's the report on those pills I left for you? Fentanyl?' This might not be so difficult after all. I was just letting my natural anger overshadow the hurt.

I'll admit it: one of the reasons I'd insisted Ken come along was that Mank wouldn't try to talk to me on a personal level and I wouldn't have to confront both how I felt about it and how I found myself acting about it, which was against my usual demeanor. So a guy had stopped dating me; did that have to mean I was going to behave like a high school sophomore whenever we met? So far, it did.

Mankiewicz nodded with a resigned look on his face. This was something he had to do, not something he wanted to do. 'Actually, no,' he said. 'Your friend appears to have been dealing Adderall to his friends. Very popular on campus, for those times you need to cram for finals, and all the other times.'

That made some sense, but I wasn't sure it made a great deal of difference. 'Enough to get killed over?' I asked.

Mank didn't pretend he hadn't gotten the report on Damien's murder. 'Yeah, thanks for getting in touch with me about that. I saw you both listed as being at the scene.'

'I figured you'd hear about it soon enough. Now you can close your file on Damien, but I'm still looking for Eliza Hennessey, and maybe the pills can lead me somewhere. Was he selling enough drugs to make him worth killing?'

Mankiewicz did the tired-cop thing with his eyes but I wasn't buying it. 'What's enough? If he was just selling to friends, probably not; he wouldn't have necessarily been intruding on someone else's territory. If he wanted to control the whole college campus, then you might be looking at another story.'

I wasn't interested in the story; I wanted names. 'Who would be threatened if someone was selling pills on the New Amsterdam University campus?'

The right corner of Mank's mouth curled, and not in an attractive or amused way. 'I don't know every drug dealer in the city, Fran, and certainly not all the way up there.'

Stupid municipal functionary.

'When I was in the basement with Damien's body, I saw Detective Brooker pick something up with a pair of tweezers and put it into an evidence bag,' I told Mankiewicz. 'Is there any mention in his report about what that might have been?'

Mank put his hands down on his desk, palms flat. 'Can we talk for a minute in private?' he asked. He looked at Ken.

Ken, without changing his facial expression in any other way, raised an eyebrow.

I dropped my arms, which had been folded across my chest, to my sides. 'Really? You want to have a private conversation when I just asked you about a police report that must be public information by now?'

'If it's public information, you can look it up. Please?' He glanced at my brother, as if it were Ken's decision to make.

'Oh, fine!' I said, because if we were going to act like teenagers I might as well go the whole way. I walked to the door and headed for a stairwell where Mankiewicz and I had held private discussions before. And yes, they were just discussions. Get your mind out of the gutter.

He followed me and we both looked to make sure there were indeed no other people on the stairs at this moment, a fair bet given that the building had an elevator. People don't like to walk up stairs when they don't have to.

'OK, what?' I said. It's a great way to begin a cordial conversation with the guy I could only now refer to as my ex.

His voice changed from the detective who had been in the precinct bullpen to something resembling an ASMR artist pretending to give you a facial on YouTube. 'Fran, I want to clear the air. I want to apologize for the way I acted when we talked in the diner.'

I'd heard this tactic before. Not from him or anyone else I'd ever dated (since to be honest I'd never *actually* dated anyone else) but I'd heard it used on other people. I wasn't ready to fall for it. 'You mean when you recoiled at finding out who I really am and then shoplifted a fork?' I said.

'I brought the fork back later. Look, what you told me wasn't in the realm of normal revelation. First I thought you were joking and then I thought you were crazy and then some things just sort of added up in my mind and I believed you, and that was hard to absorb. It wasn't just that you have a family history of illness or that you've decided you don't ever want to own a dog.' Mank looked sheepish, so I guessed he meant a sheepdog. Who'd ever said anything about a dog? 'It was something I'd never heard before.'

'It was something *nobody* had ever heard before. I was demonstrating how much I trusted you with information I'd sworn never to give to anyone, and I think you can imagine how well I reacted when you fled the building at warp speed.'

He leaned back against the ancient plaster wall of the stairwell, leaning his lower torso out to avoid the metal banister. 'I know. I reacted emotionally and I wasn't thinking. I wasn't thinking about how you must have felt. It was just a reflexive thing because I didn't know how to react.' Mank is a good few inches shorter than I am and I did appreciate him craning his neck to make eye contact. 'But as soon as I could think straight, I did try to see it from your point of view, and I did everything wrong that I could do. So I want you to know that I'm very sorry and I hope you can forgive me, but I understand if you can't.'

For a moment I almost reverted. This *was* more like the guy I'd been dating and thought could be trusted with my secret. 'You haven't told anyone else?' I said.

'Of course not.'

I made sure we were looking each other in the eye. 'Because you respect my privacy or because you were embarrassed to be dating a woman with a USB port under her left arm?' I asked.

He smiled a bent smile. 'The first one.'

'You're doing better,' I told him.

'I'm glad to hear it. Can we go back to being friends?'

Friends. 'Was that what we were?'

Mank must have felt the flood waters rising around him because he straightened up off the wall and put his hands in his pants pockets. 'It was when we started,' he said.

Now, that wasn't even accurate. The best you could have said was that we were friendly colleagues, given that I was a private detective and he was a cop. Then we were immediately dating, and trust me, that was different. I have never once kissed Emil Bendix for three hours in a row. Although 'friendly colleagues' would be a stretch with Bendix.

'What do you want to happen?' I said. I didn't offer choices because I wanted to hear which ones he'd come up with on his own.

'I'd like to work back toward where we were and maybe some more,' he said. 'But I know you were hurt and I'm not sure if that's what you want right now.'

Good answer, Mank.

I nodded once, as if we'd just concluded a business deal. 'OK. So why don't we start by you telling me what was in Brooker's report about the evidence he found on the basement floor?' I pushed the door open and walked through. I made certain not to be looking at Mank's face, because I honestly didn't want to know how he had reacted to my changing gears so abruptly.

Audibly, he betrayed nothing. No gasp, no cough, no change in tone. Mank was a good detective because he observed but didn't betray his own thoughts except when he wanted to. I admired the way he was acting now.

'There was nothing in the report about significant evidence being found on the floor of the basement,' Mank said. So he *had* read the report, even if the body was found in a precinct more than ten miles away. 'Brooker made a note of a small tuft of hair that he bagged next to the victim's head but it turned out not to be significant. It was his own hair.'

We were almost back to Mank's desk. 'Damien's or Brooker's?' I asked.

Now Mankiewicz did betray a feeling, just by turning and giving me a look that indicated he hadn't thought my remark was humorous. (It hadn't been intended as such.) 'The victim's,' he said.

'How did his hair get on the floor?' I asked.

Mank sat down behind his desk, where Ken was still standing, almost at attention, and watching. Only I would have recognized the amusement in his eyes. 'What?' Mank said.

'Damien was strangled with an extension cord,' I reminded him. 'What part of that process would have caused a small tuft of hair to fall off his head?'

Richard Mankiewicz was a classy enough man not to put his feet up on his desk to show me how relaxed he was. 'I honestly have no idea,' he said. 'What difference does it make?'

Something here was wrong and I couldn't figure out what it might be. 'Are you guys even trying to find out who killed Damien Van Dorn?' I said. 'That's a major inconsistency and you have no suspects that I'm aware of, so why don't you want to know about the only piece of physical evidence you have besides the body and the murder weapon?'

Mank looked like he'd been personally insulted, which I suppose he had, but indirectly. Ken continued to look lightly amused. I have no idea what I looked like because I was looking at them.

'Fran, in the past day I have had to call Van Dorn's mother and tell her what happened to her son. I've had to explain to her that we don't know yet who might have killed her son but that he might have been selling illegal drugs to people on campus, a little fact she obviously had no knowledge of before. And I've been given a really effective dressing down by my captain, who thinks I loafed on the missing person case to the point that the missing person got killed. So yeah, I'm trying to find out who killed Damien Van Dorn, and if you think I'm not, my guess is that you're not paying attention.'

It was the most I'd ever heard Mank say without interruption, and it had the reverse effect I think he was intending. I was becoming convinced that something about this investigation – maybe even involving Mank – was wrong, perhaps intentionally so. Why would the NYPD not want to find out who had killed Damien?

'I'm sorry to have given you that impression,' I said. I sounded meek even to myself. Was I back to caring what Mank thought about me?

He shook his head and became more like the man I'd known again. 'It's OK. It's just been a day, and it's still early.'

I said goodbye, Mank made some comment about talking later, I didn't respond to that, and then Ken and I left.

Once we were back out on the sidewalk, my brother looked over at me and said, 'Good thing you brought me along.'

FOURTEEN

Just because I couldn't think of anything else to do, I sent an email to the last address I had for my mother and then sat there for twenty minutes waiting for a response I was certain wouldn't come. I hate being stuck on a case.

Eliza had not posted on any social media site since before she had vanished. That would be too easy, I suppose.

Rainbow Zelensky was, according to Instagram, living in New York City (but had not posted a picture of herself, which I thought was odd), so that meant I had only to eliminate 8.468 million people to find her. The job was practically done before I began. Laura Rapinoe was pretty much dried up as a source of information and was probably mourning Damien full-time, so there was no point in calling her again. I felt awful for having broken the news to her and angry that no one else had ahead of me.

Ken and his mastery of online interconnectivity had not yet broken New Amsterdam University's student records other than the most basic ones, so we had no lead on Rainbow. But then, even with more than 8.4 million people living here, how many Rainbows could have been living in New York City?

Instagram seemed like it knew Rainbow better than anyone else I could reach, so I left a message for her on her Instagram page. She didn't answer any faster than my mother.

With no other brilliant ideas, and with Ken still trying to track down Malcolm X. Mitchell, I headed back to the campus of New Amsterdam University and went to the office of records and transcripts. Sometimes stat heads are the best people to ask. Especially when you can't think of anyone else.

On the subway getting there, though, I was thinking about Eliza. I had no idea if she'd left her father's apartment because she felt stifled there, or worse, or if Damien's pill business went deeper and she was somehow caught up in it. I felt like Rainbow Zelensky might be the key to it all. The trick was going to be finding Rainbow.

It's possible that my ruminating on all that was the reason I didn't notice the man in the WHO t-shirt sooner.

On first glance I thought he was advocating for the band. You don't see that logo a lot anymore, but it does pop up and some people just like retro clothing. So I didn't register the periods between the letters: 'W.H.O.'

Not until he approached me at the 42nd Street station did that logo make it into my brain, and it was too late. Before I looked at the man – thirties, mop of curly hair, medium height and weight – I heard him. He spoke in hushed tones, not an easy thing to make audible as people are heading for the exit on an MTA subway car.

'Look in Spain near Madrid,' he said. 'That's where they ought to be.'

And with that he ducked out of the train, half a second before the doors closed again. But I couldn't stop myself from calling after him: 'Malcolm?'

He was in the station and walking away at a brisk pace, so not only couldn't he hear me, but even if he did, he couldn't respond. I'd probably never see him again.

The only thing left to do was text Ken: *I think Malcolm X. was on the subway with me.*

I was in the subway so there was no way of knowing when he'd answer. I got out and walked to the New Amsterdam offices.

'So you're telling me there is no such person as Rainbow Zelensky.'

Don't get me wrong: I'm not against the occasional emotional outburst to get the information I need on a case. But I knew for a fact that Harold Lembeck, the assistant dean of students in charge of records, was *not* telling me there was no such person as Rainbow Zelensky. I knew what he was telling me was that he couldn't confirm or deny whether such a person was a student at New Amsterdam University, but I was tired of people not confirming or denying things. And the fact was, I didn't have anywhere I needed to be right now and I could easily outlast Harold until it was time for him to go home and explain to his wife why he hadn't been taking her phone calls all afternoon, that he'd had to deal with the enormous crazy lady.

'No, Ms Stein,' he said with slightly less patience than the time before. 'I am telling you no such thing. You have no authority to access our student records and so I'm trying to explain as plainly as possible that I can't give out that sort of information.'

The records office was not exactly a hub of wild activity. There was a central office, through which I had entered, and then two smaller private rooms, one that was assigned to Harold and the other, if the nameplate could be trusted, that housed Felicia Carteret, Ph.D. I bet it rankled Harold that he had no such degree listed after his name. No one else had been in the outer office when I'd gotten here, and there didn't seem to be any sound coming from outside now. So Harold had time to talk to me whether he liked it or not. And he didn't. Like it.

'I'm asking whether a person exists, Mr Lembeck,' I told him. 'I'm not asking for academic transcripts, disciplinary records or even Rainbow's middle name. I just need to find this person because the life of another one of your students is on the line and I think Rainbow can help me find her. Do you want to be responsible for withholding valuable information while the clock is ticking on Eliza Hennessey?'

(For the record, I had no idea if a clock was ticking on Eliza or if she was snorkeling off the coast of Aruba. But if I'd suggested the latter, I was fairly sure Harold would have been a little less motivated to help.)

'You're trying to manipulate me emotionally, Ms Stein.' Well, Harold definitely had my number. 'It's not my fault that Ms Hennessey is missing and my telling you anything that is clearly protected information will not change that. Under city and state law, I'm not allowed to give you any information, including letting you know whether a person by some random name you mention is or is not a student at this institution.'

My phone buzzed and there was my brother texting a response to my message from underground. Sometimes subway texts take a while to reach their destination, which is a metaphor for the subway. *What? What did you say to him? Should I come to where you are?*

Ken thought I was in danger when I could have easily flung Malcolm X. Mitchell on to another subway train from across the tracks if there had been a need for it. And if I were still on the subway and Malcolm was in some way threatening me. I texted back *No* and put my phone back in my pocket.

'I have information that has already been shared with the police,' I told Harold, 'that would indicate there was an active trade in certain prescription medications being sold on the black market on this campus, and that a young man who was a student here was not only doing some of the dealing, but ended up murdered yesterday. There is a sense of urgency here and I'd hate to have to let the *New York Post* know what I know.'

Harold, despite the black-rimmed eyeglasses and the short-sleeve dress shirt that was dying for a pocket protector, was not going to be a pushover. 'I'd prefer that to you telling them I gave you protected information I was not authorized to share,' he said.

The Force was strong with this one. I changed tactics. I coughed drily, in case I needed it. 'I'm willing to bet that if Rainbow Zelensky was *not* a student here, you'd be thrilled to tell me that so I would go away,' I said. I cleared my throat audibly.

'You are free to bet on anything you want, as long as it's legal in the state of New York.' Now he was being a wise-ass. That was a condition to which I could relate.

But he also had a stance from which he would not break. I broke into a coughing fit, leaning over and making the most grotesque noises. When I took in a deep breath, I looked over at the man behind the desk, who looked a mite alarmed. 'Water,' I croaked.

'What?' He truly hadn't understood. I'd been overplaying my role.

'Water,' I said more audibly and then coughed loudly again. This had better work or my throat would spend the next two days being scratchy for nothing.

'Yes, of course.' Harold got up and didn't exactly run (thanks a lot, buddy) but did walk briskly to the door and out into the hallway. I was glad he didn't have a bottle of water on his desk.

As soon as he was gone I rushed behind his desk, pulled a thumb drive out of my pocket and stood behind his screen (sitting in his chair seemed too much a violation of his privacy). I don't have Ken's computer skills, but I could find student records easily enough. I hustled what I thought were relevant files on to the drive and rushed back to my chair just in time for Harold to find me 'catching my breath' while looking what I hoped appeared to be anxiously toward the door. He was carrying a bottle of spring water and held it out to me.

I nodded gratefully as if incapable of speech, opened the bottle and took a long drink. What the hell, I'd been thirsty anyway. 'Thank you,' I breathed out when I came up for air.

'Not at all. Are you all right?' Maybe he wasn't such a bad guy after all.

I had to remember that I'd just had a major coughing fit and was probably hoarse as all get-out. I nodded. 'I think so. That happens sometimes.' Not to me, but I'm told it happens sometimes.

'You should see a doctor,' Harold said. 'Is there anything else you need?'

It was necessary to maintain the illusion that I had not just stolen the information I'd been nagging him to give me. 'How about Rainbow Zelensky's student file? I don't need to know her grades, just some contact information.'

'I am not permitted to confirm or deny any information about a person, whether they be a student here or not.' It was so comforting to have things back to normal.

'You can't blame a girl for trying,' I said.

'Sure I can.'

FIFTEEN

'So . . . wait,' Ken said. 'You saw Malcolm on the six train and he told you to look in Spain? For our parents?'

I was sitting on Ken's bed in our apartment and he was at his little pull-down wall desk (really a shelf) looking at his laptop screen. But we were at cross purposes here because I wanted Ken to perform his magic on the files I'd just . . . borrowed . . . from Harold at New Amsterdam, and all he wanted to talk about was the alleged WHO representative who somehow knew which subway train I might be taking and, for that matter, what I looked like. I preferred not to think about that for the time being.

'He wasn't that specific,' I told him for the third time. 'He said to look near Madrid because that was where they ought to be. He wasn't clear about who or what should be there, or why, or why he was telling me that, or at least fifty other questions I could have asked him if he hadn't disappeared into the Forty-second Street station. Sorry I hadn't expected to find our mystery man on the train this morning. I guess my paranoia isn't what it used to be. Now, how about Rainbow?' I pointed to his screen, as if he wouldn't have known where to look.

'I can hold two thoughts in my mind at the same time,' my brother said, which put him at least one ahead of what I'd have suspected. But he did start to click away at his keyboard and I saw things moving around on the screen. It's not that large a screen and I didn't want to lean over his shoulder because it makes Ken cranky. You wouldn't like Ken when he's cranky.

'Rainbow,' I reiterated.

He continued clicking away. 'Are we sure Rainbow is her real name?'

'The only thing I'm sure of today is that we're sitting here in this room trying to figure out two things at the same time,' I told him. 'Don't hold me responsible for anything else.'

'There's something like twenty-three thousand students in these files,' he grumped. 'Don't expect instant results.'

'How many Rainbow Zelenskys can there be?'

'Why would Mom and Dad be in Madrid?' Ken asked. But he was using the touchpad to do something on the screen, so I could assume he was still involved in his task.

'Maybe they're into bullfighting all of a sudden,' I said. 'We don't know that this guy is for real and we don't know why he'd be wanting us to look for our parents for any reason other than to help him find them. The last thing I want to do now is search Madrid. And while you're at it, look for Damien Van Dorn and Laura Rapinoe.'

Ken groaned a little for effect. We love each other, don't get me wrong, but a little sibling irritation is natural – far more than we are, now that I think of it. 'You sure you don't want me to find the Ark of the Covenant and the Holy Grail while you're at it?'

'And our parents, if you get a minute.'

'I don't think they went to New Amsterdam,' Ken said. But he was engaged in the task, staring at his screen with a look of complete intent. 'I did some pretty deep searches into Malcolm X. Mitchell and guess what I found.'

He didn't sound happy. 'I'm going to guess nothing,' I said.

'Right. First time today.' He pointed at his screen. 'Now this might be something.'

I didn't want to, but I leaned forward to look. Ken needed to get a bigger laptop. 'What am I looking at?' I asked.

'There is listed, in a survey of European literature class, a Janice Zelensky.' Ken was already splitting the screen to compare two pieces of data I couldn't have even located in front of my eyes. 'Janice would appear to be about the same age as Eliza, about a year younger than Damien.'

'They're college students. How much different are their ages going to be?' OK, so it was a cheap shot, but I didn't want to get my hopes up.

'Janice appears to live in Jersey City, not in the city, and doesn't take any classes with Eliza or Laura,' Ken said. 'In fact, she only takes two classes, which makes her a part-time student. I'd be surprised if she wasn't just a coincidence, but I'll keep checking.'

'Thanks,' I said, because I agreed that Janice probably had no involvement and therefore he could check in on her so I wouldn't have to. (It turned out later she was taking classes remotely and worked at a local movie theater in Jersey City. Ken called her and her response was, 'Eliza who? I never go to campus.')

'Well, I can search for Rainbow all you want, but so far there hasn't been a . . . hang on.' He did not point this time. He just pursed his lips in an expression that anyone else would have determined to be my brother kissing the air an inch in front of his face but I knew meant he was thinking.

'I'm hanging on,' I said after a few seconds. I didn't want him to forget.

'Laura said that Rainbow lived in Queens, right?' he asked out of nowhere.

She had, so I acknowledged that, wondering where he was going with it.

'Real-estate records are public information.' Ken started back on his keyboard and the information I'd done such a convincing job of fainting for left his screen. 'Queens gives us a lot less space to cover, and the fact that they're all college students means they'd have rented pretty recently. So . . . there.'

'Where?' I asked, but I was already kicking myself for not having thought of this before.

'In Long Island City,' Ken said. 'Here.' He pointed at the screen.

Sure enough, against all odds, there was a lease agreement that had been filed in Long Island City (which is not on Long Island but in Queens and don't ask me why) between a holding company and one Rainbow Zelensky, dated eight months earlier.

'So there really is a Rainbow Zelensky,' I said.

She was not living near the college, probably because that neighborhood would have been pretty pricey for the vast majority of college students. In fact, Rainbow was living in an apartment in Long Island City, in Queens. I'd have to change trains at Grand Central Terminal and would probably be keeping an eye out for Malcolm X. Mitchell the whole way. The life of an investigator. OK, this investigator. 'You want to come with me?' I asked Ken.

'Not really. Do you need me?'

I wanted to say I did, but I couldn't make a convincing case of it. If the guy I'd seen on the subway this morning had in fact been Malcolm, I could literally take him with one arm tied behind my back. He wasn't exactly imposing. Ken wasn't necessary for backup. So why was I nervous about this guy who had appeared from nowhere? Was it because of the last time (see *Ukulele of Death*)? 'No,' I said to my brother and the pause between the question and the answer compelled him to look me in the eye.

'You sure?' he said.

'I'm sure, but thanks. I'll keep in touch.'

'Yeah. Send a postcard.' Our touching moment was over. I picked up my bag and left.

I had learned that when I wanted to check behind myself on the street without being obvious about it, I could FaceTime someone and look at the part of the screen that showed my own image. But I'd just left Ken and I didn't want to call Mank right now (I was sorting out a few things there). Aunt Margie was working a shift at the radio station, reading news copy every twenty minutes and preparing it the rest of the time, so she was rarely accessible.

So I broke my own rule about not nagging people and called Shelly Kroft. For one thing, I wanted that rear-view mirror, but I also wanted Shelly to know I didn't just call her when I needed someone with access to the federal government to help me. I only had a three-block walk to the train and I knew Shelly wouldn't mind if I kept it quick. She answered on the second ring.

'I haven't found your buddy Malcolm X. yet,' she used as an opener.

'I'm just calling to talk,' I said. 'I don't know anything about your life anymore.'

'We talked about that a few months ago,' Shelly said. 'My life has changed so drastically in that time; I have a husband and three kids. Are you walking to the subway?'

'Guilty,' I said.

'That's OK. But I can't report much. I'm still marshaling like it's going out of style.'

I grinned, and I know that because I could see my face. I had to angle the phone backward more efficiently. 'Are your bosses still misogynists?'

'No,' she answered. 'They're just sexist. They don't hate women; they just think they're better because they're men.'

'Come to New York and be a private investigator,' I offered. 'I won't be the least bit sexist if you work for me.'

Shelly laughed. I hadn't been a hundred percent kidding. 'I lied before. I actually do have something on your alleged WHO guy.'

Malcolm! 'You don't have a picture of him, do you?' Then I'd know if my 'pal' on the train had been who I'd thought he was.

She laughed again at my enthusiasm. 'Afraid not,' Shelly said. 'Most of what I can tell you is negative. He's not in any way an employee of the World Health Organization, although I don't have complete access to their employment data, and he is not an employee of the federal government, at least not the ones they keep on the books, like me.'

Damn! All I could find out about this guy was who he wasn't. 'So he's probably using a fake name?'

'Or he's an accountant from Milwaukee who wants to have some fun with your brother's head,' Shelly suggested. 'He probably has no idea at all what he's talking about. But I do have one lead to follow and I'm giving it to you because I know you don't have enough to do yet.'

No one behind me seemed the least bit suspicious and I was getting tired of holding my phone up near my head. 'You're too good to me,' I said.

'I know, but it's OK. Here's the lead. There is, believe it or not, a Malcolm X. Mitchell who lives in New York. I'm guessing it's the person your guy saw listed online one day and decided to use his name.'

I stopped at the subway station because reception in the tunnel is just impossible, no matter what the MTA says. 'Who is he?' I asked.

'As far as I can tell, he works at a Duane Reade.'

OK. 'The drug store?' Why not? He claimed to know about health care. Maybe he was a pharmacist.

'No, Duane Reade the ice-cream counter. Yes, the drug store. As far as I can tell, he's there stocking shelves as part of a cooperative employment program.'

'So he's got some kind of a disability?' Probably not the guy I saw on the subway, then.

'Yeah. It's not clear but it seems like a developmental issue. Even I can't dig into HIPAA files.'

Shelly was probably right; this version of Malcolm probably was not the one who had contacted Ken or unsettled me on the train. He'd probably just seen the name somewhere and thought it would be fun to use it. But you have to follow up on every lead you have until you get an answer. 'Where does Mr Mitchell live?' I asked.

'I told you I was giving you the lead for *you* to follow up on,' Shelly said with a grin in her voice.

Just for that I walked down the stairs into the subway. I'd text Shelly when I got to Queens.

SIXTEEN

I didn't bother telling Ken about the possibility of a Malcolm X. Mitchell in the city before I went to find Rainbow Zelensky. The lure of finding the guy that our guy stole his name from (after yet another guy, who clearly wasn't involved in this case) wasn't exactly tantalizing.

Long Island City wants you to think it's on Long Island, which it isn't. It wants you to believe it's as chic as areas of Brooklyn, and hasn't quite gotten there yet. It *really* wants you to buy in on it being as cool as Manhattan, and let's be real.

I got off the seven train at Hunters Point, which is the seat of gentrification in Long Island City. Pretty soon we riffraff who don't have millions at our disposal won't even be able to have dinner at a restaurant in Hunter's Point. You already can't buy an apartment there unless you have a very large amount of working capital on hand.

Wine bars, coffee bars and just regular bars were everywhere, but the building in which Rainbow Zelensky was living wasn't all that different from the one in which Ken, Aunt Margie and I lived. It had four floors, because if you have five you need to install an elevator and that's expensive. That's if your building was put up after 1960. Before then, you could have all the floors you wanted and tell people they were getting exercise when they brought groceries home.

The information Ken had given me indicated Rainbow was on the third floor of the building just two blocks from the subway, which would have made it easier for her to commute to New Amsterdam. Long Island City is as close as you can get to Manhattan without actually paying Manhattan rents, but it didn't offer the same rates as say, Sandusky, Ohio, either.

Their building was brick, no surprise there, and had a door with very serious locks, which also wasn't a shock. Luckily Ken had given me the apartment number because there were no names listed on the buzzers outside the main entrance. I pushed the one for 3-C and waited.

Nothing happened. Perhaps Rainbow was out. On the other hand, the way this case had been going I had to recall that the last time I looked for a friend of Eliza Hennessey's he had recently been strangled with an extension cord.

I was probably strong enough to force the door open, but that would set off any number of alarms and I didn't need to be surrounded by cops today. The paperwork is excruciating and they tend to get antsy around the sight of a larger-than-life woman. Or so I've found.

The usual option is to wait for someone to walk out of the building and hold the door when they open it. But it was a quiet part of the day, just after lunch for most people, and traffic in this area was not exactly hopping right now. I could wait an hour for someone to exit or enter.

Of course, the time-honored ploy is pushing all the buttons and hoping someone in one of the apartments won't buzz down to find out who you are and instead simply unlock the front door. That's not as effective as it was pre-pandemic, because people were in their apartments and angsty, and those feelings have not entirely vanished as the rest of the protocols have loosened up. But it was worth a try.

There were twelve buttons and I pressed all except the one to Rainbow's apartment, which I'd already tried and come up dry. No one buzzed me in, which I found a disheartening commentary on the state of community in New York City. I mean, not one person took a chance that their doorbell had beeped because someone needed something other than to commit breaking and entering. I mean, that *was* what I was trying to do, but they didn't know that. I tried again, and once again got no response. People just don't trust people anymore.

I didn't take the time to lament this fundamental deterioration of comradery in my town because there was still the problem of getting into Rainbow Zelensky's apartment and seeing if Rainbow was, you know, alive and home at the same time. So I assessed the building again.

It was a brick building, fairly unremarkable, with the usual concrete foundation and concrete extensions a few inches out under each window to support people's window boxes, air conditioners or the occasional pie on the sill (back in the day the building was designed). There was a basement apartment, which as I studied the building seemed to make the plan forming in my brain more plausible. But that would only work if there was the same configuration at the back of the building.

I walked around the corner, casual as could be, and noted with some relief that the building stood alone, not attached to the one next door or in the back. Behind it was an alley that didn't have any direct view from the street or the far side. I could operate with a decent expectation that I wouldn't be seen.

As I've hopefully made clear, Ken and I are bigger and stronger than most. I do belong to a gym to help tone my muscles and keep them strong, but I go easy on the weights because I don't want to attract attention. I knew, though, that my arms and legs were sufficiently strong to accomplish my task.

The windows of each apartment were visible, and a few of them were open, but there was another one at the end of each hallway that would become my target. I didn't want to barge in on someone in their living room, or worse, anywhere else in a New York apartment.

Standing at the far side of the building to keep my visibility low, and using a wooden box that someone had helpfully deposited in the alley, I started to execute my plan, remembering that under no circumstances should I look down. I have a thing with heights.

You guessed it.

The basement apartment actually started me off well because there was that thin protrusion under each window to use as a foothold. I put my left foot on the box and pushed to give my right some momentum. Then it was half-jump, half-lift to the next concrete protrusion on the floor above, and my feet were on the window sill and off the ground. I was up to the first floor. Two to go.

I've never done any rock climbing – because of the height thing and because it just doesn't appeal – so I didn't have any experience to (pardon the expression) fall back on. My instincts told me to keep looking up and not jump to the next level so much as motivate myself toward it. Although some spring in my knees did help propel me, I won't lie. I was equally buoyed by the fact that I'd worn jeans today. A skirt would have been, let's say, awkward. I also had the knowledge that no one was directly below me. Or there hadn't been when I started. I wasn't looking down now.

The climb actually went pretty smoothly. I did scrape my fingers and palms up a bit and put my hand into something that I'd prefer not to identify, but I made it to the third level, where Rainbow's apartment would be, before realizing I could have climbed to the first-floor window, let myself in, and taken the stairs. I might be a large person but I'm not necessarily a giant intellect. And the fact of the matter is I probably wouldn't have done it anyway because the first-floor window was closed and I wouldn't have wanted to break the window. Some poor super would have had to replace it. I climb up for the working man.

My luck held when the stairwell window on the third floor was open. I was holding myself very close to the wall because falling was not an option, so being able to open it with just my right hand was especially useful. I made it into the stairwell without a major incident but was lamenting my lack of wipes to get whatever that was off my hand. I had slung the straps of my bag over my head so I wouldn't have to do without any of my other things. I put my feet down on the stairwell and heaved the traditional sigh of relief.

Inside it was cooler and I suddenly realized I'd been sweating pretty heavily on my climb. Even superbeings react to exertion. I reached into my bag after I released it from my neck and pulled out a packet of facial tissues, which were sadly inadequate to the task on my hand but blotted the perspiration from my neck just a bit.

I walked down the hall until I saw the door marked 3-C. I stopped at the door for a moment and thought about what I might find. I do better if I prepare for the worst and then adjust up if possible. If Rainbow was dead, that meant someone had it in for this whole group of students and Eliza was either already gone or could be next. If Rainbow simply wasn't home, my only option was to wait until she got here. I didn't climb up a building to go back to the seven train and head home.

The first move was to knock as if I was just there to visit.

Whoever was inside would know they didn't buzz me in, but one must at least try to respect social norms. And breaking down the door with one kick, even after the climb, would have been easy but way too loud. So I knocked.

You'll be shocked to find out that no one answered. But I could hear someone moving around inside there, trying to be quiet. A person with normal ears wouldn't have known.

I knocked again, more insistently. 'Hello?' I said.

A voice came from inside, muffled as you might expect. 'No one's here.'

It seemed silly to point out that I had evidence to the contrary, specifically that someone inside the apartment had said there was no one inside the apartment. I decided not to sound threatening, but knocked again. Then I decided that probably had sounded threatening.

'Can I come in?'

'She's not home.' That could mean a lot of things. I decided to press on.

'My name is Fran Stein,' I said. 'I'm here to help.' That seemed general enough. I could have been there to help with their internet connection.

'Go away.' That was direct.

'I really can't. I need to talk to you. That's all I'm going to do, I promise. Can you open the door so we don't have to shout?' It's baby steps. Rainbow probably had a chain on the door. Get her to open it and you can talk more quietly and soothingly than you can through wood. Investigator 101.

There was no answer, but after a moment I heard the locks being opened in the door. There were three, at least one of them a deadbolt. You think that's unusual. That's because you don't live in New York.

What I wasn't expecting was for the door to swing open; I'd expected the conversation-through-the-chain thing, and had promised myself I would push the chain off of its screws with my palm. It was a little disconcerting because there was no one in my direct line of sight when the door opened. It had been left to swing into the room in order to give the person who opened it time to get out of the way, and out of my eyeline.

I don't carry a weapon with me, although Ken owns a gun

and sometimes takes it with him when we're on a case. I wasn't wishing I had one now, because I can generally take care of myself without help, but I did start to understand the feeling of (probably false) comfort that could come with having something in my hand. I stepped inside carefully, like I'd been taught at the police academy before my very brief job at the NYPD.

Of course, the NYPD would have been disappointed with me for not having a gun. That's only one of my complaints about the NYPD.

'Hello?' I said again when I was inside. I closed the door behind me, which was likely foolish; suppose I had to get out in a hurry? Climbing back down after jumping out the window didn't seem like the best plan.

'What do you want?' The voice was indistinct in so many ways, but the one certainty was that it was scared.

'Can I come in to wash my hands?' I thought that would get me in to look around and get my hands clean. Win-win.

'No.' Lose-lose.

'I'm not here to hurt anybody.' Was that a bad choice? Why even bring it up if you're not going to do it?

'Uh-huh.' The voice was coming from another room, maybe a bedroom in the back. It wasn't a large apartment and the living room I was in took up most of it. There was a galley kitchen to my left and a bathroom behind it. The only other room had to be the bedroom and it was quite probably close to microscopic. I could hear a cat complaining about being behind the closed bedroom door. I'd been in apartments like this before.

'I'm really not. I'm a private investigator. I've been hired to find Eliza Hennessey and I thought you might be able to help me. Her father is very worried.' That last part was in case Eliza had indicated that Brian was a less than sympathetic character.

'Why?'

OK, that was a stumper. 'Because Eliza's been missing for days now and he doesn't know where she is. Because a friend of hers from school is in a lot of trouble for dealing pills and he's afraid she might be involved. Because he wants to help and he doesn't know how.'

You'll note I did not mention Damien's murder. This was already a terrified person and they would have had no idea whether

I was involved in what happened to Damien or not. No sense complicating the situation if it wasn't necessary.

'I don't believe you,' the voice said, but it was from the hallway to the bedroom. And it was being said from behind a pistol. That was all I could see at the moment. Moving quickly seemed like a remarkably bad idea, so I anchored my feet to the floor and put my hands down at my sides so they could see I was holding no weapon.

'Everything I said is true,' I reiterated. 'Can you help me?'

The figure in the hallway took a step into the living room, and therefore into the light. And the gun was the least stressful thing I had to deal with now.

'You're Eliza Hennessey,' I said.

'I know that,' Eliza answered. 'Wow. You're really big. What are you doing here, really?'

SEVENTEEN

'You don't need the gun, Eliza,' I said. That seemed reasonable. To me.

'I don't know that just because you say so.' Her voice was getting out of terrified mode and more into something approaching swagger, which seemed inappropriate if she wasn't planning on firing that pistol. 'He hired you to get me and bring me back.'

'Not if you don't want to go,' I told her. 'Only if you do. But it'll help if you'll tell me where Rainbow is and why you're here. It would also really relax the situation if you'd put down the gun. As you can see, I'm a lot bigger and stronger than you so, believe me, I can take it away from you if I want to.'

'Only if I don't shoot you first,' Eliza said. It was a valid point, but not one I preferred to dwell on at the moment. Ken and I are strong but we're far from invincible.

'What reason would you have to shoot me?' I asked. I thought the question made sense.

'What reason would you have to try to grab my gun?' she countered.

'Not getting shot,' I said. 'It's a life goal for me not to get shot.'

Eliza gave me a very interesting look, one that indicated she was taking me seriously and weighing the point I was making, which had started as a way to lighten the mood a bit. She was a thin girl with relatively short hair, not surprising since she'd just come out to her father a few months ago, and a very generic face. She was wearing makeup, perhaps just a bit too much but that's a matter of taste. Her arms looked like she worked out fairly regularly and her gaze held no trace of nonsense. She was a serious person, probably in a desperate situation. But I didn't know if she was aware of that.

After that long moment she put the gun down on a table next to the sofa and sat on the sofa, where it would be within arm's length if I decided to rush her, I guessed. 'OK,' she said. 'What are you really doing here?'

I kept standing. For one thing, the sofa was the only seat in the room and plopping myself down next to Eliza like we were going to watch Netflix seemed unbusinesslike. Also, emphasizing my height advantage seemed like an intelligent ploy. I ignored the fact that my palms had small dots of blood on them from climbing up the building. A little antibiotic cream would do all that was needed.

'Just what I told you,' I said. 'Your dad hired my firm to find you because you haven't been home and you're not answering your phone or your email. He's worried about you. I told him you were above the age of majority, legally an adult, and I wouldn't try to bring you back if you don't want to go. But I need to know why you're here and what your plans are, because there are some very bad people out there who might very well be looking for you right now.'

Eliza's eyes went dead, emotionless, which made her look angry. 'You're just trying to scare me,' she said.

'I promise you I'm not. Look. I didn't want to have to dump this on you, but Damien is dead. Someone killed him.'

She stared at me. For what felt like a very long time. When her voice came it was like a hiss. 'You're *lying*.'

'I wish I were, but I'm not. Laura Rapinoe says he was planning on ambushing two guys who were following him around and threatening him. He went to an apartment building in the Bronx and my brother and I found his body in the basement. Someone strangled him.'

Eliza wanted not to believe me; I could see that on her face. But she knew what I was saying at least held the circumstances of the truth. I knew about Laura. I knew of the two men following Damien. Did she know about the building in the Bronx? She might. So she couldn't banish the thought just because she didn't trust me.

'Why?' she asked finally, in a small voice.

'I don't know yet. I don't know who it was. I'm told there's someone named Julio but you're not supposed to call him that. Do you know anything about him?'

She shook her head. 'Not really. I wasn't really involved in any of the stuff Damien was doing. He was just my friend from school. He understood . . . about me.'

'About you being trans?'

Eliza looked me right in the eye, probably expecting me to disapprove and getting ready to defy me. 'Yeah.'

'But Damien wasn't a trans man, was he?' I asked.

'No. He just knew what it meant for the world to tell you you're different when you know you're just you. He was mixed race and lived part-time with both parents so he thought he never belonged anywhere.' She shifted on the sofa, away from the gun, which I was pleased to see. She wasn't thinking about it anymore.

'Is that why you felt you had to leave home?' I asked. I thought I was making a smooth segue. 'Because you thought you belonged somewhere else?'

As ever under such circumstances, I was wrong. 'That wasn't my home; that was my father's home, and I'm not who he wanted me to be. I never was!'

'I'm not doubting that,' I told her. I was keeping my voice even, hopefully calming. I wasn't going to say that I understood how she felt, because even though I know what it is to be different (believe me!), I had no idea what it was like to be Eliza. 'Was your father difficult about it? Is that why you didn't tell him you were leaving?' From Brian Hennessey's perspective, Eliza's move was unpredictable and somewhat cruel. He thought he was coming around to being very understanding about his daughter. Eliza clearly had other opinions.

She spoke very slowly, considering each word. 'My father . . . thinks I'm going to change back, like I wasn't me from the day I was born. He and my mom assigned me this identity that wasn't ever me. He's not going to get over that.'

I nodded, not necessarily agreeing with her assessment of Brian but indicating that I was sympathetic to her situation. 'Maybe you're not giving him enough credit.'

'I *knew* you would say something like that! He's paying you, so you're on his side!' She glanced at the gun, but I knew she wasn't contemplating shooting me.

'I'm not on a side,' I told her. 'Yes, he hired me and he wanted me to find you. I found you. I don't have to bring you back, and you don't have to go back, but I think it's common courtesy to let someone who loves you know that you're OK and maybe keep the lines of communication open, or leave it so they can be.'

I couldn't read Eliza's face for two reasons. 1. She was being enigmatic and 2. I didn't have time. There was loud banging on the apartment door as soon as I was finished speaking.

'NYPD! Open up!' It sounded, if I remembered correctly, like Merchant.

Eliza's eyes turned to slits. 'The cops. Why did you call the cops?' She leaned back toward the gun, which is exactly what you don't want when the police are outside your door.

'I didn't call them. You should put that gun away and let them in. You haven't done anything illegal.' I took a second. 'Have you?'

Eliza had looked at the gun with some fear when I'd told her to hide it, something that probably wouldn't have gone over well with the NYPD anyway. She picked it up and stuffed it under the sofa cushion, which was the equivalent of putting up a sign over the couch that read 'GUN HERE.' With an arrow.

'Um . . . no.' The least convincing denial I'd heard in quite some time. 'Not really.' Worse.

I took a step forward to loom over her more efficiently as the banging on the door resumed. I spoke quietly but with, I hoped, authority. 'Your best course of action is to let those cops in and tell them absolutely everything you know,' I said. 'You're only making it worse if you don't.'

She gave me a look that could curdle milk that had just left the cow. 'You think that's how it works for trans women?' she said. 'They put us in jail cells with *men*! They think we're *men*! I'm not giving into the cops!'

It was quite probable she had a point; the NYPD doesn't have a great record when it comes to LGBTQ+ issues. Neither does any other police department. Eliza probably wasn't in physical danger, but that wasn't certain and they weren't here by accident. They'd decided she was a suspect in Damien's murder and figured they could find her in Rainbow's apartment.

Or had I led them here by accident?

'I've gotta get out of here,' she said. She sounded like a child. A very frightened child.

There just wasn't time to think. If somehow my investigation had led the police to what turned out to be Eliza's door, this was at least partially my responsibility. And this suspect wasn't going to be especially sympathetic in the eyes of the law or a jury of her peers, if they could find any.

'Will the cat be OK if you leave for a while?' I asked.

'The cat'll be OK. It's not my cat.'

I walked to the window and opened it. 'OK,' I said, pointing to my shoulders. 'Climb on.'

EIGHTEEN

For the record, climbing down a building with a 19-year-old on your back is not easier than climbing up all by yourself. Thank goodness the apartment's bedroom window (the one we'd chosen after a moment's thought) faced that back alley and not the street or I'd have been on the front page of the *New York Post* the next morning, after a night of watching myself inch down three floors on some 24-hour news channel or another.

Eliza, for the record, was not crazy about the mode of transportation she took to the ground, but when it turned out that the apartment did not contain a rope and the pounding on the apartment door seemed likely to lead to a broken lock, she found herself without options and did as I suggested, which ended up as me hoisting her over my shoulder in a fireman's carry and doing the climb up in reverse. Less jumping, because I could hang by my fingers and that got me fairly close to the next ledge. The last floor I just lowered her down and then jumped.

Once on the ground, the question of where to go became most urgent. Taking Eliza back to Brian's apartment did not seem to jive with her preferences, and probably would have led to another visit from the cops if they were truly after her in connection to Damien's murder. Going back to my apartment with Ken, if I had unintentionally led the NYPD to Rainbow's door, seemed equally ill-advised. I texted Ken as soon as we were around the corner and trying to look nonchalant while walking to the subway.

Need a place to crash with a friend for some time. Ideas?

Immediately my brother, who wasn't actually born in a sports bar (or anywhere else) but should have been, sent back, *So you and the cop are back on good terms?*

He's hilarious. Just ask him; he'll tell you.

Serious.

That got him in the right mode. I could tell because Ken didn't answer right away. I was trying to keep Eliza from being noticeable, and walking by my side it was a decent bet people would be concentrating on me. But we were not, by any stretch of the imagination, blending in.

Igavda's place. That was my brother's suggestion, to go to the apartment of our one employee, a woman he'd been ogling surreptitiously since she was hired. It didn't seem like a great set-up, but I was in a hurry and it was unquestionably a place no detective would think of looking.

Send me the address and then delete all these texts. Yes, it would be possible to drag this conversation out of the bowels of my iPhone if things went that far, but any obstacles you put in your adversary's path will at worst slow them down and that's never bad.

That was what had happened in the past ten minutes. The police – all police – had become my adversaries. I'd have to text Mank later and tell him we were enemies, in case he thought that we weren't now.

We got on the seven train and headed toward Manhattan, which admittedly is not exactly a long trip. Luckily we were heading in that direction and not the other, because the seven going toward Flushing was going to be packed with Mets fans heading to Citi Field for tonight's game. You have to get there early to avoid the lines at Shake Shack. I'm told.

Igavda lived in Washington Heights, up near the George Washington Bridge, so we changed to the four train and headed uptown. I hoped Ken had sent Igavda home with her key because there was no way Eliza and I would be able to look inconspicuous in her hallway, assuming we could even get inside the front door. No more building climbing today. It was a hard-and-fast rule.

All that proved to be moot when we walked out of the subway and walked west to a spot about a block from Igavda's place. I'd been educated in criminal justice, I'd been trained and employed as a New York City police officer and I'd been a private investigator for a while now.

I knew unmarked cop cars when I saw them, and they were flocked around Igavda's building like paparazzi near the British royal family. (Someday someone will have to explain that fascination to me.) I felt my stomach clench up a bit.

'Stop,' I said to Eliza. 'It's not safe there.'

She looked at me, wondering. 'How is that possible?'

'The only plausible explanation is that at least my, and prob- ably both of our cell phones are being monitored,' I told her. Reflexively I put my hand on my front jeans pocket, where my phone was betraying me even as I spoke. 'You need to turn yours off. We might end up having to destroy them or at least throw them away.'

Eliza looked positively stricken. 'What?' I'm not young enough to be of the generation that can't conceive of life without a smartphone. But I'm close.

'They can find us if we use them, and maybe if we don't,' I told her. 'You can't get in touch with anyone right now or the police will know where we are within seconds.'

She blanched.

'Who have you been in touch with since we left Rainbow's place?' I asked Eliza.

'Nobody,' she said, and the way she looked directly into my eyes convinced me she was lying.

There was no sense in arguing with her; what was done was done. 'Well from now on you can't get in touch with *anybody*,' I told her, trying to put the authority of adulthood into my voice. (Even though she was technically an adult, I was clearly the authority figure here; at least I thought so.) 'Even Googling something at this point would connect with a tower and if we connect with a tower they can come close to locating us. If they've read my texts, they can read yours. So we have to be extremely careful.'

That, of course, was the moment I pulled my mobile phone out of my pocket and started texting Ken. Eliza's jaw dropped a couple of feet and her eyes screamed, 'TRAITOR!' even as I explained, 'I'm not going to say anything that will help them, and we're going to leave this place *now*.'

But I had to get in touch with Ken. I took a picture of Igavda's building and sent it to him with the caption: *Not safe. Heading to that place.* He'd know what that meant. But I had to add: *Bring charge.*

Because my energy had been waning since the climb up Rainbow's building, and if I didn't plug in soon I would completely run out of gas.

NINETEEN

I turned my cell phone completely off as soon as we turned away from Igavda's building and headed for the subway, but I insisted on two things: that Eliza turn her phone off as well (which was not the most popular suggestion ever), and that we head for a different subway, one completely on the other side of the island.

She complained most of the way and especially when I saw her pull ear buds out of her pocket and reach for her phone. 'No music,' I said.

'You're not my mother.' The classic response.

'No. I'm just trying to keep you out of jail.' Luckily we were on the six train on Lexington Avenue and absolutely no one was listening to us. (Most, to be honest, had ear buds in.)

Never let it be said that a 19-year-old woman can't pout as well as a 14-year-old girl, because Eliza still had her chops. She might not have looked like a girl back then (or maybe she did; I had no idea) but she was identifying that way and that was all that mattered.

We got off the train at Bleecker Street and started walking south. I knew where we were heading but felt no obligation to mention that to Eliza, who was reaching into her jacket pocket regularly until I noticed how low that side of her jacket was hanging down on her hip.

No. She didn't.

I spoke loud enough for her to hear but not for anyone else. Someone passing by would have thought we were having a casual conversation. 'You brought the gun with you?'

Eliza looked at me as if I'd asked whether she had brought her legs. 'Of course I did,' she said. 'Feels like we're in a pretty dangerous situation, don't ya think?'

Both boys and girls are harmed by the image of John McClane taking on a small army with a handgun and winning. Worse, they are bombarded with images of schools being shot up with automatic weapons and think the only way to stop that is to outgun the shooters. This is not going to stop any time soon, and it had clearly gotten deep into Eliza's thought processes.

'We're not going to be in a shootout with anyone,' I said. 'You only made it more dangerous for us by taking that thing with you.' A thought struck me. 'What do you know about Damien's business that you're not telling me?'

She sniffed like a society matron being told a homeless man had walked into the gala. 'I told you I didn't use any of that stuff.'

'Yeah, but you didn't say that you weren't involved.'

'Well, I wasn't.' She couldn't even make that sound a trifle sincere.

'Who's after you besides the police?' We were getting near the spot to meet Ken. It's only because I know my brother is actually a very intelligent, resourceful man that the thought was comforting. Also that he could easily beat up anyone who came after Eliza. Not that I couldn't, but you like to have two of us when you can.

'Nobody,' Eliza answered. She didn't trust me, which wasn't terribly surprising seeing as how, from her point of view, I'd shown up and brought the cops to her door. On the other hand, I'd literally put her on my back to get her out of the situation, and you'd think that would count for something. I kept forgetting she was still a teenager, and one who'd been through a lot more than most.

'I get why you're lying, but you're still lying,' I told her. 'I can't explain to you why, but I understand what it's like to feel that the world thinks you're not who you know you are. I know you feel like you can't open up to anyone. But I'm telling you that right now I'm your very best shot at not going to jail or getting killed. So the sooner you learn to trust me, the easier it's going to be for both of us.' I didn't add, 'Come with me if you want to live,' because I wasn't sure if she'd seen the second *Terminator* movie.

'People don't think I'm me.' Eliza spoke quietly, which for normal people would be hard to hear on a street in lower Manhattan. 'Do you know what *that* feels like?'

'I'm sorry. I shouldn't have suggested we have the same

circumstances because we don't.' I pushed open the door to a tiny, as nondescript as possible corner coffee shop and indicated she should walk inside.

'That's where we're going?' She couldn't believe we'd come all this way on the train to get to such an ordinary place. What she didn't realize was that the lack of outstanding features was the point. Nobody would be looking for us here.

Ken was already seated at a table as far away from the windows as he could have managed in this place. It wasn't crowded but it wasn't empty either. My brother, ever the gentleman, did not stand when we approached. In reality, that was probably a smart move. People notice when Ken stands up.

As soon as we sat down and I'd introduced Eliza and Ken, he pulled a small paper bag out of his jacket pocket (which was probably why he was wearing a jacket on a warm day) and handed it to me. I knew it would hold the charger I'd need to keep my body's energy at a workable level once I found a place with an electrical socket. Worse came to worst I'd sequester myself in the diner's women's restroom and give myself a boost there, but I'd rather not for any number of reasons.

I got Ken up to date on the odyssey Eliza and I had undertaken, and why. He listened carefully and didn't act like a giant frat boy when I was talking, so I knew he was on his best behavior on Eliza's behalf.

He looked at me when I was finished. 'So you think they were there to arrest her for Damien's murder? Based on what?'

It was a good question, and I had time to think about it because the server, clearly an NYU student trying to pay for her dorm, came to ask what we'd like to order. I got a turkey club because that's what I get at a diner when I haven't bothered to look at the menu. I'm sure Ken and even Eliza ordered food as well but I honestly don't remember what their preferences might have been. My mind was elsewhere.

The server headed for the kitchen and Ken looked expectantly at me. 'All I have is that Brooker and Merchant were asking about Eliza more than they should have and even Mank brought up her name once Damien was dead. I can't imagine they have any actual physical evidence.' I turned toward Eliza, who was staring sort of dreamily at Ken. She probably thought he was the brain in the family now. 'You weren't down in that basement in the Bronx with Damien, were you?' I asked her.

'What? No.' Ken probably could have told me that her respiration had risen a bit and her breathing had gotten shallow. I knew some of that, but didn't need to know it to understand that Eliza was lying again.

I looked at my brother with a little request on my face and he caught it: I wanted him to respond instead of me because Eliza would respond less defensively. Maybe.

'You didn't even go down there to bring him coffee or something?' Ken said.

I knew Eliza hadn't been aware of Damien's death because she had proven to be a bad liar and she'd been shocked when I'd told her about it. So I was sure she hadn't been present when Damien was killed. But if she'd been there earlier, her DNA could be found on the premises, and that would be bad.

'No,' Eliza said, then her eyes opened wider and she bit her lip. 'Well, maybe.'

Oh, boy.

'Maybe?' I said. Eliza shot me a glance that indicated I could take the rest of lunch off.

'I mean, I wasn't on the stakeout with him or anything,' she went on. 'But I did go there when he was deciding where he was going to wait. I didn't *do* anything.'

'That's true,' Ken said. He was taking back over because he was getting better results. I saw the wisdom in it but it annoyed me. Who'd climbed down a building with that girl on their back, after all? 'But your presence there could be detected and it could lead the cops the wrong way.'

Eliza looked sad, which made a good deal of sense. 'It's all crazy,' she said. That didn't tell me anything but how she was feeling, which was valuable but not helpful at the moment.

Our lunch orders came, and I suppose we started to eat. I had more questions than I could deal with at one time. Why were the cops focusing on Eliza? *Were* they focusing on Eliza, or were they looking for Rainbow Zelensky? After all, they'd come to Rainbow's apartment. What did Damien's murder have to do with either of them, and why didn't Julio want you to call him Julio? Who was monitoring my cell phone? Did the NYPD have that capacity so quickly? Wouldn't they have had to get a search warrant or an order by a judge? Why didn't this turkey club have any mayo on it?

'Tell us about Rainbow,' I said to Eliza.

'What about Rainbow?' Because the question had come from me and not from Ken, Eliza sounded suspicious.

'Just what she's like, how you know her, how did she know Damien, stuff like that,' Ken said. I decided to keep an eye out for the server to get some mayonnaise and let my brother handle the questioning. Was I being petty? Yeah, probably. But I'd already had a rough day and it was just lunchtime.

I remember now that Eliza was eating an Impossible burger with a side salad. She was determined to be healthy and not harm the Earth. And the cops thought she had strangled Damien Van Dorn.

'Rainbow doesn't have anything to do with any of this,' Eliza said. Oddly, she looked amused when she said it.

After a bit I managed to attract our server's attention and mayo was allegedly on its way. I turned my attention back to Eliza (after checking the diner's windows for any sign of encroaching cops) but let my brother continue the interview.

'Did you introduce Rainbow to Damien?' he asked.

Eliza looked more amused. 'I don't think Rainbow ever met Damien.'

That was news. 'So Rainbow wasn't tied to whatever Damien was up to?' Ken asked before I could.

Eliza shook her head, looking at him like she'd lost confidence in his intelligence, which I could understand. 'No, that was Laura. She was the one who was all into Damien.'

Laura Rapinoe. 'Were they a couple?' I asked.

OK, so I probably shouldn't have spoken, but just try to sit there and be silent when you're on the run from the police. I dare you. '*I don't know*,' Eliza said emphatically. 'They didn't tell me about their sex life.'

'Laura told me you were "obsessed" with Damien,' I told her.

Eliza's eyes became fiery. 'That's a *lie*.'

'So it's possible Damien and Laura were involved.' I just wanted to lock that down, all the while wondering if Laura had lied about it to shield herself.

'I *don't know*, I said!' Eliza glared at me and, frankly, it was a little intimidating, given that she was about a foot shorter than I am.

'How about you?' Ken asked. He's so subtle. 'Are you involved with Rainbow, or someone else?'

'I am *not* involved with Rainbow,' Eliza answered. She chuckled at the very idea. 'I'm single right now. Why?'

'We don't know what we're dealing with yet,' Ken said. 'The more information we have, the better off we are.' Eliza nodded, accepting what he said. Go figure.

It seemed to me that attraction is attraction and if Rainbow were interested in her, Eliza would have known it by now. But it was that rare moment when I was disciplined enough to keep from blurting out what I was thinking. It took enormous effort on my part.

'We have to focus on the present situation,' I said. 'Right now the police are after you and, if they know about me, they're after me too. We have to assume they are because they knew we were going to Igavda's apartment by monitoring my phone.' I looked at Ken. 'How could they do that so fast?'

He shrugged. 'Think your pal Mankiewicz turned you in?'

No. That couldn't be. Mank hadn't dropped a dime on much more explosive information about me, even to the point that Ken didn't know he was aware of it. Besides, that just wasn't the kind of guy Mank was. 'I don't know,' I said. 'Maybe.' But I felt sick saying it. The mayo came and I didn't even want it anymore.

'Who's Mankiewicz?' Eliza asked.

I shook my head. 'He's not our problem,' I told her. 'Right now we have to make decisions. I'm guessing that you don't want to do what I think you should do, which is go back to your dad's place and then answer any questions the police have when they find you there.'

Eliza looked like I'd suggested she go out on a date with my old pal Count Dracula. 'God no,' she said. 'The cops are no better to trans people than the maniacs who track us down and kill us just for existing. And my dad . . .' Nothing followed that. I guessed there was still considerable unfinished business between Brian and his daughter.

'Is it OK if I at least get word to your dad that you're OK?' Ken asked her. 'He's really worried about you.'

Eliza gave that some thought. 'If that's all you tell him, it's all right,' she said. 'I don't want him doing anything crazy.'

'Like hiring detectives to find you?' I said, but nobody laughed. 'You'll have to be *extremely* discreet,' I told Ken.

'No kidding.' This just wasn't a good table for me.

I decided I'd talk to Ken and let Eliza listen. This was a business conference, one area in which I was definitely in charge. 'We're going to have to find a place to stay,' I told him. 'Our apartment and Aunt Margie's are definitely out of the question. Now so is Igavda's place. I don't want to put anyone else I know in legal trouble. You have any ideas?'

'A real-estate agent friend,' he said. I waited, but nothing followed.

'You have a friend who is real estate?' I asked.

Eliza, in time-honored young-woman tradition, rolled her eyes in anguish.

Ken, now in his role as the grown-up, decided just to press on. 'I have a friend who is *in* real estate,' he said. 'She was telling me about a building that's not quite ready to go on the market yet, you know, still doing construction on the upper floors, that kind of thing. She said some of the apartments are finished and they're almost ready to be shown, but not yet. Maybe you can stay in one of those for a couple of days.'

To be fair, he was playing that grown-up role pretty well.

But the setup sounded just a little fishy to me. 'Your *friend* is just going to let us live rent-free in a brand-new apartment because you ask?' I said.

'Well, I won't know until I do ask. But I can't pull my phone out with you two here, and I can't get in touch with you when I hear back. We have to figure out how we're going to communicate until this whole thing blows over.' Ken was just picking at a steak sandwich, a sign that he was indeed thinking deeply. Or that it wasn't a good steak sandwich.

'You've gotta go old school.' Eliza, of all people, was tearing through her plant-based burger and pointing at Ken with her fork. 'We need to stay off the grid. We have to act like it's 1994 and none of this stuff has been invented yet.'

For someone who had practically gone into a coma when I'd told her she had to turn her phone off, this was an amazing turnaround. 'So we just prearrange to meet every day, or maybe twice a day, in a designated spot?' I asked. That's what it had come to; I was looking for operating advice from the girl I'd been sent to find.

'That's one way.' She sounded less than impressed, which wasn't at all surprising. 'But there's the idea of a drop-off point, and I think that might work better. It's not tied to a particular time of day.'

'To drop off what?' Ken asked. I was glad he had, because if I'd said it the eye rolling would no doubt have returned in force. I was starting to realize that being a fugitive from justice was only making me whiny.

'Notes,' Eliza said. 'Paper notes. We should probably have a code figured out, too, in case someone finds them. A million years ago people would have taken out personal ads in newspapers to communicate like this, but we can't do that because we can't go online.'

'Maybe we can once in a while,' I said. 'We can use the internet at the public library as long as we get out fast enough that we won't be traced while we're still in the building.'

Eliza looked at me with something resembling respect. 'Not bad,' she said.

'But the first order of business is this alleged apartment you're going to find for us,' I told Ken. 'It's supposed to rain tonight.'

We spent the next fifteen minutes working out drop-off points near the diner, near the apartment building Ken's friend had told him about (and I was betting she was more than a friend, but Juliet didn't know about her) and near, but not too near, the office of K&F Stein Investigations. Getting near our apartment just seemed too risky. We set up elaborate schedules to check the drop-off points, all written down on the paper napkins our server had supplied. I even ate a quarter of the turkey club.

TWENTY

scanned the windows around the diner again, saw no one who might be watching us with suspicion, and we parted, Ken for parts unknown and Eliza and me for the nearest branch of the New York Public Library. I needed a restroom in a more public place (that would have more space and fewer people knocking on the door) to charge my batteries.

Even as Eliza and I walked with purpose toward Mulberry Street, I was feeling myself run down. Stress can use my energy as much as physical exertion and I'd had both today. I wasn't in danger of passing out or anything, but I was feeling the urgency.

It's not easy being a manufactured superbeing. Yeah, boo-hoo to you, too.

And I realized Ken and I had not discussed Malcolm X. Mitchell or our parents while we were seated with Eliza. It was going to be especially hard to track down that lead while I couldn't communicate with anyone but my brother and Eliza.

This whole being-wanted-by-the-cops thing was not turning out to be fun. 'I wasn't kidding when I said your best plan might be to talk to the police,' I told Eliza discreetly while we walked. 'They can protect you and I'll make sure that's what they do. I have a few friends in the department.'

She just shook her head. I didn't know what it was like to be a trans woman in New York and she didn't know what it was like to have to plug yourself into the wall to stay awake. There was no point in trying to explain it either way because we could only understand on an intellectual, not a basic emotional, level.

'OK,' I said, and we walked on.

We reached the Mulberry Street Library only about ten minutes after we left the diner. If you weren't looking for it, you'd think it was the ground floor of an apartment building or an office facility, or maybe a bookstore. Not every library in New York has statues of lions outside guarding the place.

Only the book drop and the sign over the door reading 'New

York Public Library' gave it away. Inside, it was quite a lovely facility, but I was mostly interested in the restroom, which required a key that had to be borrowed at the desk. It took a few minutes but I did manage to get plugged in with the charger Ken had furnished.

The problem, of course, was that any electrical outlet in the library bathroom was going to be in no proximity to the stall, which meant that I had to stand to one side of the restroom, reach under my shirt (I never wear anything sleeveless because of the port) and plug myself in. And then . . . stand there. Usually a charge can take forty-five minutes to an hour. I obviously wouldn't have that kind of time until Ken found us a safe haven, but I could take fifteen minutes or so to top myself off.

I couldn't even turn on my phone to check emails.

It gave me time to think, which I had in fact been doing for some time now. Eliza had left her father's apartment at least partially because he'd had trouble accepting her as herself, although her reasoning was a little cloudy so far. She'd gone to stay with Rainbow, whom I had still not met, and at some point in the past three days had been in the Bronx basement with Damien, but said she had not stayed long. Then, having a gun within reach, she did not seem at all shocked when the police showed up at Rainbow's door. She said she didn't use any of Damien's product but clearly knew about his business. She was upset that Damien was dead, but not *that* upset.

A lot of her story was just barely adding up, and I needed to get much clearer answers. Obviously the library wasn't the place for such a conversation, particularly if Eliza had logged herself into one of the pubic computers, but hopefully Ken would find us a landing spot and we'd have some time to talk. Probably a lot of time.

OK. Only fourteen minutes of charging to go.

I wondered what communications I was missing. Was Mank trying to find me, and if so, was it personal or professional? Was Aunt Margie losing her mind with worry? (Ken would be able to give her heavily coded messages very soon.) Had Shelly found out anything more about Malcolm X. Mitchell? Was Malcolm still following me around? Was he behind the appearance of the cops at Rainbow Zelensky's door?

I don't mind having a lot of questions. It's the lack of answers that gets on my nerves.

OK, so I gave up after twelve minutes out of nerves and boredom, if such a juxtaposition is possible, but I was sufficiently recharged to get through the rest of the day easily. A charge usually lasts at least three or four days, so a fraction of one can offer a normal level of energy for an analogous period. In short, I was OK for now. It wouldn't last.

It didn't take long to find Eliza because I'd already located the public computers and there was no chance she'd be anywhere else. Sure enough, she was reading her emails and thereby making herself visible to anyone plugged into the city's computers, like for example the police. We were very much on borrowed time, but I'd expected that.

'Three minutes,' I said to Eliza as I sat down next to her. I wasn't going to wait long enough to get access myself; Ken was going to be my eyes and ears for a little while. And no, that wasn't my first choice, but it was my only one.

'I just got started!' she protested. 'I've been out of circulation for a long time.'

'It's been two hours. And now you have two minutes. I'm not letting the cops or the bad guys or anybody else find us here. Do what you have to do.' I pointed at the screen just in case she had thought I believed she needed to do something other than check her emails.

Eliza made a scratchy noise in the back of her throat to communicate her displeasure but she didn't argue and in two minutes and fifteen seconds we were heading for the library door. When we approached the door I felt a surge of caution – just because you're paranoid doesn't mean they're not after you – and put up a hand to stop her from barging out into the warm New York day without a moment's thought.

'Stop. Look.' Luckily the door was glass so I didn't have to open it to look outside.

There were two men across the street trying desperately not to look like they were watching the library entrance. Neither of them was smoking a cigarette, a nod to modern times. They weren't wearing trench coats, either, because it was a very warm day and this wasn't 1943. But they were definitely watching.

One of them was Detective Sergeant Louis Merchant. The other was someone I hadn't seen before.

I turned immediately toward the interior of the library again, grabbing Eliza's arm in mid-turn. She said, 'Hey!' but saw the look on my face and followed me. But she did yank her arm away and add, 'Where are you going?'

In lieu of an answer I walked directly to the reference desk, where a woman in her mid-thirties with a nose ring and three tattoos on her left arm was stationed. At the moment she was reading a mystery novel by Catriona McPherson. She put a bookmark in the page when we approached. 'How can I help?' she said.

There are times in life that, no matter how self-aware you might be, you simply can't avoid the cliché. 'Is there a back way out of here?' I asked.

The reference librarian didn't so much as blink. 'Is there a reason you can't use the main entrance?' she asked.

'Yes. There are some people who pose a danger to my . . . younger sister here, and we need to avoid them at all costs. Is there another way out?'

'I'm really her daughter,' Eliza said. 'She's just being vain.'

Our new friend ignored this ridiculous banter. She looked each of us full in the face and was clearly making a judgment. 'Follow me.'

She walked away from the station, nodding at another librarian at the main desk, who nodded back. Eliza and I trailed behind her, Eliza walking with some swagger and me marveling that this lame ploy had worked. She led us down an ornate staircase that was left over, I found out later, from when the library's building had been a chocolate factory. We went down two flights and she brought us to a door painted blue, pulled a key out of her pocket, and opened it. She held the door open.

'Go to the end,' she said. 'You'll see another door painted blue. Open it and you can walk up to the street level. Don't touch anything along the way. Good luck.'

Eliza gave a quick nod and immediately started down the stairs. I stopped and looked at the librarian, who was still holding the door open.

'Thank you,' I said. 'You've been very understanding.' I started through the door, then stopped and looked at her. 'Why shouldn't we touch anything?' I asked.

She looked surprised at the question. 'Library property,' she said.

Once I was through the door she let it close and I heard her turn the key in the lock behind me. I thought I might have heard a man's voice talking to her but I was already on my way downstairs to a floor that was clearly below the street. I didn't even touch the hand rail on the way out. When a librarian tells you to touch nothing, you touch nothing.

The floor downstairs wasn't terribly distinctive. It wasn't even like the dank basement where we'd found Damien. It was clearly a storage area, possibly for books that had been taken off the shelves to make space for others. But the stacks here were plain metal shelving and they were covering every possible space save for a slim hallway down the middle to our right.

Eliza was already halfway down that corridor by the time I got to the bottom of the stairs and she wasn't slowing down. Luckily I had considerably longer legs than she did and needed fewer steps to catch up. We reached the far end, with the blue door at its terminus, at the same time.

'You ready?' I asked.

'No. Let's stay in the library basement forever.' It was going to be fun rooming with Eliza for a few days. Assuming we had a place to room.

I pushed the blue door open and found another set of stairs with a door at the top. The door had a window and sunlight was pouring through it. We hadn't been down here a full minute and I already felt like I was digging my way out of a deep cave. We climbed the flight of stairs but once again I stopped at the top to assess the situation.

'We have to be realistic,' I told Eliza. 'If there are cops out there and they're armed and looking for us, we're going to have to turn ourselves in.'

'Maybe you,' she said. 'Not me.' Swell.

I didn't see any point in arguing, so I gave the best glance I could through the window, which was admittedly limited. I didn't see any police but that didn't mean they weren't, at least, ten feet away. It was time to just open the door and take the plunge.

I swung the door open and insisted on going out first, so I could slam it in Eliza's face if I saw anyone who might have it in their minds to shoot her. But all that drama had been for naught, which was a relief. There were no uniformed officers or, for all I could tell, plainclothes detectives outside this door to the library, which had left us on Lafayette Street heading toward Houston (and it's pronounced HOW-ston in New York, not HEW-ston, like in Texas). We made the right turn on Houston and just kept walking.

'Now what?' Eliza asked, making it sound less like a request for directions and more like a challenge.

'Now we go to the first drop-off point and see if Ken has rustled us up some accommodations.'

The problem was, despite there having been no cops keeping a watch on the Lafayette door to the library, we seemed to be walking into a rather imposing wall of men in bland suits looking at us and not, as is the Manhattan custom, at their phones or directly ahead, expressing the immense importance of their destinations.

'We've been spotted,' I said quietly to Eliza. 'Do as I do.'

I turned on my heel and picked up my pace after pivoting to a perfect U-turn. But I didn't break into a run; that's almost always a mistake if you're not being shot at. And a lot of the time when you are. I just strode somewhat more purposefully, which for someone my height can help make up ground in a hurry. But I had to make sure Eliza was with me every stride of the way.

She, trouper that she was, kept up but her breathing was getting a little labored. I couldn't use the FaceTime trick to see behind me and gauge the cops' progress. Frankly, I was surprised they hadn't called out and ordered us to freeze already. After all, they thought at least one of us was a murderer.

I figured there was no point in continuing any pretense, so I stole a glance behind me. The cops – and they were definitely cops – were following but maintaining their distance. It was more like a surveillance than a pursuit and that was weird.

'We can't go to the drop-off point yet,' I said. 'Want to stop for an ice cream?'

'Are you kidding?'

'Actually, no.'

Van Leeuwen Ice Cream on Houston Street is a very classy scoop shop with some tables for those who prefer an indoor experience. And under these circumstances we definitely wanted that, despite what would seem logical.

'The cops are after us,' Eliza stage-whispered at me as we walked in. 'Why are we going to a place where they have us cornered?'

'Because they've had plenty of chances to stop us and they've chosen not to,' I said in a normal voice. 'I have a feeling we're not running away from the police.'

I walked up to the counter – OK, the line, where I placed fourth at the moment – and waited for Eliza to join me, which she did. No one in New York had blinked in her direction. She was hardly the first trans woman anyone had seen in this neighborhood.

'Then who are we running away from?' she asked, still sort of dropping her voice to what she thought was a hard-to-eavesdrop level.

'If we let them, I imagine the cops will find a way to show us,' I said. I was now third in line and had already decided on brown sugar chunk ice cream because it had been that kind of day. 'What flavor do you want? It's my treat.'

'I'm vegan,' Eliza said, more as a challenge than a piece of information.

I pointed at the menu above the counter. 'They can accommodate you.'

She looked up and scowled because her obstacle hadn't stopped me. I get that a lot. 'In that case, churros and fudge,' she said.

Just about the time we were getting our ice cream (or in Eliza's case iced-something) cones, a large man in his twenties entered the shop and looked around. He wasn't looking at the flavor list and he wasn't searching (no matter how much he wanted you to believe he was) for someone he had agreed to meet here. He took one look around the room and focused on two people.

I'm guessing you can figure out which two.

I took a lick of the ice cream, which was excellent. 'Him,' I told Eliza.

She was looking toward the napkin holders and had to turn her head to see who I meant. Her eyes grew wide and she took in a quick breath. 'Julio,' she said.

TWENTY-ONE

Julio did not look like someone named Julio, but that didn't mean anything. You can decide to call yourself Rumpelstiltskin if you feel like it and I'll go along. I'm not the most average person either. But Julio apparently was adamant about *not* being called Julio, and his looking more like a Chip or a Harper made that only more confusing.

'Let's take a table,' I said to Eliza. 'I doubt he came here to kill us in front of every cop in New York City.'

She was standing stock still and didn't appear to have heard me. 'Julio,' she said again.

'There's nothing to be scared of,' I told her. 'If it comes to it, I can take him, but I don't think it will.'

She turned her head and stared at me. 'Are you nuts?' she asked.

'I don't really think we have time to get into my mental health issues right at the moment,' I said. A table had opened up near the door, which I thought was advantageous, and I made sure to sit down at it. Eliza, staring at Julio and looking massively panicked, followed out of what I assumed was a preservation instinct. At worst she must have figured she could hide behind me.

I was licking away with some enthusiasm while Eliza seemed to be doing the same out of a sense of responsibility. She never looked at the cone and didn't register any reaction to the treat she was having. Some people just aren't that into ice cream. And they think *I'm* a freak.

Julio strode – that's the word for it – over to our table, and I kid you not, turned a chair around and sat on it backwards. If that was his idea of intimidating, it was going to be much easier to deal with him than I'd initially expected.

'So, Eliza,' he said. 'Good to see you again. Who's your friend?' Yup, that would be me.

'I'm Fran,' I told him. 'I'd shake your hand but I have this ice cream.'

'That's OK,' Julio said. 'I'm not sure I want to touch you anyway, big lady.'

Ooh, snap! 'Good. Now why don't you tell us exactly what happened in that basement with Damien. Because there are about thirty cops outside who'd like to know and so would we. Wouldn't we, Eliza?'

'Fran . . .' Eliza was not as relaxed as I appeared to be.

'That's why I'm here,' Julio said. 'I need to get the cops off my back and I noticed they've been following you around. I was trying to figure out why, but I guess it's because they think Eliza here offed Damien in the Bronx. Did you?' Now both of us were looking at Eliza, who had absolutely no color left in her face. None. If a person could be clear, it would have been Eliza.

'What are you talking about?' she croaked. A big drip of her vegan ice cream (that's what they call it; don't blame me) landed on the table. I wiped it up with a paper napkin. 'Everybody knows you killed Damien.'

Julio, for all his size and bluster, looked insulted by the very suggestion. 'Me? I didn't have nothing to do with that. I mean, I figured the cops were following you because you did it.'

'Why would I kill Damien?' Eliza said. She was trying and failing to sound fierce, or at least calm.

'I dunno. Maybe he made a pass at you and found out you're not a girl.'

OK, that was crossing a line. 'Walk it back, Julio,' I said.

'Don't call me that!' he snarled. 'Nobody can call me that!'

When you find your opponent's weak spot, you poke at it. 'OK. I'll respect who you are as long as you respect who Eliza is. That a deal?'

Julio, massive intellect that he was, took a moment to process that. 'Yeah. OK.'

'What's your name, then? What should we call you?'

'My name is Jules,' he said with a completely straight face. Eliza just nodded.

'OK,' I said. 'Now we've established who everyone is here.' I took another lick of the ice cream because Jules wasn't worth losing any of it. 'If you didn't kill Damien, Jules, you can solve all our problems at once. Who did?'

Now, I'm not naïve. I knew exactly what Jules was going to

say. He would deny any knowledge of the events surrounding Damien's murder. But that wasn't going to help anybody in this room and it wasn't about to make all the officers of the law, who were out in the street hoping someone would come out shooting, go away. But in order to get the answers you need as an investigator, it is sometimes necessary to go through the motions in order. It's a ritual of sorts. And that was what I did.

'How the hell do I know?' Jules said. 'I told you I wasn't there.'

I was almost down to the cone itself, which was of the waffle variety and looked delicious. I sat back in my chair to show how relaxed and unimpressed I was by Jules's answer. 'Come on, Jules. Lying isn't going to fix anything.'

'I'm not—'

'Yeah, you are. We know you were Damien's supplier for his little pill business on campus. We know that you sent some of your . . . friends . . . to follow him around and threaten him, to the point that Damien thought he could make one last stand against you. So he went to that basement and somebody wrapped an extension cord around his windpipe. OK then, explain how you had nothing to do with Damien being killed.' I took a bite of the cone. Heaven.

'I wasn't there,' he repeated.

'Don Corleone wasn't there when all those people got killed, and yet you knew he had a little bit to do with it,' I said. 'You didn't have to strangle Damien if you could get someone else to do it for you.'

Jules didn't even pretend to be insulted. He just shook his head. 'Not in my best interests,' he said. 'Damien was a good customer. He's dead now and I don't have a distributor in that area. It's bad business. Nope, I didn't want Damien dead.'

Eliza's eyes were down to slits. 'Yes you did,' she hissed at Jules. 'You went after Damien with some other guy because he was supposed to owe you money or something, and that's why you told that guy to kill him. You said Mr Martin was coming for him. Who's that?'

Jules let his face go cold; no longer was he the amiable, misunderstood guy who could be reasonable. His eyes bore into Eliza's and his mouth went straight across the lower part of his face in a horizontal line.

This was Julio.

'You don't know what you're talking about,' he growled. 'I don't know no Mr Martin. And the cops ain't chasing *me*. They're chasing *you*.'

He stood up and regarded me. As with many such men who hope to have some factor of intimidation over women, he regarded me mostly below the neck. Mistake after mistake, Jules. 'I didn't have nothing to do with Damien getting killed,' he said to me. 'If you want to talk about it, you let me know, hotness. But don't bring this *boy* with you.'

Jules wanted to turn and walk out, having delivered his exit line, but I didn't care for the way he'd treated us. I stood up and in one motion grabbed Jules by the belt and the shoulders and hoisted him over my head.

He was loquacious enough to let out a 'Whoa!' as he ascended. Eliza looked astonished, as did many of the patrons of the store, who turned to watch. Nobody had the wherewithal to get out their phones and start a video feed yet, which was good with me. I had to move fast.

Holding Jules over my head, I shook him a little. A small gun and a switchblade knife (a throwback!) fell on to our table. Eliza quickly confiscated them. But Jules was not taking this quietly, letting out a tirade of invective that would have made a Cockney footballer blush.

'Hey, there are children here,' I said to the man over my head, although there were perhaps two kids in the store. 'You need to leave.'

I carried him, full arm extension, over my head to the street, where four cops, none with a weapon visible, were standing and chatting. They turned when they saw us and gaped.

Even Eliza, who had ridden down a building on my back, stared with her mouth open. 'What *are* you?' she said.

'We don't have time for that now.'

With one last grunt I tossed Jules into their midst, turned and grabbed Eliza's arm. I did not say, 'Let's go!' because that's stupid. Eliza knew we weren't staying for another cone. It was a shame to leave the two we'd had behind, though.

Before the NYPD officers knew what had (literally) hit them, we were around the corner and gone.

TWENTY-TWO

The coffee shop where we'd met earlier today was across the street from a small bodega, above which were three floors of apartments. Eliza and I, having assured ourselves that no officers of the law were on our tail, walked over to the bodega casually. 'Go in and get a bottle of water,' I told her, reaching for my bag.

'I can pay for water,' she told me, and turned to stomp inside the store.

'Pay *cash*,' I said.

Given a minute to myself in a place I wouldn't be staying for more than that minute, I felt it was safe to check my messages. There were many from Ken, from before the diner meeting. There were two from Aunt Margie, who didn't sound frantic, so they must have been from early in the day. There was one from a client wanting to know if her birth father was living under the name Pollitzer in Peoria, Illinois. And there were five from Mank, the gist of which came to: *Where the hell are you and what have you gotten yourself into?* But the last one included the disquieting addition, *Turn yourselves in and I can help.* I answered none and turned the phone off again. At least I was saving battery time.

I walked to the northwest corner of the building, where there was a loose brick in the façade, courtesy of my brother and his strong hands. Ken and I had agreed this would be one of our drop-off points for messages and, sure enough, when I pulled the brick halfway out I found a small piece of yellow paper, probably from one of the office's legal pads, stuck behind it. My brother had come through with a note, if not a safe haven. That was yet to be seen.

I was unfolding the paper when Eliza walked out with a bottle of spring water and a Red Bull. Apparently she was in need of some energy. 'Here's your water.' She held out the bottle and I took it, because that wasn't a ruse: I actually wanted the water.

'We're heading uptown,' I said. 'My brother's real-estate friend has actually come through.'

'Imagine,' Eliza said.

We decided – OK, *I* decided – not to take the subway because it's too hard to extract yourself from a train if you find yourself in an untenable situation. Walking left us a lot of options. Eliza complained a little about the distance because we walking from the West Village to East 62nd Street, but she gave it up pretty quickly when she saw that I didn't especially care if she was complaining; I just kept walking. If you can't irritate someone, there's really just no point.

It was something of a trudge but I didn't want to have deep important conversations in the streets of Manhattan, particularly when it felt like every cop in the city was hot on our trail. You'd think they would have left a few guys out to track down jaywalkers or something. I nattered on for a while about how this was a great time of year to be walking in the city while Eliza studied her pink Skechers and opted not to answer.

When I finally took a breath Eliza seized on the opportunity. 'How come you can lift a guy over your head and throw him at a bunch of cops?'

'I work out a lot.'

She took her eyes off her every step and gave me a withering glance. 'Come on,' she said.

'Fair enough. I'm not really like other people,' I said. I knew that wouldn't suffice, but I thought the implicit message 'Not now' might land.

It did not. 'No kidding,' Eliza said. 'I work out but I can't do that. How come you can, and you can carry people down the side of an apartment building?'

Subtlety was not my top priority on East 21st Street. We still had a way to go and I was definitely not in the mood to unburden myself like I had to Mank, especially given how well *that* had worked out. 'Not here and not now,' I said.

Eliza gave me an interesting look that blended a certain loose familiarity with something like understanding. 'You're not out yet,' she said.

That would be how she'd see it, and she wasn't wrong. 'That's it,' I said. 'And I might never be.'

She looked sympathetic. 'It really frees you up,' she suggested.

'It's not the same thing. You know that.'

We shut up and kept walking until we got near our new digs. I checked in my bag for my wallet and found all of four dollars in cash. 'I guess we're not buying groceries,' I said. 'We'll figure out food.'

Eliza reached into her jeans for her thin wallet. 'I can go to an ATM.'

'No. You can't. They'll find us in about four minutes.'

She looked like something smelled bad. 'Oh yeah,' she said.

When we got to the building on East 62nd we walked to the southeast corner as Ken had instructed in his note. Sure enough there was a mailbox there, one of the old blue ones that the Post Office put up for collection that virtually nobody uses anymore. I followed the note's instructions and opened the hinged slot at the top. You used to be able to open the box and put in something larger than a number-10 envelope, but people being what they are put all sorts of disgusting things in mailboxes and the USPS installed narrow slots in the boxes and made you go to the post office for everything else. People.

A testament to how often these boxes are used now was the small white envelope Ken had taped to the inside of the hinge on the slot cover. I pulled the envelope out and walked toward the building, which was fully constructed for the first eight floors but clearly not yet completely habitable. There were fences around it and many of the upper floors were still boarded up. I reached into the envelope and found a key card and another note.

This will get you in. I'll see about getting you food later. And keep in mind the electricity and the bathrooms don't work yet. Swell.

Thank goodness it wasn't February, because I was willing to bet the heating units weren't up to speed yet, either.

We went to what was clearly the construction entrance and found no one guarding it. There's security and then there's a building my brother knows about. The apartment he'd secured for Eliza and me was on the third floor, which appeared to be about halfway up the part of the interior construction that had been completed so far. I hadn't wanted to be on the ground floor, which was mostly lobby, anyway, just so we would have a view of the street if anyone discovered where we were hiding.

The key card got us in through the front door and then, strikingly, the apartment door was unlocked, because the same key card was apparently going to be used for the locks, and there was not yet any electrical power to the apartments. I guess they figured nobody was going to break in to steal the nothing.

It was a valid point; Eliza and I walked into what I'm sure was becoming a very expensive luxury apartment and found walls and a ceiling. The place was clean enough, given that it was a construction site, but there was no furniture, no rugs, no light fixtures. We had to figure out how to get some cash soon or it would be pitch black in this place within a couple of hours. And we'd be sleeping on the floor.

Still, it was not open to the elements and I could pretty much bet the few dollars I had left to me that the NYPD or whoever was after us would not think to look here. I was here and *I* wouldn't think to look here.

'Home sweet home,' I said to Eliza once I had done the one and only thing I could do, which was sit on the floor. Eliza, being more resourceful than me, hiked herself up on the kitchen countertop and sat in a cobbler's pose there, looking not nearly as serene as her online yoga instructor might hope. (I was guessing.)

'Yeah,' she said. I was lamenting the lack of a bottle of wine until I remembered that I don't drink and buying Eliza any alcohol would be illegal for another two years. 'Now tell me.'

'Tell you what?' Was she wondering what my plan for a next move would be? Because I definitely didn't have one I liked yet.

Eliza's voice was measured and calm. 'Tell me why you can pick up a great big guy like Julio and carry him out to the street so you can throw him at the cops.'

It was a fair question and not a surprising one. But I'd spent decades not telling anyone the answer, and I wasn't the least bit comfortable giving my most closely held secret to a nineteen-year-old I'd met that day.

'I'm bigger than most people,' I said. 'You can see that. It's genetic. Ken is bigger and stronger than almost anyone else, too. The luck of the draw, I guess.'

Eliza raised an eyebrow in an expression that was not, to be honest, very accepting. 'It's more than that and you know it,' she said.

I lay down on the floor because the day had been more than enough and I hadn't charged up as much as I'd wanted to. In this place without electrical service that was going to be something of an issue. And I didn't want to answer Eliza. 'I'm gonna take a nap,' I said.

'Coward.'

I can't tell you why, but that got to me. I sat up. 'Coward? I carry you down the side of an apartment building, keep you away from the cops even though I think you should turn yourself in, toss a guy into a crowd to keep him away from you, and find you shelter for the night, and you think I'm a *coward*?'

A lot of people would have been intimidated by someone who looks like me yelling at them. Eliza was not a lot of people. Her tone remained even and unperturbed. 'I had to tell *everyone I knew* about who I really was after I'd spent my whole life pretending to be who they wanted me to be. I didn't know how any of them would react. Some of them accepted me right away. Some of them took their time and then sort of accepted me. There are more than a few I never heard from again. So you tell me about being brave, OK? I lost people that I thought loved me.'

For reasons I can't begin to identify or explain, that made me think of Mank. I deflected. 'Did you tell anyone on the day you met them?' I asked.

That got to her; she blinked and looked away, despite there being remarkably little to look at. 'Not when I didn't have to. My only ID has my deadname. Anyone who sees it is someone I just met and came out to at the same time. I don't always get the choice.'

'OK. My bad. I get that. So I'll prove I trust you but you have to trust me, too. How about that? I'll tell you as much as I possibly can without putting you in more danger, but you have to tell me everything you know about Damien's little side hustle and what happened to him in that basement by Yankee Stadium. How's that?'

She really didn't want to go that way; I could see it in her face, in the way she refused to look in my direction. It wasn't getting dark yet, but the windows were already losing the direct sunlight they'd had when we'd arrived less than an hour before. I hoped Ken was at the supermarket because I was getting hungry. And I needed to find a place with working electricity to charge my battery. I couldn't dare turn on my phone to push my brother. This was all coming down to trust. I needed Eliza to trust me.

She was thinking about what I'd said and the only indication she'd reached a decision was that she came down off the counter and sat on the floor across from me. 'OK,' she said.

I waited. 'OK, what?'

'OK, you tell me what you can and I'll tell you what I can about Damien. I figure they're chasing us because of that and so you need to know.'

'Good.' I waited some more. 'So?'

'So, you go first.'

I should have seen that one coming. But she needed the gesture and I had offered it; there was no way of backing out now. 'OK. Ken and I were changed by our parents, even before we were born, to be bigger and stronger than other people. Our parents were geneticists and they wanted to protect us from the harder parts of life. They felt that making us strong and unusually agile would do that.'

Eliza sat and stared at me for a very long moment, making me worry that perhaps I'd said too much and she now saw me as a freak. If she didn't trust me, that was going to make a very difficult situation even harder to navigate. She seemed to take a moment to collect herself, or at least that was my impression, and then she said, 'And?'

'And, what?'

'Well, aside from the idea that your parents seemed to dabble in eugenics and *that* really needs to be addressed, you're obviously holding something back from me. I can see you're big and strong, but that's not something you have to hide from the rest of society. I had to come out as trans. You don't have to come out as big and strong.'

I hated it when she was logical.

I especially cringed at the use of the word *eugenics*. Was that what Mom and Dad had done? Ken and I joke about being superbeings, but we're really not. We're essentially the same as everyone else but with . . . *differences* our parents gave us. Were they actually contemplating creating a race of champions? There was no evidence they ever 'made' anyone other than Ken and me, and Aunt Margie always insisted they went to the lab for us because they couldn't conceive and had problems with adoption. That last bit might have had something to do with my father's four arrests protesting apartheid when he was a college student (in Ohio, not Johannesburg).

'That's true,' I acknowledged, because what choice did I have? 'Although I think "eugenics" is a little overstated. But see, they didn't manipulate us in the womb or try to change our DNA.' How far could I go without going too far? 'They developed some parts of us organically because they couldn't conceive children of their own.' I'd never said it that way before, but it was technically true without being graphic.

Eliza looked at me as if I were a new breed of dog she hadn't encountered before and she couldn't decide whether to pet my head or back away before I bit her. 'They never heard of adoption?' she asked.

'They had issues.' That wasn't any of her business. 'Now how about you? When do I get to hear what you know about Damien?'

It was starting to get dark and that was a worry. We couldn't turn on our phones to use the flashlight apps and pretty soon the only light we'd have would be from the construction team's overnight facility. It was something, but it wasn't enough and it was going to be coming from only one direction, below us.

But none of that made a difference to Eliza. She was being backed into a corner and clearly wasn't happy about it. So few are. 'What do you need to know?' she asked carefully.

'Everything. I can't help solve this crime and get you out of a boatload of trouble if I don't know what I'm dealing with. So, spill.' I looked at as much as I could see of her in the shadows and tried to use my most penetrating gaze to get her to talk.

She stood up, which I wasn't expecting. Some people like to pace when they're in uncomfortable conversations. I didn't know if that was the case with Eliza, but she walked over to the window and looked out, which blocked more of the light coming through.

'I wasn't in love with Damien,' she said. 'I think Laura was, but I wasn't. He wasn't my type and I'm not dating anybody right now. So I was just around for some of the stuff.'

'Then just tell me what you know,' I said, because she had stopped talking for a bit.

I didn't so much see Eliza nod as I noted that the light from the construction klieg brightened for a moment and then dimmed. It was getting very difficult to see in here. 'Damien was kind of sketchy right from the beginning,' she said. 'I met him in my first semester, when I was still pretending. He thought I was a dude and I let him think it because I didn't care what he thought at first.'

Aha! Perhaps a breakthrough! 'At first?'

'Damien was funny,' she said, still staring out the window, probably to avoid looking at me. Not that she would have been able to see me that well. 'He didn't tell jokes or anything, but he made you laugh. Somebody, you know, just in a crazy conversation, asked him once who decided that thing you serve gravy in should be called a boat, and he said, "The gravy navy." That cracked me up.' She chuckled just thinking about it, and had a hard time saying the words without laughing.

'So you got to be friends.' If I didn't move this along we'd be discussing the gravy navy all night.

'Yeah. And Laura was always around, too.' Her voice sounded sour and displeased.

'I thought you were friends with Laura,' I said. 'You were into Mary Shelley.'

She actually turned to face me so I could see the contempt on her face, except that I couldn't because she was backlit. 'For class,' she said. 'We didn't hang outside of class until she was involved with Damien and his pill thing, and all of a sudden he was like a hundred percent into that. After a while he stopped going to class.' Eliza walked back over toward me but did not sit down. She stood there and stared in the direction of the door.

'It would be a really bad idea to bolt,' I said quietly.

Eliza's head swiveled quickly and she stared at me. 'I wasn't going to . . . You know, you don't know me nearly as well as you think.'

'You're right, I don't,' I told her. I didn't have time for a deep character study because someone was dead and other people were coming after Eliza and me. 'So how did Damien get involved with Julio? Did you believe Jules when he said he didn't kill Damien?'

'Jules,' she said with an edge. 'Now he thinks his name is Jules.'

'Now? That's a new thing?'

'I dunno. He's always been a pain about his name. I think it's really Eric.' She sat down. 'What are we going to do about food?'

Because I apparently live in a movie, there was a sudden knock at the door, and both of us started as if we'd heard a gunshot. By the time I'd managed to get to my feet, the knocking had stopped. Had Jules found us? It seemed unlikely that knocking would be his style. He was more a kick-down-the-door kind of guy, which would be a shame because it was a nice new door. But it was a door without a peephole, largely because there was a security monitor already installed over the top of the door, which would have been very handy if there were electrical power in the building.

Feeling a little drained and wondering if I could lift Jules into the air again, I very carefully turned the knob and opened the door, suddenly remembering it had never been locked and anybody could have walked right in on us.

Maybe tomorrow we'd have to find a new place to crash.

I pulled the door open quickly, thinking I might be able to startle the person/people in the hallway and get the drop on them. But I needn't have worried.

There was no one standing in front of our door. On the floor outside the apartment there were three reusable tote bags full of groceries. And on top was a box indicating it held a battery-operated electrical charger.

My brother had come through for us again.

TWENTY-THREE

Things are so much easier once you've eaten.

Eliza and I sat on the floor of the bare apartment with two candles Ken had left for us (to be completely accurate, I was certain he would have stayed away and gotten someone else to deliver the groceries, possibly Igavda, maybe his real-estate friend, who would have had a key card), sitting in plastic cups and effectively lighting our small part of the room. I'd just as soon not have tons of light in here to alert anyone who looked up that there were people in the building under construction.

I felt like we'd relaxed a bit once Eliza had eaten a veggie sub and I'd had one of the turkey variety, to complete a turkey-centric day. So I propped myself up on one elbow and said, 'Did you always know—'

She cut me off and her face bordered on angry. 'There's nothing to know. I was always this, even when I was three and trying to play by their rules. I'm Eliza. This is me. There was no change that took place; I didn't used to be who my father thought and then become who I am. This is my true identity.'

'I was going to ask if you'd always known Damien was dealing pills,' I said.

Eliza looked sheepish and then grinned a little. 'Sorry.'

I waved a hand. 'You spent enough time being sorry about who people thought you were. That's over now. But we need to know who killed Damien. Was he selling on campus when you first met him?'

'No,' Eliza said after a sip of the spring water she had been supplied. I was trying to be careful about the fluids because Ken had said the bathrooms weren't working and he had not provided any in the grocery bags. 'That just started maybe a month ago. I tried to talk him out of it but he wanted to pay the rent on his apartment himself and not take money from his mother.'

'He couldn't wait tables like everybody else?' I said.

Eliza closed her eyes for a moment and then looked at me. 'I don't know who, but somebody must have approached him with this idea. Julio used to say he was Damien's supplier, but someone was supplying Julio. He wasn't smart enough or connected enough to do it himself, and one time Damien had to wait a couple of days for pills because Julio had run out.'

'You have no idea who the supplier was?' I asked.

She shook her head. 'I mean, the truth is that we never really talked about it that much once it got going. I didn't want to have anything to do with it and Damien wouldn't listen to me about it. I think he was only telling Laura because she thought it was a great idea.'

A lot of this was the direct opposite of what Laura Rapinoe had told me, but I tended to believe Eliza more than Laura, whose story had changed a few times in the short period I'd known her.

'What about this Mr Martin you talked to Jules about? Who's he?'

Eliza looked a little shaken. 'I've never seen Mr Martin. He's somebody they threaten you with, like when your mom tells you to wait until your dad gets home. I don't know anything about him.'

That was something to file away.

'Was Laura the supplier?' I asked.

Eliza laughed. 'No! Laura wouldn't have been able to find pills at a Walgreen's. She just thought Damien was great and anything he did had to be great, too.'

'So our first order of business should be finding out who was selling the drugs to Jules that he was selling to Damien, that he was selling to everybody else,' I said. My head was getting a little hazy and there was just no denying it. 'I'm tired. I'm going to go into one of the bedrooms and sleep for a bit,' I told Eliza. But on my way I picked up the little charger.

'What's that?' Eliza asked.

Dammit. 'Shaver,' I said, and turned back toward the hallway, carrying my candle and the charger.

'Can I borrow it?' I looked at Eliza again. She was wearing just enough of a mysterious grin that the candle could make it visible.

'Um . . . I'm kind of personal about stuff like that,' I said. 'We'll find you another one tomorrow.'

I was three steps into the hallway when I heard her say, 'It's because I'm trans, isn't it?'

Turning myself back toward the living room had become a habit. 'Of course not!' I started.

But then Eliza burst out laughing. 'You're so easy,' she said.

I didn't turn back this time; I just kept walking until I was in the completely bare bedroom with a candle, a tiny battery-powered charger, and a long note my brother had snuck into the grocery bags along with $200 in cash.

> *You can charge with this. It'll take a long time but it'll do the job. There are some backup batteries in the bag if you need them.*
>
> *Aunt Margie knows you're OK but nothing else. We're living proof that she can keep a secret, but she's also a mad gossip and told me she doesn't want to know where you are in case she's asked. I think that was a good plan.*
>
> *We have a lot to do. I'm working on finding out who this Julio guy is.*

That's the problem when you're communicating by notes; whole news cycles go by without an update.

> *Mankiewicz calls about every two hours and asks the same questions. He seems surprised when he gets the same answers.*
>
> *I'm guessing you told him about us. I'm not mad at you, Frannie. I've wanted to tell someone but I don't ever get close enough to trust. But if something's going on between the two of you and it's a danger, you need to tell me. Trust runs both ways.*
>
> *The incident report of Damien's murder naturally doesn't give any really helpful details; I looked it up. It's public record and that means there's nothing in it the cops don't want you to know. No mention of physical evidence that Brooker might have picked up off the floor except some hair, which doesn't make sense, and not a word about fingerprints on the extension cord or anywhere else. For a spontaneous crime, this one seems to have been really well planned.*

Brian Hennessey has been calling the office. I've told him that Eliza isn't in danger but can't come home now. He doesn't want to accept that but, as you know, I can be fairly stubborn. He's not going to find out anything else until Eliza wants him to.

I did some checking in places I shouldn't have been and found some medical records on Eliza. She's taking some hormones but isn't yet on a path to surgery. If she goes without her meds for too long things could start to reverse themselves.

Also checked on Rainbow Zelensky, who appears to have vanished into thin air. She leased the apartment where you found Eliza six months ago and has been paying the rent in cash to the super, a guy named John Cassidy. Nobody seems terribly concerned about Rainbow, which makes me concerned about Rainbow.

Leave me a note in the fourth drop spot tomorrow morning and I'll leave you what I can there. In the meantime, try not to get killed or arrested. You're not leaving me that detective agency all to myself.

K

That was a lot to unpack. So were the groceries, in which I had found basic unperishable foods that didn't require a can opener or utensils. There was bread but no butter. There was soda and bottled water but no juice or milk. There wasn't anything to make a sandwich out of, which made the bread, a store-bought whole-wheat loaf, seem kind of lonely. There had been two bagels included, one with cream cheese for me, one with lettuce and tomato for Eliza. They'd survive long enough to serve as a breakfast in the morning. Although again, Ken had been unable to provide us with a working bathroom. We'd be having lunch out early to find a restroom. We'd pay in cash.

There was also a pen and a legal pad so I could respond to Ken's note. I'd do that after I charged up. The little charger, which luckily included a USB cable and instructions, didn't provide the same tingly rush that a real one, plugged into the wall, would, but I could feel myself getting stronger . . . very . . . slowly. Ken was right; this would take a while. Best to think about next steps.

I hadn't had time to process all that had happened. Eliza and I had been moving too fast and too often to evaluate. But now, lying on the bare floor in a bare room in a bare building that still needed a good deal of construction before it could be called habitable, I had nothing but time. And a bagel with cream cheese for the morning.

Start at the beginning, Aunt Margie always says. So I avoided blowing out the candle, no matter how I might need it again, so I wouldn't fall asleep, and I thought about the scene in the basement across from Yankee Stadium. I forced myself to mentally look at Damien's body with the thick extension cord coiled around his throat.

Had I seen what Brooker had picked up? I was pretty sure it wasn't hair; Merchant or Brooker was covering something. It was small, certainly, and floppy, if I remembered correctly. Paper? Maybe, but probably not. Was there anything on Damien's body that could help? Surely Brooker and Merchant had been all over the photographs from the scene with a fine-toothed comb and had the benefit of having read the full ME's report. What was I missing? There was no doubt in my mind that Eliza had not killed Damien, and for reasons I couldn't begin to justify I didn't think Jules had done it, either.

It's amazing what you can recall when you're in a room that is one step away from a sensory deprivation tank. In that dim space something struck me: Damien's mouth had not been open. His eyes were not bulging. I lay back, just starting to feel a little more strength return to my muscles and my brain, and considered the conclusion I'd just drawn for myself.

Damien Van Dorn had not been strangled.

TWENTY-FOUR

First, we decided to save the bagels for at night because we both needed a restroom and didn't want to stiff the wait staff at the nearest breakfast place. I felt fully charged after a good six hours of battery boost and had come up with a plan, which Eliza had agreed to reluctantly, only because it was my plan.

For the first time since we'd met, Eliza and I separated. We both needed to communicate with important people in our lives and that meant visiting libraries. I felt it was best if we were not in the same building when we made ourselves vulnerable to surveillance, so Eliza took the subway to the Kips Bay Library on Third Avenue and I walked all the way to the Columbus Library on Tenth Avenue in the low 50s. I just needed the walk, and I put all my effort into it, feeling fresh from my charge. My legs are longer than most, so what should have been a forty-minute walk took me just under half an hour. We'd agreed to meet on 28th Street at the Lexington Avenue line in two hours. And I'd insisted Eliza promise me not to spend more than twenty minutes online in the library. I figured that gave her thirty minutes online in the library.

The Columbus branch is a short, two-story building that seems determined not to draw attention to itself. It does have a sign by the door identifying itself, but it looks more like a small school or an ancient office building (it's more than a hundred years old) than a library until you get inside.

I found the public computers on the lower level, used the code the librarian had provided (in exchange for a scan of my driver's license, which I have never used and hoped would not become visible to the authorities for at least the twenty minutes – really twenty minutes – I expected to spend here), and started checking in on what until yesterday had been my life.

The publicly available version of the medical examiner's report on Damien Van Dorn was remarkably skimpy. The cause of death was listed as asphyxiation, which I thought might have been true or not, brought on by strangulation, which I very much doubted.

The extension cord was almost certainly a prop to distract investigators. Details were, let's say, limited. In other words, the real ME's report wasn't available to the public yet.

I check in on my email immediately after looking at that. Aunt Margie and Ken were no longer attempting to communicate that way. I had chosen the Columbus branch because the message drop spot Ken had directed me to was near it, and that would be my next stop. Paper notes were not the quickest form of communication but they were efficient and would be until the first time it rained.

Mank had continued to frantically email, and I assumed he was texting as well but my phone wasn't going to be activated so I wouldn't find out. I responded to the last one of his emails:

> *The cops are chasing the wrong suspect. Eliza wasn't there. Check on possible inaccuracies in the ME's report. I can't respond by phone. But I've decided not to hate you, so there's that. Talk to Ken. He doesn't know where I am but he can get me information. Don't ask for anything else.*

That was probably more than I should have said, particularly the part about not hating Mank, because it still stung when I thought about how he'd reacted to the real me. But Eliza was giving me some insight into the dangers of showing people your true self, and even if she hadn't really forgiven Brian yet, she wasn't openly angry at him. Maybe there was a lesson to be learned.

Technically, Ken did know where I was, or at least where I'd been, but I didn't need Mank knowing that. He's a nice cop, but he's a cop. He'd do cop things, which would include closing in on a suspect in a homicide and the woman who'd helped her escape. In a weird way I couldn't blame him, but then there were all the normal ways.

I sent an email to Shelly because I couldn't call or text her. Basically it said that while I was still interested in finding out about Malcolm X. Mitchell, it wasn't my top priority at the moment and I appreciated her help. I did not suggest that she ignore any bulletins she might have seen about me because I was hoping there hadn't been anything that would have traveled as far as Portland, Oregon.

But I added a quick paragraph asking if she knew anything about a guy named Julio, or Jules, or Eric, who might have been involved in a drug trade in the Bronx. She'd tell me that was an NYPD matter, but it would gnaw at her that I'd have bothered to ask and she would do some digging. People look down on passive-aggressive behavior, but it can be really effective.

Then I checked with a friend of mine in Texas named Luci who'd helped on some of my criminal justice studies to inquire about possible reasons a man could look like he was strangled when in fact he was, you know, not. Luckily I knew her email from memory because my iPhone was proving to be an attractive little bauble that, if used at all, could send me to jail for a very unpleasant number of years.

I'd been checking the clock obsessively and it was time to leave before the entire police department of New York City came to escort me out of the building. That would have been so inconvenient.

The phone was still out of the question, but before I left I had just enough time to log on to my cell phone provider's website and check on messages. The expected pleas from Mank, a few quick confused tries from Ken before he got my last text, and some from Igavda confirming that I could use her place to crash, which was sweet but completely dangerous now.

Then there was one at the bottom that I almost overlooked because I thought it was a scam. But the address, which was not familiar, seemed to be from an official agency. I glanced at it. *Contact me re: Important business involving the World Health Organization. We need to meet.*

It was signed, which texts never are, 'Malcolm X. Mitchell.'

I sent back, *You're not from WHO. Who are you really and how did you get my number?*

There was no point in waiting for a response. I needed to be away from this building as quickly as possible. I logged out, stood up and grabbed my bag. I was at the door to the library in the same time it takes The Flash to do anything.

Because I'm paranoid, I stopped at the door to check for the people who might be hunting me, which at the moment would encompass the entire Eastern Seaboard. And again, my irrational fears turned out to be absolutely rational.

Leaning on a car I would have bet my entire bank account wasn't his was Detective Sergeant Louis Merchant, barely even trying to look casual. I mean, at least he could have been looking at his watch or tying his shoelaces. He wasn't wearing a wristwatch and his shoes were slip-ons. Merchant was a real class act.

Having learned my lesson at the first library, I had gone online and checked the layout of the Columbus library, so I knew exactly where the (publicly accessible) back door of the building was located. I walked back into the library itself and headed for the other door, plotting in my head what to do when Brooker was leaning against (I decided) a tree and looking at his phone because he really did want to blend in.

But when I reached the door and checked through the glass, no cops were to be seen. Brooker wasn't there and neither were any of his academy classmates. Merchant must have been staking out the library on his own.

That suggested two possible explanations and neither of them was calming. It could have been that Merchant had followed me from the subway somehow and decided to wait until I came out, maybe checking in on the library computer records, to arrest me.

Or it could have been that Merchant had been monitoring the Columbus library computers on his own and didn't want any other cops to be around when I exited the building.

I decided I liked the second scenario even less than the first, and I wasn't crazy about the first.

But the first order of business was to check again, thank my good luck that this door wasn't being monitored, and get out of Dodge before Merchant considered the concept of multiple exit portals. He wasn't the brightest cop I'd ever met but he'd probably heard of back doors.

I walked out, wholly expecting to hear someone tell me to freeze after two steps, but there was nothing. If I were stupid enough to walk around the block and check out the front entrance, I'd probably see Merchant still leaning on that car not doing anything but looking like a cop.

Ashamed as I am to admit it, I was more than two blocks away and heading for the message drop point before my stomach clenched and I realized why Brooker hadn't been watching me.

He was trailing Eliza.

TWENTY-FIVE

T he spot where I could find a communiqué from Ken, on Ninth Avenue, was on the way to my planned meet with Eliza, where I'd find if she was already in custody or if Brooker was as bad a tracker as his partner. I was walking much more quickly than usual and starting to work up a sweat. I wished Ken would have included my exercise clothes in with the groceries but, being Ken, he had not thought of clothing. (And in all fairness, there wasn't enough space in the grocery bags for that sort of thing). I was going to need a shower sooner than I'd anticipated, and that presented yet another in a series of problems, and not the one I needed to concentrate on immediately.

That would be Eliza. Running to 28th and Lex would have taken too long even for me because getting across town from West to East is untenable, so I made it as quickly as possible to the Port Authority Bus Terminal on 42nd Street at Eighth Avenue. There I could catch the S train or the 7. As it turned out, the 7 train got me to Grand Central Terminal, only six blocks from where I'd told Eliza I'd meet her, and I even took the subway from there because it was only one stop.

All along the way I castigated myself for creating a plan where we'd split up. I should have known better than to let Eliza, the focus of many investigations, out of my sight. If she wasn't at our rendezvous point, I'd have to begin an entirely new search, frantic all the time that she might be arrested, or dead. The cops had clearly wanted to shoot at her when we'd been exiting from our ice-cream excursion.

But my fears proved, for once, to be baseless, because Eliza was pacing at the entrance to the Lexington Avenue line at 28th Street, just where I'd told her to be. And a fast scan of the area showed no evidence of law enforcement activity. Apparently Merchant wanted me and only me.

I wasn't sure if that was bad or good.

'Did anybody follow you?' I asked the minute I was close enough for her to hear without my shouting.

She looked blankly at me for a second. 'How would I know?' It was a good point.

I told her about spotting Merchant at the library. Eliza said she hadn't seen anyone at all suspicious where she'd been. Then I pointed to the subway entrance. 'Let's go,' I said.

'Where?'

'Uptown.' There wouldn't be any going back to the construction site now; there would be workers all over the place who would see us. We needed to find a safe haven. At the very least, we needed to find a place to have lunch.

'I don't think we can go to libraries to get online anymore,' I told Eliza once the 6 train was loud enough to cover our voices, which was immediately. 'They've found us both times we tried it. Someone is tracking us better than I would have expected.'

Eliza looked thoughtful, stared at her Skechers for a moment, and then directed her gaze at my face. 'They haven't found us,' she said. 'They've found *you*.'

That was entirely true but it wasn't what I wanted to hear at this moment. 'What did you find out in your library?' I asked. That wasn't exactly changing the subject, but it was close. I'd think about the implications of the cops looking for me and not Eliza later.

Eliza gave me a quick look that indicated she saw what I was doing but didn't comment. 'I heard from Laura,' she said.

Finally, something that resembled a development we might be able to use! 'What did she say?'

'I'm not going to tell you anything that will get anybody in trouble,' she said in a hurry.

'You were already staying in someone else's apartment and if I'm not mistaken you're still carrying Rainbow's gun,' I pointed out. 'Everyone you know is already in trouble. This is about getting us all out.'

We stopped talking when the train stopped at 51st Street, then waited until the doors closed and we started moving again.

'Does Laura know anything about Damien's murder?' I asked. 'Truth, now. This is no time to protect someone if it puts us in more danger.'

'Laura definitely wasn't there when Damien got killed,' Eliza answered. 'But she knew about staking out the basement and probably found Damien's body before you did. She got scared and ran and that's why I hadn't heard from her for a couple of days.'

'That and us not turning on our phones,' I said.

Eliza looked displeased.

We went through the same routine at 59th Street and I gave a glance to the subway map in our car even though I knew the 6 train by heart. 'Let's get off at Sixty-eighth,' I said.

Eliza's eyes widened a bit. 'That's New Amsterdam,' she said.

I knew it was the stop nearest her college. I nodded. 'We have people to see.'

'I don't know if that's a good idea.' Her shoes became objects of great interest again. I almost never look at my shoes but then they're very basic designs. It's hard to be creative in my size.

'It's the only good plan to have. We don't have access to physical evidence and the cops have clearly already decided you did it, although that becomes less likely with every passing minute. I don't even really know how Damien died.'

Eliza's eyes shot up to look at mine. 'He got strangled, didn't he?'

I told her about my analysis of Damien's body and how asphyxiation seemed to be almost impossible. 'I think maybe he was poisoned to make it look that way, something that would cause him to lose the capacity to breathe.'

'That's crazy,' Eliza said. The train was slowing down and she looked more panicky.

'Show me something about this whole business that isn't,' I answered.

We stopped at 68th Street and without a coherent plan in my head I sort of insisted that Eliza get off the subway and come with me to the center of the New Amsterdam University campus, which is the common area of separate buildings. It was where I had last spoken to Laura Rapinoe.

While we were walking toward the campus, I asked Eliza if there was anyone besides Laura who would have known about Damien's comings and goings, who he was dealing with and what he was doing. Even though the most obvious explanation of his murder was that it was related to his pill business, it's always a mistake to go with the most obvious explanation and not investigate anything else. 'Laura was probably in love with him, from what you've told me, but she said it was you who were interested in Damien,' I said. 'It sounds like he didn't reciprocate. Is there someone else he might have been involved with?'

'It wasn't me.' Eliza didn't want to go where we were going and she was retreating into her less communicative self.

'I get that. If it wasn't Laura either, who could it have been?'

'I dunno.' I thought I'd made progress with Eliza. Clearly coming here had been a mistake on that front, but we might still get some useful information and that was worth a few hours of Eliza hating me again. Maybe I'd send a note to Ken so he could meet us for lunch. She liked Ken.

'Do you know where to find Laura? Would you two have a class together today?' Maybe Laura was the key. There didn't seem to be anyone else except the elusive Rainbow, about whom I still knew next to nothing.

'No. Let's go.' Did she think it was going to be that easy?

'Not just yet. Let's find Laura.' Skimpy though it was, my plan consisted of confronting Laura Rapinoe with the fact that she'd been lying to me whenever we'd spoken, that she'd been at least in lust with Damien Van Dorn, and that she needed to come clean about what had been going on around him before his murder. Hey, I *told* you it was skimpy. But right now it was all I had.

'I don't want to find Laura.' Eliza was reverting to a pouty ten-year-old. That wasn't going to work on me, either.

'Well, if you have a better idea, I'm listening.' I kept walking in the direction of what could be called a quad, except it was all concrete and had its own subway stop. There's quads and there's *quads*. Eliza was following, but not really keeping up.

'Julio knows who did it. We should find him.' The voice was coming from behind me.

'Jules *doesn't* know who did it or he wouldn't have come looking for us. Laura's our best source at this point. She might have been in the room with him waiting for Jules and his buddy for a while. I doubt she was there when he was killed.'

Eliza didn't answer me, probably because I made sense and she couldn't argue with it. I made a point of not giving her a smug I-told-you-so look. I'm classy.

'Besides,' I said, 'this is where Damien was doing his business. Maybe you'll recognize other people around here who were buying from Damien. Now, I know you're not a narc and neither am I. I'm not interested in knowing who was buying Damien's pills. I *am* interested in finding out who killed him, and every thread you pull on can lead to something. Does that sound right to you?'

Again there was no response and this time I didn't think it was because I was being so brilliant. That was never a good position from which to begin for me.

I spun around and my worst fears were realized. There were any number of people of undergraduate age milling around, some in a hurry, heading to or from class or with some other business at the college.

But not Eliza. Even after I scanned the area, she was nowhere to be seen.

TWENTY-SIX

After all was said and done and I had kicked myself around the block mentally, there was nothing to do but to go home. I trudged up the steps to my building and then up two flights to my apartment and by then was so emotionally ragged that the only way to cheer myself up was to remember that I'd be able to take a shower soon. And what kind of comment on a person's life is that?

It was a decent bet that Merchant would show up at the apartment soon because Eliza was right about one thing: he did always seem to know where I, and not she, was. I was fully charged and could handle him easily enough if it came to that, but the shower was definitely at the top of my priority list, and if he tried to arrest me while I was doing that, the NYPD would have a really serious lawsuit on its hands.

But when I got inside I found my brother and Aunt Margie, who normally weren't here this time of day. Still, I'm willing to bet I didn't look as surprised to see them as they did to see me.

It was one of those TV sitcom moments when everyone said, 'What are you doing here?' at the same time. But then Ken added, 'And where's Eliza?' So that took some explaining, during which I felt like an idiot who needed a shower.

Once my demoralizing tale had been told, Aunt Margie told me to sit down next to her, which I did, and she patted my hand and told me it wasn't my fault, except that we all knew it was. I should have been keeping a closer eye on Eliza. I'd fooled myself into thinking we trusted each other.

'Why'd you come home?' Ken asked. 'The cops can be at our door any minute.'

'I didn't come straight home. I went to Rainbow's place in Queens because I thought Eliza might go there, but nobody was home. The door's been fixed, though.' I put my head back and closed my eyes. I wasn't tired but I was weary. Closing my eyes was the next best thing to a shower. 'Then once I couldn't find her and had no idea where to look, I figured I'd come here. The cops don't think *I* killed anybody.'

Aunt Margie had spent decades as a radio crime reporter, so when she looked pensive it got my attention. (I'd reopened my eyes by now.) 'No, but they'll call you an accessory after the fact, they'll say you harbored a fugitive from justice and they'll squeeze you for information on where Eliza could be.'

Closing my eyes again seemed like the way to go. 'If I knew where Eliza could be, I'd go there and keep harboring the fugitive,' I said. 'Let them come and try to squeeze me. I've come up with a few defensive moves over the years.'

'We've got to find her.' Ken was focused on the task at hand. 'She's out there, she's going to feel the temptation to use her phone and she'll get picked up in a nanosecond.' He turned to me. 'What can we do?' Ken talks a nice game but he knows I'm the more experienced investigator in the firm. He got his license because I'd grilled him for days on the questions that would be on the exam.

'First thing is to report to her dad,' I said. 'Actually, the first thing is for me to take a shower. It's been days.'

'You took one yesterday morning,' Ken pointed out. 'You used up all the hot water.'

Was that only one day ago? It seemed like weeks. 'Trust me. I need another. I'm going to do that right now.' And, fool that I am, I stood up to go to my room and find a robe.

Before I could make it out of the room, Ken said, 'I still want to know how we can find Eliza. She's out there alone.'

'That kid is good at taking care of herself,' I told him. 'We'll look for her, of course, but at the moment I'm more worried the cops will find her than her being on her own.'

I walked into my bedroom and took off all the clothes I'd been wearing, as it turned out, not for a week but only since the day before. Then I got an especially fluffy terrycloth robe from my closet, lamented that it wasn't really my size and therefore fell well above my knees, and opened the door to finally have that promised shower.

And when I was two steps from the bathroom door, just in the line of sight of the living room, Aunt Margie and Ken were sitting in a chair and on the sofa, respectively, just as they'd been when I'd walked out.

Except that in the other side chair now was seated Detective

Sergeant Richard Mankiewicz of the New York Police Department.

At least he wasn't still holding that damned fork.

There was a brief (I'll say) moment of panic and then I turned to run back into my bedroom and at least put on underwear, but it was too late. 'Fran,' I heard Mank say. 'Come on in. We should talk.' Like it was his apartment or something.

'I need to get dressed,' I said.

'Don't worry about it.' That, dear reader, was my brother, who at the very least was finding some aspects of my current situation amusing. 'It's fine.'

'No, it's *not*,' I said, and fled to my bedroom.

I locked the door. It wasn't that I thought anyone was going to try to force their way in, but it gave me that sense of safety that at the moment was more an illusion than a reality. Hey, they're my emotions.

What were my options? I could climb down the fire escape and try to, you know, escape, but the window squeaked loudly when you opened it and Mank would know before I made it out. Besides, the whole idea of coming home was that I had nothing to run from without Eliza by my side. And overpowering a New York City detective to run out into what might very well have been a small army of other cops didn't seem like such a good idea, either.

My best choice – and it wasn't great – was to let Mank book me and go through whatever process it would take to get back to where I was now, only without cops chasing me. It wasn't much but it was something. Don't ask me what.

I put on a pair of jeans and a very bland khaki t-shirt that was, amazingly, a little too large for me (I bought it at a men's big and tall shop) to keep from being too revealing. Because I'd just walked out into the hallway wearing a bathrobe that covered at least fifty percent of me. No sense sending false signals.

There was a series of deep breaths, which my martial arts sensei had taught me as a means of finding my center (which I always thought was right around the bellybutton) and then I opened the bedroom door and walked out again, fully dressed and prepared to meet my fate.

My fate, at that moment, was sipping from a glass of iced tea Aunt Margie had certainly provided (Ken can cook but it would never occur to him to offer someone a drink other than a cold beer) and looking as causal as if he had dropped by to discuss an upcoming police fundraiser. Why the police need fundraisers with an annual budget of $11 billion is something of a stumper, in my opinion, but perhaps that's beside the point.

'What can I do for you?' I said when I got to the living room. I sat on the sofa next to Aunt Margie, who is the safest person I've ever met.

'I'd like to know where you've been for the past twenty-four hours,' Mank said in a tone so conversational he might have been telling me about a movie he'd seen on Netflix the night before.

'Any number of places,' I told him, which was undeniably true.

'Can you tell me what some of them were?' he asked.

Ken looked amused, which pissed me off beyond the usual scale. Aunt Margie looked at Mank as if she thought he was a nice young man, which served to infuriate me even more. Didn't my family understand that this man was the enemy?

'Are there any rights I need to be made aware of?' I asked Mankiewicz.

He had the temerity to look surprised. His eyebrows practically left his forehead and circled over him like one of those banner planes that carry advertisements over the Jersey shore. 'You think I'm arresting you?' he said. 'What for?'

The one advantage of Mank being here was that I no longer had to worry about the cops being able to trace me; they clearly knew where I was. So I could break out my poor neglected iPhone and fire it up. It had eighteen percent power left and needed a charge. I could empathize, but I didn't need a boost right now. 'You've been texting me pretty much on a quarter-hour basis,' I told him. 'One of those messages read, *Come in and let me help you.* Isn't that what cops say when they want to arrest you?'

'It's also what friends say when they want to help,' Mank said softly. 'Fran, I get where you're coming from. You were trying to keep Eliza safe and there were officers everywhere you turned up. So my being here must seem awfully suspicious.'

'Ya think?'

Mank stood up and approached my end of the couch. 'Let me explain. The Van Dorn case is not in my precinct. I have no connection to it. I'm not here to arrest anybody because I haven't been assigned a case. I'm here as a friend and I'm trying to figure out how to help get you clear of all this stuff that's been going on. I'm not here as a cop.'

'You caught Damien's case,' I reminded him.

'As a missing person. The murder took place in the Bronx. I can consult but I'm not the lead on that one.'

It was municipal red tape but it might mean I could trust Mank a little. But oops. I immediately powered down my phone. 'I probably shouldn't have turned that on,' I said. 'Detective Merchant will show up at our door in about three minutes.'

This is how my family works: Ken immediately curled his hands into fists and stole a look at the apartment door. He stood up to check if it was locked, and it was because we live in New York.

Aunt Margie's face took on a stony look. Anyone who might possibly be a threat to Ken or me has to get through Aunt Margie first, and they're not going to be happy they did.

'It's not that easy to trace a cell phone that's just showing someone's text messages,' Mank told me. 'Nobody's coming to your door just yet. Now tell me, where is Eliza Hennessey and what does she know about the murder in the Bronx?'

I didn't want it to happen or consciously try for it, but my eyes narrowed. All of a sudden Mankiewicz was asking me questions about the fugitive I'd been keeping from the NYPD for more than a day. 'I thought you weren't here as a cop,' I said, and there was a definite edge in my voice.

'I'm not. I'm here as a friend.' Mank squatted down just a touch to look me in the eye. The fact was, he probably could have done it standing up, but the man has some pride. 'You have a problem and it's tied to Eliza. You don't have to tell me where she is, but it'll help if you tell me what she knows and what her plan is at the moment. Because you're right, Merchant and Brooker definitely want to talk to her, and they think she's violent. There are some reports she's carrying an unlicensed gun.'

Ken glanced at me. He knew about Eliza's gun but neither of us was aware the police had known about it. 'I don't know about that,' I said. It was true; I had no idea if the gun Eliza was carrying was licensed or not.

Mank shook his head to indicate it didn't matter. 'What did Eliza tell you about the murder? Does she know who killed Damien Van Dorn?'

I told him what Eliza had told me, up to a point. That she hadn't been there when Damien died. That she didn't know who had killed him, although I left out her suspicions about who it might have been because they seemed to have included everyone. But I did tell him about Jules.

'The guy they call Julio found us getting ice cream in the Village,' I said. 'He told us he didn't have anything to do with Damien's murder because it would have been bad for business. He also told us to call him Jules.'

'Yeah, we know about him,' Mank said with a wry smile. 'I believe you threw him to a number of officers outside the ice-cream place.'

'He was using inappropriate language in front of both the ice cream and some young children,' I said. 'I didn't see an alternative.'

Aunt Margie's mouth had dropped open. 'You threw a man at some police officers?' she said. 'You disappoint me, Frannie.'

That cut deep. I lowered my eyes. The coffee table looked sad. 'I'm sorry, Aunt Margie.'

'Did you at least yell "fore" or something before you threw him?' Aunt Margie has a wicked sense of humor that still fools me to this day. I lost interest in the coffee table and looked at her for the silly grin and then to Mank.

'Where is Eliza now?' he asked.

'You said you wouldn't ask me that,' I reminded him.

'I said you didn't have to tell me. I didn't say I wouldn't ask.' Everybody was being a wiseguy today.

'The plain truth is that I don't know where she is,' I said.

'I'm not here as a cop,' he repeated.

I stood up because my legs needed stretching. This had the effect of making me look like I was taking Mank in to buy his first suit. 'I'm not kidding,' I said. 'I lost her in the crowd outside New Amsterdam University about two hours ago. I have no idea where she is and I'm worried about her.'

Mank had gotten out of his squat to face me but it was an uphill battle no matter what on his part. He was looking into my neck, which at least was the gentlemanly thing to do. 'Fran, we've got to find that girl,' he said.

'OK,' I answered. 'Got any ideas?'

TWENTY-SEVEN

We didn't go anywhere until I had that shower. That was not negotiable.

Because I hadn't accessed my emails or sent a text, and because I'd charged and set my phone on airplane mode (no contact to a cell tower) before turning it off, Merchant had not materialized at my apartment door. It was a blessing and a curse. I would have liked to have looked him in the face and asked him how it felt to try and track down a nineteen-year-old girl. I doubt Merchant would have taken the point well, however.

Instead, I'd sent Ken (that is, I suggested that he go) to the construction site just to watch. If Eliza showed up he could follow her or at least confirm that she'd made it back inside for the night.

I didn't want to recruit Mank into my merry band of investigators, but he insisted I would need backup, Aunt Margie was probably not the right choice for that job, and besides he would have followed on his own because he already knew where I was and what I was doing. It was very much a no-other-choice situation.

As it turned out, the NYPD also had the last known address for Eric 'Julio' Sanderson, something I had not been able to turn up on my own. I'll admit it. So we were off to East Harlem to check in on good ol' Jules and see to his welfare.

Mank, not used to the private investigator lifestyle, had wanted to drive up to 118th Street but I felt that a police car, however unmarked, double-parked in this neighborhood, would have been just a little too obvious to avoid detection. So it was the subway, however less personal the transportation might be. Because this was my operation and I was calling the shots.

'Can we talk about that morning at the diner?' he asked around 68th Street.

My face must have betrayed my discomfort with the question.

'OK,' he said, 'let me rephrase. *Why* can't we talk about that morning at the diner?'

'It was humiliating and disappointing, just to start,' I told him, looking up at the ads for slip-and-fall lawyers and weight-loss treatments. 'Why would I want to talk about that?'

Mank exhaled extravagantly, but it was not for effect; it was genuine. He felt badly about the way he'd acted. 'I can't apologize enough,' he said. 'I wasn't thinking.'

'That's true.' Why hadn't we reached the 116th Street station yet? 'You had no idea how you were making me feel.'

I braved a glance at Mank; his face was drawn and pained. 'I know,' he said. 'It was a lot to hit me with and I had no way to be prepared. That's not an excuse, it's an explanation.'

'I figure you see me as a freak now.' I don't know where that came from. I hadn't planned on saying it. Amazingly, the other MTA passengers were not paying attention to our heartfelt exchange. I tried to concentrate on what we were going to do when we found Jules and that wasn't going very well.

'I see you as someone who I care about and who was hurt by my actions and I am very sorry about that.'

As apologies go, that wasn't bad at all. I looked at Mank. I don't cry much and I wasn't crying now. But it was possible I was blinking a little more than usual. You can't let your eyes dry up, you know.

'Do you know a guy named Malcolm X. Mitchell?' I asked.

Now it was Mank who was blinking a little too much. 'What? Um . . . no. Who's that?'

'It's an excellent question.'

We didn't talk much the rest of the way, but when we reached 116th Street, Mank let me walk off the train ahead of him and we went up the stairs somehow more relaxed than we had walked down. There's nothing like a nice soothing ride on the New York subway.

People still looked twice at us on the street. For some reason men are supposed to be taller than women, according to society, and that was clearly not the case here. But we were not appearing as a couple; we were on a case and we were working. So they needed to lose their prejudices and calm down (which would have been equally true if we were out on a date).

The building at E. 118th and Second Avenue wasn't terribly interesting to look at. It was a five-story brick building that had been renovated in a halfhearted fashion. It was clean enough but hardly stylish and the front door had been propped open by someone with a two-liter soda bottle, which was convenient for Mank and me but a serious problem for the people who lived in the building. I removed the bottle after we walked in. Let the person who left it there bring a key next time.

We walked up to the second floor and found the door to Eric/Julio/Jules's apartment. I saw Mank reach into his pocket for his badge and shook my head; he wasn't here in an official capacity. For this moment, right now, he was an operative of K&F Stein Investigations. If the subject came up.

'He won't know you, will he?' I asked quietly. Mank shook his head. 'Then let's keep it that way.'

Mank put the badge away. But I noticed when he did that the windbreaker he didn't need in this weather was concealing his service weapon. I wasn't sure how I felt about that. So I knocked.

It took a long moment but the door opened. I thought someone in Jules's line of work might have a peep hole in the door but he didn't. Maybe the landlord wouldn't approve. The toughest people in New York live in fear of their landlords.

Jules took one look and tried to slam the door but I'd already straightened my arm and held it with my palm flat. 'We're just here to talk, Jules,' I said.

'You are a crazy lady,' he said. I thought that was unnecessarily harsh. 'You threw me at cops.'

'You were using inappropriate language around small children,' I told him. 'I really felt that you needed to be taught a lesson. We're coming in. Are you going to try to make it hard for us? Because I can still lift you.'

He stepped back with a sheepish expression on his face, although to be honest he didn't look a thing like a sheep. He looked like a guy named Eric. I walked in first and Mank followed me without saying a word. Smart Mank.

The place was a little beyond functional. It appeared to be a two-bedroom apartment with the usual Manhattan tiny kitchen but a decent living area with a flat-screen TV mounted on the wall. The furniture was tasteful and clean. The place didn't need

painting. It must have cost a fortune in rent every month. I knew
that because my apartment wasn't nearly as nice and it cost a
fortune in rent every month.

It was, without question, not what you'd expect from a guy
who had supplied Adderall (and probably other pharmaceuticals)
to Damien Van Dorn.

'Nice place,' I said. 'You must have quite the day job.'

Jules was a lot of things, but quick on the uptake was not one
of them. 'Thanks,' he said.

He clearly wasn't going to offer us a cold drink or some
Adderall so I just plowed right through. 'OK, how about you tell
us the name of the guy you sent to intimidate Damien Van Dorn
and we can start with them instead of you.'

You could say this about Jules: he had nerve. Nerve enough
to look surprised when I said that. 'What you talking about?'
On top of everything else I was going to have to give him grammar
lessons. This day was getting exhausting and it wasn't that late
yet.

'If you mean, "What am I talking about," then I think you're
shortchanging yourself, Eric,' I said. No reaction to the use of
his real name. 'You sent your men after Damien because he was
behind to you for some money. They threatened him and he
decided to retaliate by ambushing them in an apartment building
in the Bronx. Now I will grant you that as a strategy that leaves
a lot to be desired, including a strategy, but those are the facts.
So let's start again. What is the name of the man you sent after
Damien, the one who wasn't you? The one who has a birthmark
on his face.'

'I don't know nothing about that.' Jules was sticking with his
pose even though it wasn't the least bit convincing. It's not hard
to defeat people like that but it takes time. I was thinking that
my original plan of picking him up and throwing him to the cops
might have been the best strategy after all.

'So you do know something about it?' I asked. If I was going
to play schoolmarm I might as well go the whole way. 'You
employed a double negative.'

'I don't employ nobody,' he said. 'I'm an entrepreneur.' That
word he could get right. He'd clearly used it frequently.

'Look, Eric,' I began.

'It's Jules.'

'OK, sure. Jules. Damien Van Dorn was murdered in the basement in the Bronx or he was murdered somewhere else and brought there. You are clearly the most logical suspect in that murder because you had a grudge.' I sat down on his expensive sofa to show him I could. 'Damien owed you money in your drug operation on the New Amsterdam University campus. So the cops are watching you. You want them to stop watching you because they're making it harder for you to sell pills to college kids. So I'm offering you a way to make things better – for you. Tell us who your musclebound buddy was and we can feed them to the police instead of you. Because you're not stupid enough to have killed Damien yourself, so surely he did, didn't he?'

For the record, I didn't believe a word of what I was saying. Damien had been hiding out in the basement waiting for his two pursuers to come home so he could confront them. They had no reason to suspect he was waiting there for them. So it was unlikely one of them was the killer. But they had been around and they knew about it, and let's be real, so did our friend Eric/Jules/Julio.

'No way,' he said, betraying the fact that he had indeed sent anyone after Damien. 'Nobody was supposed to get hurt and everybody knew it. Look, there are people following *me* now. I see them whenever I walk outside, pretending not to follow me. So no, I didn't want this. I didn't tell nobody to kill Damien. We didn't touch that guy.'

'*Who* didn't touch that guy?' Mank was impatient with all the dancing around the point and I didn't blame him. 'What is his name, Julio?'

'*Don't call me that!*' Let's-call-him-Jules's arms tensed up and he shifted to the balls of his feet as if he were going to lunge forward.

'Why not?' I asked. 'What's so much better about being Jules than being Julio? Your real name is Eric. Why not use that?'

Whatever-his-name-was's face twitched and he relaxed his posture. He remembered that I could easily toss him around the room and decided to be our friend again. 'Because who's afraid of a guy named Eric?' he said.

'OK, Jules,' I said again. 'You don't want to give up your men. I respect that. But I need to know who's putting Eliza's life in danger. She's my focus. The cops can find out who killed Damien and I'm OK with that. I need to know, right now, why anybody thinks Eliza had a part in Damien's death and, more than that, I *really* need to know where she is at this minute. So tell me that. Where is Eliza?'

'I thought she was with you,' he said, and he seemed so confused that I believed him. 'Last time I saw her she was with you.'

'Well she's not with me now. Where would she go?'

Jules made a show of thinking that wasn't in the least convincing, proving to me that he didn't think very often because he didn't know what it looked like. He put his hand to his chin and rubbed it. He must have seen that in a movie. 'If she's not with you she must have gone to take care of Rainbow.'

'Rainbow Zelensky?' I said. No, like there were fifteen people named Rainbow in this bizarre caper. 'Why does Rainbow need to be taken care of?'

He stared. 'You don't know?'

I think people should never say, 'You don't know?' Because it's clear you don't, and it makes you feel like you *should* know, and if you don't, you're either a fool or someone has been keeping something from you. It's just rude.

'For the sake of argument, let's say I don't know,' I answered. 'What don't I know?'

'Rainbow is a cat.'

TWENTY-EIGHT

It took a full forty minutes to sort that one out. This was largely because Eric honestly didn't know the answers to such questions as: Why was Rainbow's last name Zelensky? Rainbow was a cat. Whose cat? And whose apartment was that where Eliza had been staying, unless the cat was paying the rent? And the one question I was smart enough not to ask Jules, particularly when Mank was around: Whose gun was Eliza carrying around?

Once we got past the fact that Jules couldn't answer any of those, we focused on the ones he *could* speak to, which didn't actually garner me much in the way of information. 'Tell me who you sent after Damien,' I said for the umpteenth time. 'Eliza's in danger and I need to know if it's from them.' Truth be told, for all I knew Eliza was living on a beach in Bimini and learning how to sport fish, but that wasn't going to get Jules to tell me what I needed to know.

'I'm not giving up my boys,' he said. 'But if she's in trouble, it ain't from me. I didn't send nobody out after Eliza.' On the spot I decided to buy Jules grammar lessons for Christmas.

'But they killed Damien and they know she knew him. Is Laura Rapinoe in trouble too?' That was Mank asking. He's much more a cop than I am and it was showing. Jules had undoubtedly been around cops enough that he could spot one, but on the other hand, by now he might believe that everybody talked like that.

'Who are you, anyway?' It was, startlingly, the first time Jules had thought to ask.

'Call me Rich,' Mankiewicz said, which was both accurate and misleading. But he wasn't here for the NYPD, I kept reminding myself. He was here for me. 'I'm one of Fran's associates.' On that night, that's exactly who he was. 'Now tell me if I need to worry about Eliza and Laura Rapinoe. And I promise, if you tell us who was after Damien to get your money, the cops won't hear about it from us.'

That was a fairly bold promise to make, considering that if Mank heard it, at least one cop would know. But Jules wasn't buying under any circumstances. 'You don't get names from me,' he said. 'I take care of my own.'

'OK,' I said, wresting the conversation back from Mank, who was probably itching to yank his detective shield out of his pocket, the last thing I needed. 'Tell me who you were buying from. You're not making Adderall and whatever else you were selling on your own. You supplied Damien but you have a supplier yourself. Who is it?'

Jules looked at me with a combination of disbelief and pity. 'Are you nuts?' Just as an aside, does anyone ever answer that question in the affirmative? *Sure, I'm crazier than a bedbug. Thanks for asking.*

'What, you're going to tell me you don't know nothing about pills? You think that on top of your horrendous double negatives that you can pay for this apartment doing . . . what? Working as a cashier at Target?' I mean, seriously. If people can't use language properly, or at least creatively, what hope do we have for world peace?

'Half the time I don't know what you're talking about,' Jules said.

'Only half?'

Mank chose this moment to play bad not-a-cop to my good not-a-cop. He pushed Jules up against the well-painted wall, which was impressive, given that Mank was also a good three or four inches shorter than Jules. 'We have to come away with something that helps,' he rasped at Jules. 'You're not giving us anything that helps. We want to find Eliza and we need to know who killed Damien Van Dorn. So let's assume you want to hold on to this apartment and all the nice stuff in it. What do you have to offer in exchange for keeping your place nice and neat?'

Now, that wasn't the tactic I'd have employed. I use force on occasion, but only when I think I have no other choice, or if someone is threatening me or a person I care about. This was Mank (sort of) roughing up Jules to get him to talk. Later on I would discuss this with Mank and tell him it wasn't company policy. He wouldn't care because he was a cop, and I probably would only say something if this didn't actually work. People make compromises all the time.

'Back off, man,' Jules said, employing exactly the attitude I had expected. 'I'm not giving up anybody I do business with. I have a legit bodega I own on 112th Street and that's how I pay the rent. So I don't have to tell you nothing. Back off.'

Mank wisely did stand away from Jules and lower his hands. 'We mean no disrespect,' he told Jules. 'We're worried about Eliza.'

'You oughta be,' Jules said. 'From what I hear, that girl's in a whole lot of trouble.'

I didn't care for that. 'You mean the cops are after her,' I said hopefully.

'No, the cops aren't her problem. She crossed somebody – and I don't know who – talking about Damien to people, and now I hear she's being squeezed for more information. Somebody wants to take over Damien's business and they don't want to do it the right way.'

It was worse than I had thought: Eliza hadn't just skipped out on me at New Amsterdam.

She'd been taken.

TWENTY-NINE

I still couldn't use my cell phone, buy luckily Mank wasn't being monitored by any law enforcement agency so he could text Ken. (My brother's phone was showing no signs of being watched, evidenced by the fact that he'd had it turned on the whole time I was at our apartment and no hostile law enforcement officers had shown up.)

'Ken says nobody's come back to the construction site,' Mank reported.

'Of course not, because Eliza didn't just run away, she was taken.' I thought that had been obvious. 'She's not going back there because the choice isn't up to her.'

Mank looked serious as we walked back to the Lexington line. 'You think when Jules said she was being squeezed, that someone took Eliza and they're trying to get some information out of her? That's ominous, but it's a bit of a jump.'

'It fits the facts we have and that's the frustrating part because Jules didn't know who might have taken her and that leaves us with no leads to follow,' I told him. 'That girl is in all kinds of trouble and it was supposed to be my job to keep her safe.'

Mank stopped in his tracks and it took me a few steps to realize it. I turned finally and looked at him, walking back over to stand right in front of him. Which probably had been the point of his stopping in the first place.

'Your job, as I understand it, was to find Eliza and see if she wanted to come back to her father's place,' Mank said. 'You did that. She didn't want to go back. All you need to do is report to Brian Hennessey what you know and your job is done.'

'Wow. That's cold.'

'I'm speaking technically,' he answered. 'I understand that you feel a responsibility to ensure Eliza's safety, and that it might actually entail figuring out who killed Damien Van Dorn, but don't make this about how you haven't done your job. You did your job as soon as you walked into the cat's apartment.'

It all just kind of hit me at once. I'd been operating on adrenaline for long enough now that the reality of the situation felt like being run over by a freight train. I felt myself sort of wilt, my knees to soften up. I didn't crumple to the ground, thank goodness, but my shoulders sagged and I had to put effort into holding up my head. 'Mank,' I said, 'she needs me and I don't know what to do.'

Mank reached over and put his arms around me. Some women might have felt that was a condescending mood in a post #MeToo world, but I knew Mank, and it was exactly what I needed at that moment. If he'd been Aunt Margie I would have wanted the same thing. 'We'll figure it out,' he said so that only I could hear him. 'Come on. You haven't eaten and that makes a person weaker. I know a place.'

Had Mank been another kind of man, he'd have taken me back to the infamous diner where we'd had our most recent meal together. Sort of. (I hadn't eaten.) But he wasn't trying to recreate the dating experience we'd been building then; he wanted to make me feel better. So we took the train all the way downtown and went to Yonah Schimmel's Knish Bakery on Houston Street. The ultimate comfort food.

It was a nice early evening, and we decided to order the knishes and sit outside two blocks away where we found the first possible place to sit, the steps of a brownstone that didn't seem too busy. We opened our bags of food and I, for one, dug in, realizing I hadn't eaten in about nine hours and Yonah's are the best.

'Could she have gone back to the cat's apartment?' Mank said, eating from a kasha knish, which is fine but potato is really what it's all about.

'Don't call it that,' I said. 'I'm still trying to figure out how Rainbow is a cat and not a person, the way everyone talks about her.'

'Nonetheless, I ran a search and the lease is in the cat's name,' Mank said. 'That indicates to me that the real lessee doesn't want anyone to know who they are. Records show they pay the rent in cash to the super every month.'

'It's legal to put a lease in a cat's name?'

Mank pursed his lips. 'It's not illegal.'

'Maybe it's worth going back there, but the last time I went nobody was in the place,' I said.

'I texted Ken. He's on his way there now.'

I looked at Mank for a long moment. He wasn't being a cop now, but he was using his cop skills to help me because that was the best way he knew. I started to remember why I'd said yes to dinner with him the first time we went out. 'Thanks,' I said. I would have said more but that was a really good knish.

'If Eliza isn't there, and someone did take her away, the only way to know where to look would be to know who it was that took her,' Mank said. He was (correctly) avoiding anything emotional in our current situation. He wanted to focus on the task at hand. Making me like him again would come later, I was sure, and I wasn't that certain it wouldn't work.

'If it wasn't Jules, we don't have a lot of candidates,' I noted. 'It's not her dad because she'd just be back at his apartment, and I'm pretty sure he couldn't keep her there. It's not Damien's mom because that would be too rude for her to consider. It's not Laura Rapinoe because she doesn't have a motive.'

'Could it be a hate crime?' Mank suggested. 'A transphobic thing?'

I shrugged. 'That's always a possibility. But there's so much going on around Damien, who wasn't trans, and the little side hustle he had that I can't imagine someone just randomly abducted Eliza on the street because she's trans.'

Mank looked a little embarrassed. 'That's fair.'

But it had struck a nerve somewhere in me and I was just starting to work it out. 'That's the thing, isn't it?' I said. I took the last bite of knish, drank from my bottle of water and stood up.

'What's the thing?' Mank, being male, had downed his knish in about three bites and was already on his feet. He could see the look on my face and realized I was formulating something in the general vicinity of a plan.

'Damien's pill business. It was a little side hustle. It wasn't the biggest enterprise on the upper east side. It was something he was doing to pay the rent and probably only for people he knew.' I started heading back to the subway and Mank followed along looking intrigued but not at all understanding.

'So what?' he asked.

'So how come it was a big enough deal to get him killed and Eliza kidnapped?' I said. 'Who's so worried about little Damien Van Dorn that they had to kill him and then track everyone involved with him for days?'

Mank caught up with me as soon as the sidewalk was wide enough for us to travel astride. He was having a tiny bit of trouble keeping up with my pace because my legs are demonstrably longer than his.

Some men like that.

'What do you mean, everyone involved is being followed?' he said. 'Eliza's been taken and Jules said people were following him, but we don't know if that's even true. Who else?'

The food had helped clear my head, but it wasn't doing a thing for my speed. Knishes are wonderful but they're not the lightest food in the world. I kept moving but I was thinking about it. 'First of all, Jules *is* being followed. I saw two guys outside his apartment pretending to be changing a tire, except the tire on the car was fine. Second, there's Eliza and then there's me and Ken. We're all being monitored one way or another and, as evidence, I submit that I can't turn on my cell phone to call my brother and find out that he didn't see Eliza at Rainbow's apartment. And while we're at it, whose cat is Rainbow?'

'You know who's monitoring you and Ken,' Mank said. 'You're being followed by the New York Police Department.'

'Exactly,' I said. 'And that's what worries me.'

THIRTY

B ecause I couldn't think of a better idea, we ended up at
Mank's apartment. I wasn't completely comfortable with
that, although I'd been there before, because no matter
what else he was – and that was a number of good things – Mank
was also a cop and we'd demonstrated very clearly that the cops
were after me.

'You think a police officer had something to do with Damien
Van Dorn's death?' he asked me once we sat down in his small
front room. Cops are paid well in New York, but the real-estate
market is still what it is in Manhattan. Many officers live in
Queens or Staten Island to keep costs low, but Mank liked to be
in the middle of things and he wanted to live in Manhattan, about
twenty blocks north of where my apartment building was
standing. Last I saw of it.

'I think we at least have to consider the possibility,' I told
him. 'No matter where I went yesterday, cell phone turned off
and operating like it was 1987, there was one face I saw at every
stop. And it was Detective Sergeant Louis Merchant.'

Mank flopped on to a chair that I hoped had been sprayed for
bedbugs before he'd swiped it off the sidewalk. The place was
not exactly ready for a spread in the *New York Times* style section.
'I have a hard time believing that. I mean, I don't know Merchant,
but that's a big leap to make. The department thinks you're
involved in a murder. That's reason enough for them to be monitoring your movements so they can bring you in to be
questioned.'

I sat back and thought about closing my eyes. This had been
another in a series of really long days. Luckily the little do-it-
yourself battery charger that Ken had sent me the night before
had turned out to be really effective, and could be an addition
to our arsenal, the ability to charge anywhere. So I sat back but
didn't close my eyes. I was thinking.

'That's a reason for the NYPD to be looking for me, but

Merchant seems to be taking it personally. He was outside both libraries and the ice-cream store.' A thought hit me and it wasn't a comforting one. 'I can't say for sure that he wasn't at the college when I was going back to talk to Laura Rapinoe and Eliza got snatched.'

'You also can't say for sure that he was,' Mank pointed out. 'Look, I'm not saying it's impossible, but so far all you've got on Merchant is guesswork.'

'That's why we're going to take an hour right now to rest up and then you're going to find out where Merchant lives so I can pay him a visit.' I hadn't even known I was going to say that before I said it.

Mank stared at me, thankfully not in the way that Bendix does. 'You can't be serious,' he said.

'I don't even have to go,' I said. 'Seems to me all I need to do is turn on my phone and Merchant will appear at your door.'

'Not if he has Eliza with him.'

He had a point. I hated that he had a point, but sometimes there's nothing you can do about it. 'All right, we go back to Plan A,' I said. 'You find out where Merchant lives and I go there.'

Mank stared at me as if I'd suggested I might jump into a pit of asps. '*You* go there? On your own?'

'You're a cop. You can't be spying on other cops unofficially. You could get fired.' I pointed at the laptop on his desk, which was on a card table in one corner of the room. 'So go find his address. I bet he lives in Queens.'

Mank walked over to the desk, his face clearly looking for an alternative plan that would get him involved in the hunt, and then stopped after he sat at the keyboard. 'If I do this there'll be a record of it,' he said. 'I can't log on to my NYPD account, search for a fellow officer's home address and not be detectable. If this goes south, they'll have a clear trail back to me.'

I actually had not thought of that. 'OK. Don't do it. Ken always says to start with the simplest online search. Let's google Merchant.'

As it turned out, Louis Merchant was not in the least interested in keeping his online information private. There were four different mentions in his official biography on the NYPD site (which appeared to have last been updated in 2015) and more personal areas to his apartment complex, whose owner had apparently been the target of a lawsuit Merchant had brought due to the landlord's refusal to install soundproofing that would have muffled Merchant's drum practice and stopped his neighbors from complaining to him and the landlord. The lawsuit was settled out of court and apparently Merchant sold his drum kit on eBay.

But his address was plainly listed, and it was on Staten Island, not in Queens. The worst possible location for a Manhattanite because the best way to navigate Staten Island is by car, and we generally don't have those, no matter what the traffic around the Holland Tunnel might suggest.

'Do we even know that Merchant is the one who has Eliza?' Mank said as we got out of the subway near the entrance to the Staten Island Ferry dock. 'Or that he'd be stupid enough to take her to his own apartment?'

'He was stupid enough that we found his address just by googling his name,' I pointed out. Mank nodded to concede the point. 'If you've got a better idea, I'd be tickled to hear it.'

He stood there, obviously trying to form a better plan in the next six seconds, then gestured with his hands, a kind of shrug, to indicate he had nothing. 'You can't even keep in touch,' he said. 'I'd give you my phone but that wouldn't help.'

'I'm fine,' I told him. 'Don't you remember? I'm a muscle-bound freak.'

Mank reached over and embraced me, which I was not expecting. 'If Eliza's there, turn on your phone,' he said quietly in my ear. 'You'll be surrounded by cops in minutes.'

'Every girl's dream.'

He stood back and looked at me as if I were embarking on a trek down the Amazon rather than a free ride to another borough of the city that was twenty-five minutes away. But I knew how he felt.

'I'll do what I can,' I said, and started on to the ramp. I was, naturally, unarmed, but if there were metal detectors I couldn't be sure the USB port on my left side might not cause trouble. Fortunately, there was no such security in place that night – apparently it's intermittent – and I was on the boat and on my way in just a few minutes.

There's not much to the ferry; you just stand there (or sit on a bench) and wait to get to the least-remembered borough of New York City. Staten Island itself most closely resembles its closest neighbor, New Jersey. It's basically suburban. But it's bigger than you think it is and I had to flag down a cab at the Staten Island side, glad that I still had some of the cash Ken had supplied in his grocery bags.

Merchant's address was near Old Town, a historic area of the island that was about as close as you could get to the Verrazzano-Narrows Bridge, which would take you into Brooklyn. It was, in short, a ridiculous place to live for a cop who worked in the Bronx. I couldn't imagine what Merchant's daily commute must have been like.

I got the cabbie (not an Uber driver because I still couldn't use my phone) to drop me off a block from Merchant's building. If the man was holding Eliza hostage in his apartment, I really preferred not to give him advance warning I was on my way. I asked the driver to wait at least a half hour for me and gave him twenty dollars. There was no way I'd hail a cab here without my phone. I hoped the driver was trustworthy.

But that was a lot of ifs. IF Merchant had killed Damien. IF he had abducted Eliza. IF he had chosen to take her to his apartment. IF they were still there.

I was starting to feel like I'd jumped at the easiest possible solution and was operating more on hope and less on smart deduction.

The building was not a large one, not even as big as the one I lived in. It appeared to have as many as six apartments, one of which I would bet belonged to the landlord/super. You'd think a guy who lived in the same building as Louis Merchant would have been tickled to make renovations that would have made his drumming less audible. But then, Merchant had gotten rid of the drums, hadn't he?

It was the usual issue with getting inside the locked building. Nobody had supplied me with a nice heavy soda bottle keeping the door open this time. I figured that Merchant wouldn't have seen me coming. If I could buzz his downstairs neighbor and get inside, I wouldn't have alerted the man I'd come to see. And oddly, that happened.

From the mailboxes marked outside, I gathered that Merchant lived on the second floor in Apartment E. That turned out to be one flight up and down a corridor.

It seemed stupid but my first move was to knock. Yes, that might have given Merchant some advance warning and he could hide Eliza if she was there, but kicking in his door would have been louder and probably afforded him the same opportunity. There was no answer so I waited. A little.

There was no sound from behind the door. Eliza surely wasn't being tortured, even with a gag in her mouth. No movement. It was hard to know if getting inside was even worthwhile; Merchant was pretty clearly not home.

But seeing where he lived could be instructional if I could get in without causing too much damage. Climbing the house was pretty much out of the question; I'd be seen in this neighborhood, which was far too well lit and too well populated. The door was the issue and I'd have to deal with it.

I've seen people pick locks and a guest lecturer in one of my criminal justice classes in college (a former burglar) had once attempted to show me how, but you need equipment, and practice would probably be a good thing; I had neither.

But I had that whole superhuman strength thing going. And Merchant, the ever-vigilant NYPD detective, appeared to have only one lock on his door. If Eliza was inside it would be worth doing a little damage. If not, this was payback for shadowing me all over New York City. There was no downside, as long as I didn't get caught.

Someone as strong as I am – a group that includes all of two people on Earth – doesn't need to overwhelm a lock to break it. A well-placed palm pushed slowly (that's the key, pun unintended) against the lock will eventually force a deadbolt to smash its way through its mount and push out the wooden stud that keeps it secure. I had to exert a good amount of force for more than a minute, but the lock gave way with a minimum of sound and I was inside before one of the other tenants could look out of their apartments to see what the noise was about.

I had decided by now that Merchant was holding Eliza, but not in this apartment because nobody could be that stupid. It was as standard a place as you're likely to see, a garden apartment set-up in what had once been a private home, perhaps a three-family, cut up into six units. The front room, currently dark, housed a sofa that Merchant had probably inherited from his mother, over-upholstered and worn at the armrests, an armchair from the same collection, a coffee table of dark wood that held a TV remote and a package of Chinese takeout (which he'd eaten with a fork, sitting nearby) and a fairly small flat-screen TV on a table across the room, a decent distance from the sofa.

Between the coffee table and the TV, on the rug clearly bought on clearance, lay Detective Sergeant Louis Merchant, a bullet hole in his right temple. His eyes were open but they weren't seeing anything. The gun that presumably had fired the bullet was still in his right hand, stretched out at a ninety-degree angle from his body. I could smell the gunpowder in the room. This hadn't happened very long before.

I didn't move my feet at all. I just reached into my pocket, pulled out my phone, and turned it on. The cops would be here soon enough.

THIRTY-ONE

I texted Mank and Ken to let them know what I'd found. There wasn't going to be anything incriminating there. But the broken door and the smashed frame were not going to look great for me.

The first officers arrived ten minutes after I phoned the police. Two more came five minutes later once it had been phoned in that the victim was a New York cop. They were all professional and clearly over their heads; the first two were both young and might not have dealt with a gunshot death before. They immediately started treating it as a suicide.

I waited until Brooker showed up to express my opinion that it was anything else. The only facts I gave the two rookies (who probably weren't rookies) was that I had indeed broken into the apartment because I thought Merchant might have been holding someone hostage, and that I had found him as they had without touching anything inside the apartment. All of that was true.

Brooker, whom I had not called, arrived about twenty minutes after the first two, when the Staten Island detective, a woman named Peabody, was already assessing the scene and holding off the EMTs who wanted to put Merchant in a body bag and drive him to his not-exactly-final destination. One of the two original cops left and I asked him to tell my cab driver that I wouldn't be back. I figured Brooker was giving me a ride home.

'So you found him like this? You didn't move him in any way to see if he was alive?' Brooker asked me.

'Look at him,' I said. 'Do you think I believed he might be alive? I didn't touch him because I knew you and Detective Peabody would want to see him exactly as I found him.'

'You were right about that,' Peabody said. She was using an iPad to take pictures of the body and the room. 'The lights were out when you got here? Did you see him right away?'

'It took a few seconds, but not too long,' I told her.

'That was after you broke in the door,' Brooker noted. 'Why did you do that?'

The night's key question. 'I had reason to believe that Merchant was holding Eliza Hennessey against her will,' I said. 'If that were the case, he wasn't going to come to the door just because I knocked. I needed to see what the situation was, and if you want to charge me for discovering his body, I know a couple of lawyers.' OK, one lawyer. I have malpractice insurance and he watches out for me. I don't think we've ever met.

Brooker cocked an eyebrow. 'What reason?'

Was he speaking in code? 'Huh?' I was at my most eloquent.

'What reason did you have to think that Lou was holding Eliza hostage? He was a cop assigned to find a suspect in a murder. Why wouldn't he just arrest her and bring her in?'

'There was evidence that he had his own reasons to do that,' I said. The last thing I wanted to do was tell a detective I thought his partner had committed a murder.

'That doesn't answer my question,' Brooker said.

'I know. Should I call my lawyer? Or is he monitoring every move my phone makes the way you are?'

Brooker held up his hands as if surrendering, in an effort to signal that somehow I was being unreasonable. Peabody, on the other hand, had a dead body in the room and wanted to ask me about it, which I thought was at least more immediate.

'You said you didn't touch him?' she asked again.

'Are you serious? Of course not.'

She walked to the spot where Merchant lay, probably minutes from being carted away once Peabody signed off on it. 'So his right hand was like that when you came in.'

'Yeah, and so was the left. I know enough not to touch a dead gunshot victim before the police show up.'

From behind me I heard Brooker mumble, 'But not enough that you wouldn't commit breaking and entering.' He was making a list of things he could charge me with. This was going to be a long night.

Peabody either didn't hear him or chose not to react and either way was fine with me. 'That's an odd angle for his arm to fall after he shot himself,' she said. 'It's as if he flung his hand away from his body after he was dead.'

'That's because he didn't shoot himself,' I said. It seemed obvious enough. 'Somebody he knew came in and killed him. I bet if you look in his pockets you won't find his key to the apartment. The killer took it and locked the door.'

Brooker nodded. 'That's what I thought when I first saw him,' he said. 'I mean, Lou just wasn't the type and was showing no signs of depression. He just leased a new car.'

Peabody looked at the remaining uniform with the iPad. 'You got all the pictures?' she asked. The kid nodded and she looked at the EMT. 'OK. You can take him.' So they started getting Merchant into the body bag.

'You and I are going to be dickering around about jurisdiction, but your partner died in my precinct,' Peabody told Brooker. 'Whatever case you were working doesn't change that.'

He did his 'surrender' motion again. 'You'll get no argument from me, but the murder he and I were investigating happened in the Bronx because a drug dealer thought another drug dealer owed him money.'

Peabody nodded. 'Your case,' she said.

There was probably another hour of them asking me why I broke the lock and did I touch the body and, strikingly, my answers remained the same. Brooker *really* wanted to know why I thought Merchant was holding Eliza and I *really* wanted to know where Eliza was. The difference was that I knew the answer to the question he kept asking me, and I had no idea what he knew about the one I was asking him. Cops can be infuriating.

He looked at me when the questioning was through and he'd made sure Peabody didn't need anything else from me. 'Come on,' Brooker said. 'You can have about forty minutes by my estimate to convince me that I shouldn't book you for harboring a fugitive, illegal entry, breaking and entering, resisting arrest and withholding evidence.'

'A couple of those are the same thing,' I told him.

'Get in the car.'

So we went outside and got into the car. Brooker drove, what with it being his car and all (and the fact that I haven't driven in five years because I live in Manhattan). We stayed silent until it became obvious he was heading toward the Verrazzano Bridge to get into Brooklyn and then to the lower end of the island. It was a choice, and not a terribly odd one.

'I'm sorry about your partner,' I said finally.

'We weren't close.' Brooker was staring straight ahead even more than most people do when they drive. 'I didn't dislike the guy or anything, but he was old school, and I'm . . .'

'New school?' I said.

'Let's just say "school."' Anyway, our styles weren't the same. He'd just plow ahead without telling me sometimes. Like with your Eliza. How about you tell me where she is?'

Talking to men is like talking to subway trains. They don't listen and the only sounds you get back are annoying. 'I have no idea where she is. That's why I went to see Merchant, because I thought Eliza was with him. I've told you this. More than once.'

Brooker was staying right at the speed limit, I guess so a cop wouldn't pull him over? Maybe he was just one of those crazy law-abiding drivers. 'The thing you haven't told me is why you thought Lou was holding Eliza in his apartment.'

What the hell. 'Because I thought Merchant was the one who killed Damien Van Dorn and he was taking Eliza to keep her quiet.' Go ahead. Argue with me.

Not a blink, but he took a moment. 'You thought Lou killed Van Dorn? Why?'

Since I was in an honest mood, figuring Brooker wasn't going to arrest me any time soon, I didn't hold back. 'He was at every stop I made yesterday, no matter how careful I was not to transmit my location. He wasn't everywhere Eliza stopped, just me. I figure he had something to do with the business Damien was doing on campus and it tied him to the scene where Damien died. And by the way, Damien wasn't strangled.'

That got Brooker's attention. I could tell because our speed went up by two miles per hour. 'What do you mean, he wasn't strangled? I read the ME's report myself. Death by asphyxiation, caused by strangulation. You saw the extension cord around his neck.'

'I saw pictures of strangulation victims when I was in college,' I said. 'Damien's eyes were not extended. His hands weren't clawing at the cord. His mouth wasn't even open. He wasn't gasping for breath when he died. Mostly he looked surprised.'

'Then why did the medical examiner report that he'd been strangled?' Brooker asked. We were reaching the entrance for the Verrazzano Bridge.

'That's another reason I think Merchant was involved,' I told him. 'Someone has some sway in the ME's office.'

Brooker didn't look shocked and he didn't react in an amused or incredulous fashion. Mostly, he looked angry. 'That stupid son of a bitch,' he said. I'd like to point out here that he was simply expressing the view that someone was a male dog. Words have precise meanings that people almost never use.

Wait, I guessed right? How often does *that* happen? 'Merchant knew someone he could use to fake an autopsy?' I asked.

'A preliminary report, for sure,' Brooker answered after a moment. He was gripping the steering wheel very tightly as we got off the bridge and started the trek to the Brooklyn Bridge, I figured. 'He had a cousin who worked in the ME's office. It's possible, but he never said anything to me.'

Then he drove past the entrance to the Brooklyn Bridge and started following signs to the Brooklyn–Queens Expressway and that's when my stomach sank. 'I live in lower Manhattan,' I said.

'Good for you. We're going to my precinct in the Bronx so I can arrest you for the murder of Lou Merchant.'

THIRTY-TWO

There were a number of flaws in Brooker's plan to arrest me:

1. It was Peabody's case in Staten Island, not his in the Bronx.
2. I had absolutely no motive to kill Merchant.
3. There was no evidence that I'd done anything more than break in and discover the body. (OK, that wasn't my strongest defense.)
4. No district attorney in the city would want any part of this arrest because see: 1–3.
5. He was being a jerk.

I texted Ken and Aunt Margie as soon as we were on the BQE, a road designed to slow down your progress as much as possible. They'd probably beat us to the station. Aunt Margie, who used to get cash contributions to our upbringing from our parents in the mail, would probably have saved some for bail money; now it would come in to use.

But once we arrived at the 44th Precinct on 169th Street in the Bronx, it was Mank who was waiting in the station before Brooker had even managed to present me for booking. And he looked pissed, for once at Brooker and not at me.

'Detective Richard Mankiewicz,' he said, showing Brooker his gold shield. It doesn't impress other detectives that much but it is a legitimate means of identification. 'I'm here to find out why you're arresting one of my CIs?' That's 'confidential informant' for those not in the NYPD. He was saying I was a criminal that he used for inside information. Not exactly flattering, and I'd bring that up with him later.

'I thought she was a PI,' Brooker said. 'What business do you have with her?' He looked Mank up and down, which didn't take very long. Maybe he thought they'd have a fist fight and wanted to assess his chances, which he probably thought were pretty good. He didn't know Mank.

'She is, but she's helping me on a case,' Mank answered. 'And you still haven't told me why you're arresting her.'

'She killed a cop. My partner.' It was a miracle Brooker didn't wipe a tear from his eye for effect.

Mank looked at Brooker, then at me, then at Brooker again. 'Seriously?'

'Yeah. We found her with the body in his apartment. He had a bullet in his head. What else do you need to know?'

'Maybe he needs to know that I was the one who called in the murder and that I have already told you why I was there,' I jumped in. Hell, it was my ass he wanted to throw in jail. The least I could do was stand up for it.

We stood there for twenty minutes, during which Mank noted all four of my points above about this being a bad arrest for Brooker, but it wasn't until he threatened to call Peabody on Staten Island and ask if *she* thought I'd killed Merchant that Brooker put up his hands in surrender.

'Fine. I acted rashly. But I don't like her breaking into a cop's apartment with him dead on the floor,' he said. To Mank. 'I'm gonna keep looking at this.'

'Look all you want,' Mank told him. He looked at me. 'Need a ride?'

'You know I do.' He had, after all, dropped me off at the ferry.

We drove back to my apartment in Mank's car. He said he'd called Ken and Aunt Margie and told them he'd handle the 'arrest' so they shouldn't worry. 'How did you find out I was being arrested?' I asked him. 'There wasn't time for Brooker to file it and show up on your NYPD sites.'

'Claire Peabody and I were in the academy together,' he said. 'She started going back through the case that Merchant was working, found Damien Van Dorn, and saw I was the detective assigned to his disappearance. She called me.' At this time of night on FDR Drive, there was no way to not be at or below the speed limit, but Mank wasn't being as painstakingly careful as Brooker. I notice how people drive.

'She doesn't think I shot Merchant, does she?'

Mank made an amused face. 'No. But I'd like to know who *you* think might have done it.'

'I've been giving that a lot of thought.' And I had. I mostly wasn't listening to Brooker while we drove up to what was clearly not going to be my arrest for murder and that gave me time to sort out the facts, of which there were both too few and too many. 'I believed Jules when he told us he hadn't ordered anyone to harm Damien, and as far as I can tell he didn't have any reason to want to kill Merchant.'

'That "as far as I can tell" goes a long way,' Mank pointed out. 'There's a lot you still don't know about what happened and why it happened.'

Yeah, thanks for pointing that out, Mank. 'What I do know is that I was hired to find Eliza and now she's missing and probably being held against her will. The murders are your job, you being the cops. I need to find Eliza.'

He nodded his agreement. 'If we don't know who's holding her, that becomes considerably more difficult,' he said.

'I haven't heard from Ken because he thinks he's on stakeout and probably believes I'm still observing radio silence because he hasn't checked his texts. I should call him and find out if anybody was at Rainbow's place.' I picked up my phone, my good old phone, my friend, my companion. I'd missed it so.

Mank put his hand up to stop me, the spoilsport. 'I heard from him. Ken says there aren't lights on in the apartment but he can see something flickering. He thinks Eliza might be there with a candle or something.'

'Then why aren't we headed there now?' I asked.

'Who said we're not?'

Well, the apartment was in Queens but Mank turned at just the right time to stifle that argument. 'Who leases an apartment in the name of a cat?' I said, thinking aloud. 'I mean, if that's the name on the lease, I doubt the cat signed it. Whose apartment is that?'

'Could Eliza have rented it herself?' Mank asked.

'With what money? She's lived in her father's apartment all her life and as far as I can tell has never held a full-time job. How's she paying rent in Long Island City?'

Mank cleared his throat and looked uncomfortable. 'Maybe with money she was earning by helping Damien with his little pill business,' he said.

Well, *that* wasn't a pleasant thought. 'She swears she had nothing to do with it.'

'Oh yeah, well, that clinches it. Nobody who's guilty of a crime has ever lied about it.' Mank thought he was being witty but it was coming across as a little mean. He must have realized that. 'I'm sorry.'

'That shows progress,' I said. 'But we don't have any evidence that Eliza was involved with Damien's drug business. And if she had the money, she could have rented the apartment under her own name. I think someone else rented that apartment and put it in the cat's name as cover.'

'Or as a joke.'

I texted Ken that we were on our way and got back: *So now that you're booked you can go back on the grid?* My brother, ladies and gentlemen.

I didn't get booked. Is she still in the apartment?

It took a minute. *Somebody is. I didn't see them go in.*

Maybe the cat is playing with a cigarette lighter. I could use dark humor, too. And just as badly as my male associates. Ken didn't answer that one.

We pulled up to the building I'd scaled . . . yesterday morning? Was that possible? It was dark out by now. Knowing the layout of the building and the placement of Rainbow's apartment, I waited until Mank parked (double parked; he's a cop) and led him around the back to the alley from which I'd started my ascent. Sure enough, Ken was sitting on a garbage can, feet up off the ground. Ken hates rats, even though there was no sign of any currently in the area. It was a garbage can. Everybody has their phobias.

'What's up, shamus?' I said when we were close enough, but not so loudly that anybody in one of the apartments might hear.

'Who's Seamus?' Ken, when focused, is easily confused by shiny objects.

'What have you seen?' Mank asked him. Mank isn't one of us in so many ways, and he wasn't interested in the hilarious banter.

'I've been watching from back here instead of the front of the building because Rainbow doesn't have a window in front,' Ken said, although that seemed pretty obvious. 'So comings and goings have been pretty hard to see. I almost gave up after a half an hour and that's when . . . *that* started.' He pointed up at the window.

There was a flickering light, but it wasn't natural, like that of a candle. It was the kind of light you see if you go to a concert and the people want an encore.

'She's using her phone,' I said. 'It's amazing the place isn't swarming with cops.' I looked at Mank. 'No offense.'

'None taken.'

The flickering didn't last long, and then the window was completely dark again. 'How are we going to get in there this time?' I asked. 'The apartment door's been repaired.'

Ken nodded. 'I checked when I got here because someone held the front door open for me. I thought about staying inside to let you two in, but then I couldn't watch the window and I'd be kind of hard to miss hanging around in a hallway all evening.'

That was true; Ken is hard to miss no matter where he is, but it's easier for him to hide in a large crowd. I know the feeling.

'We can watch the front door and wait until someone comes out,' Mank suggested. 'Or I can call the management office and flash my badge at the super.'

'You're not here as a cop,' I reminded him. 'You're not the primary on Damien's murder. I guess now Brooker is.'

Mank and I stood there and thought about it for a number of minutes until Ken realized that at some point he'd have to put his feet down on the pavement. 'Let's go,' he said. 'I'll break and enter if nobody's coming out.'

'There's probably an alarm system,' I warned him.

'Life's full of choices.'

As it turned out, we only had to wait about ten minutes before a young woman exited the building and Ken, chivalrous to a fault, held the front door open for her. She nodded appreciatively at him, probably not just for the door being open, and walked away. We took the opportunity to go inside in a more conventional fashion than I had the day before.

At the door to Rainbow's (or whomever's) apartment, I gestured for Mank and Ken to stand out of sight. Eliza probably would have preferred Ken's company to mine, but she was probably expecting me. If she was being held here against her will I was prepared to do what was necessary, but I didn't mind having backup.

I knocked. It seemed the thing to do. Inside, I could hear a good deal of activity. Someone was moving around. Footsteps were very clear, on a wooden floor like the one inside Rainbow's living room. Objects were being moved. I looked at Mank.

'Somebody's covering up and maybe trying to leave,' I said.

'If they can't jump out the window and hope to survive, this is the only way out,' he answered. 'There's no fire escape. This place should be shut down for code violations.'

That hardly seemed the top priority at the moment, but Mank had a point. There was no reason to go outside and wait for escapee(s). 'I don't want to break down the door again,' I said.

'I'll be happy to do it for you,' my brother added helpfully.

I knocked again, louder and more times. 'I can hear you in there,' I said.

The apartment door across the hall opened and a woman in a bathrobe stuck her head out. 'What's going on? You cops?'

Honest to goodness, Mank started reaching for his shield. 'No ma'am,' I said. 'We're just concerned friends.' We *were* concerned and we *were* friends. I hadn't lied.

The woman looked . . . well, unconvinced, but closed the door. And at the same time, the door to Rainbow's apartment opened.

Standing in the doorway, holding a taser, was Laura Rapinoe.

THIRTY-THREE

As far as I could tell, there was no one else in the room behind Laura. If Eliza was inside, she was in the bedroom or the bathroom. The kitchen was visible from the doorway. 'What do you want?' Laura demanded.

'Can we come in?' I asked. 'You don't want to tase us in the hallway, do you?'

'Us?' Laura hadn't seen Ken or Mank yet. She looked from side to side and her eyes registered anger. 'Who are those guys?'

'They're my crew,' I said. 'Can we come in?' She hadn't answered the question, after all.

'Why?'

'We're looking for Eliza. We think maybe she's in there,' Ken said. Laura turned her head to look at him and I could easily have taken the weapon from her hand, but I wanted her to have the mistaken impression that she was in charge of this situation.

'She's not here,' Laura said, to Ken. 'So you can go home.' She actually reached over to close the door in my face, but I had longer, stronger arms and I blocked the door with my palm.

'I'm afraid we're going to have to see for ourselves,' I told her. 'Stand away and let us in.'

Laura squared her shoulders to be facing me directly, and thrust the gun forward. 'I don't think so.'

Maybe it was better if she *didn't* think she was in charge. I reached over and grabbed the taser out of her hand in one motion. 'I do,' I said.

Looking astonished, Laura took two steps backward and said, 'Hey!'

I nodded to Mank. He and Ken walked in past me as I put the gun into my pocket. I closed the apartment door behind me. Ken walked toward the bedroom and Mank headed into the hall that would end at the bathroom door. 'You could have just let us in,' I told Laura. 'Now, why not tell me what you're doing in this apartment?'

She looked sincerely surprised. 'It's mine,' she said. 'Why shouldn't I be here?'

Mank walked back in, shaking his head. Eliza wasn't in the bathroom. Ken, having turned the lights on in the bedroom, came back in spreading his hands; same result. But a little yellow cat walked out of the bedroom, which smelled of kitty litter. 'The lease lists the renter as Rainbow Zelensky,' I said to Laura. 'Why would you sign a cat's name to your lease?'

'I can if I want to,' she said, a defiant lower lip turning down. She looked like she was thirteen years old. 'What difference does it make to you?'

'Seems to me that if you're hiding your identity from your landlord, it might be because there's some activity going on here that you don't want to let them know about,' Mank said. He's such a cop. 'Like selling drugs to students on a college campus.'

'I don't know what you're talking about. I didn't have anything to do with Damien's business.' Laura wasn't making eye contact. It's not the only sign, but it's a sign. Another sign was that her respiration went up a tick. Ken gave me a look that showed he'd noticed that too.

'You knew Julio had someone following Damien,' Mank said, moving closer to Laura and standing over her. She had chosen to sit back down on the floor despite there being perfectly good, if well-used, furniture throughout the apartment. 'You knew Damien was going to that basement in the Bronx to confront them. You told other students at New Amsterdam about Damien if they needed something. You had something to do with Damien's business, Laura.'

Even with the bedroom lights on, the living room was pretty dim, but I could see Laura's shoulders start to tremble. She was crying. I gestured for Mank to back off, and he did.

I knelt down to be on a level close to Laura's but she was assiduously avoiding looking at me. 'You loved Damien and you wanted to help him,' I said in a quiet tone that I hoped was soothing, but you can never tell about your own voice. 'But the only way to really honor him is to tell us everything you know about what was going on. Do you think you know who killed Damien?' I was struggling to avoid mentioning Eliza because I had been getting the impression that Laura saw her as a competitor or a threat, two things Eliza probably was not.

'I don't think it was Julio,' she said, and her voice was damp. She sniffled a bit. 'He just wanted his money. He couldn't get it by killing Damien.'

'How about Julio's supplier?' Mank asked. It wasn't the wrong question to ask, but did I mention what a cop he is? The direct approach isn't always best. 'Could he have been mad enough to kill Damien?' I had an irrational moment of feminist outrage at Mank's failure to acknowledge that a woman might have been supplying pills to Julio.

'I don't know who it was,' Laura said. She wrapped her arms around her knees and I thought she might start rocking back and forth soon. Her boyfriend was dead, the cops were after everyone she knew, and she was sitting on the floor of a cat's apartment in the dark, playing with her phone. She was spiraling at the time we needed her to give us information and I wasn't sure what to do about it.

Luckily – and this might be the only time you hear me say it – Ken was there.

He sat down on the floor next to Laura, then stretched himself out and lay on the hardwood, fingers laced behind his neck, the very picture of relaxation. He even smiled. 'Laura,' he said. 'That's a nice name.'

That seemed to snap Laura out of her fog. She looked at him sharply and said, 'What?'

'I said that Laura's a nice name. Mine's Ken.' Did my brother think he was talking to a five year old? But he was getting her to look him in the eye, something Mank and I had been failing at stupendously.

Not unreasonably, Laura looked puzzled. 'Hi?'

Ken unlaced his fingers and reached out his hand to her. 'Nice to meet you. I'm Fran's brother.'

Laura did not acknowledge his admission that he had anything at all to do with me. I was an annoyance, a pest. Ken was the calming influence. It was becoming clear to me that my brother had some strange power over female college students and I didn't want to think about how he might use it. (To be fair, he tends to date women roughly our age.)

Laura took Ken's hand and didn't so much shake it as hold it for a moment, then let it go. He went back to pretending the hardwood floor was a hammock. 'I'm sorry about everything that's been going on,' he told Laura. 'You're having a really hard time.'

She reverted a little, clutching her knees again. 'I know. Nobody seems to notice that.' Poor Laura. Eliza was probably kidnapped and wanted by every law enforcement agency in the Tri-State area. Damien was dead. Even Jules seemed scared and confused. But it was her plight that clearly seemed the most unfair to Laura. I had to remember she was still a teenager.

'I think it's a shame,' Ken said. His voice almost sounded like he was singing lightly. 'But maybe we can help it get a little better.'

Laura put her palms down on the floor and looked at him. 'How?' She was almost wailing.

'We'll find out who killed Damien and you can look them in the face and scream at them if you want,' Ken said. 'And I'll ask his mom about letting you speak at his funeral, if that's something you'd like to do, let everybody know how you two felt about each other.'

Man, I thought that was going about six miles over the top, but Laura was buying it. 'You think she'd say it was OK?' That was when I knew Ken had her reeled in.

'I can't promise, but I will talk to her.' Ken had never spoken to Helena Van Dorn in his life, but if he could work her as efficiently as he was doing with Laura, she might agree to booking Beyoncé for Damien's funeral and having Laura serve as one of her backup singers. 'But first you have to help us.'

Laura shrunk back down a little, but she nodded her head once. 'Damien wasn't looking for some drug business at the beginning,' she said. 'He just wanted to get his mom off his back about the rent at his place and getting a work/study job or something at a restaurant wasn't going to pay enough. Someone he knew – I don't know their name – hooked him up with Julio, just a little to start. But then it got bigger.'

'How much bigger?' Mank was conducting a police interrogation. I thought that was the wrong question. Our goal was to determine Eliza's role in this and figure out who was holding her, if anyone. We needed to find Eliza. Mank was investigating the murder in the Bronx without being assigned to it.

'Bigger,' Laura said. 'I don't know numbers. He started off with two or three people and by the end . . . he had a bunch. Maybe ten.'

'That's a good business but it's not enough to kill someone for,' Mank said, fingers on the bridge of his nose. 'I'm not sure that was the motive for killing Damien.'

I needed to bring this back to our real purpose. 'Right now I'm focusing on Eliza,' I said. 'Laura, you have to have some idea who might have seen her as a threat.'

Laura looked confused. 'A threat?'

Ken, ever the charmer and calming influence, sat up to make a connection with Laura. He actually took her hand. I thought that was a corny gesture, but Laura stared into his eyes like she'd found a long-lost friend. 'Someone took Eliza,' he said. 'There's been no demand for ransom, so we can only assume they have another reason. One, given all that's happened, is that she knows something that can be a threat to whoever is holding her. Now, do you have any idea who would think that, or what kind of danger she might pose to someone?'

'How do you know they're holding her?' Laura asked. 'How do you know they didn't kill her like they killed Damien?' It was an academic question, reading her face. She didn't especially care if Eliza was dead.

'She was taken when she was with me,' I said. 'Whoever it was took her somewhere else. It doesn't do us any good to think she might be dead. We need to find her. Do you know anybody who might think they had to get her away from other people?'

It seemed this time like Laura was really giving the matter some thought. She didn't look at her phone and she didn't stare at the floor in shame or whatever she'd been feeling before. She looked away, not to avoid contact but to give her brain a blank image so she could consider. It was pretty dark in the apartment, especially if you were insisting on staying on the floor.

'I can't think of anybody special,' she said finally, and the other three of us in the room let out a collective sigh of frustration that I don't think Laura heard. 'I mean, there weren't that many people involved. Damien, Julio, Julio's jerk, the guy with the birthmark, and Neil. I think he knew the supplier.'

Mank was first but he asked the wrong question again. 'The skinny dude and the guy with the birthmark – did you know their names?'

But I was already barreling through, because it was starting to come together in my head. 'Neil?' I said. 'Big guy? A little older than all of you?'

'I only saw him once, but yeah, he's pretty big,' Laura said. 'Do you know him?'

I looked at Mank, who had caught on to what I was thinking, and he looked stunned. 'Maybe,' I told Laura. 'Except I know him as Detective Brooker of the NYPD.'

THIRTY-FOUR

'**W**e've got nothing,' Mank said.

After considerable discussion and in some areas argument, I'd given Laura her taser back, she'd sat back down on her living-room floor and turned off the light in the bedroom, and then locked the door behind her after Mank, Ken and I had left. Then we'd taken Mank's car (Ken had used the subway to get to Rainbow's apartment) back to our apartment and we were working on determining a next step. Mank was trying to suggest that without proof of Brooker's involvement in Damien's drug business, we didn't have enough to do much of anything.

'We're not cops,' I said, gesturing toward Ken and myself. 'We don't need proof to act. We're not going to arrest anybody. But if Brooker is holding Eliza somewhere, we need to find out where and we need to find out fast.'

Mank is a cop (I think I might have mentioned that) and, as such, hates to believe that other cops aren't quite as upstanding and honest as he is, but this wasn't Mayberry, and Brooker wasn't Andy Griffith (I watch a lot of classic television). He was pacing the tiny floor in our kitchen while I made coffee and Ken sat around looking at us. We have extra-heavy-duty kitchen chairs for exactly that purpose.

'The only person who ties someone who *looks* like Brooker to Damien is Laura Rapinoe,' Mank said. 'She's not the most reliable witness I've ever met. That's not a lot to go on.'

'He has the same first name as Brooker, too,' Ken pointed out. I got the sense he was enjoying this because he knew the whole back story that Mank and I had, and he liked seeing us argue a point without trying to piss each other off.

'The point isn't whether we can prove it's Brooker,' I said, ignoring both men. 'We think it's Brooker. The point is where he might have taken Eliza. And I'm willing to believe he isn't stupid enough to go to his own apartment with her. What can you find out about him from NYPD files, Mank?'

'I am *really* uncomfortable digging into personal details of a police officer, even if those files are open to me as a member of the department.' Mank didn't want to believe Brooker was the culprit because that would lead to speculation that Brooker had killed Damien and Merchant, too. That was something a cop would do almost anything not to believe about a fellow officer.

'Give me your password and let me look,' Ken suggested. 'I'm not at all uncomfortable doing that.'

Mank gave my brother the look I wanted to give him except that Ken actually shut up. Mank groaned lightly and gave me a different kind of look entirely. 'I'll look, but you can't,' he said. 'I'll tell you what I think is relevant and that's all. This is not open to negotiation. Take it or leave it.'

'We'll take it,' I said before Ken could think of some way to mess up the deal.

'OK. I need a space where I can be alone so nobody's looking over my shoulder.' I was going to protest but he was right: one of us would have been trying to eavesdrop. 'I don't have my laptop and I'm not using yours, so it'll be on my phone. Probably take about half an hour. Where?' Mank looked around as if he hadn't been in my apartment before. He had.

'My bedroom or Ken's,' I said. 'Do you need to plug in your phone?' I might have cringed, thinking of the times I'd plugged in myself and not my phone in my own room.

'It won't hurt. Do you have a charger?' *Did we have a charger?*

We set him up in Ken's bedroom at Mank's insistence. Maybe being alone in my room would have projected the wrong kind of image for him, or he'd noticed that Ken's room, like Ken, is larger. Mank closed the door and I heard him knocking around inside, no doubt plugging in the charger and his phone. I figured he'd set up at Ken's desk in a far corner of the room rather than have to sit on his bed the whole time. With all the privacy contingencies in mind, I backed away from the bedroom door and headed back into the living room.

'You know what bothers me?' Ken asked when I got there.

'The fact that all women don't fall at your feet?' I suggested.

'Well, yeah, but that's not what I was thinking of. How come Brooker had time to come after you if he's holding Eliza? Can he just lock her up somewhere when he needs to go be a cop?'

I love my brother but there are times I truly can't follow the way he thinks. 'That's what's bothering you?' I said. 'Brooker's daycare situation?'

'What if he didn't kill Damien?' Ken said, digging into this devil's advocate role. 'What if he really is just a detective who's now trying to figure out who staged his partner's suicide while working on a murder in the Bronx? What if there's someone we're overlooking?'

'Like who?' I sat in the side chair to consider my brother, who had walked into the living room and deposited himself, sideways, across the sofa, his feet hanging over the arm.

'What about Laura?'

'Well, we just left her and Eliza definitely wasn't there.'

'You're talking about a woman who signed her cat's name to a lease because she thought it was funny,' Ken pointed out, as if that proved something.

'What motivation did Laura have to kill Damien? Or especially Merchant? She loved one and probably never met the other.' Dammit, I was going to keep logic on my side.

Ken didn't sit up, because there's nothing he loves better than lying all over the couch (extra long, for three people), but his face did get a little more thoughtful. 'OK, I can't answer that,' he said.

'Now, if we could find this "associate" of Jules', maybe he had a grudge with both guys, but I can't think of a reason he'd kidnap Eliza, because he'd only do what Jules told him to do.' Everywhere I looked in this case there were questions that had answers that led to more questions. 'And if Damien wasn't strangled, what killed him?'

'And what about Malcolm X. Mitchell?' Ken said out of nowhere.

I sat back on the chair and let myself be overwhelmed for a moment. 'Yeah, what about him?' I said.

The door to Ken's bedroom opened and in walked Mank, putting his phone back into his pocket lest either of us see the web page he might have been looking at a minute ago. Mank knows Ken and I can do things he can't, but he's not really clear on what. Seeing back through time is not one of them.

Mank looked troubled, which led me to believe he'd found

something that made a fellow officer (likely Brooker) look bad. That might have been bad news for him but not for me. People have different priorities.

Nobody said anything until Mank sat down next to me on the side chair rather than try to displace any particular section of my brother. 'OK,' he said. 'There is something that took a little digging to find out, but as city employees officers are required to list investments that might cause a conflict of interest.'

Investments? Did Brooker list a campus drug business as a side business for him? I didn't think he was that stupid.

'What kind of investments?' I asked, because saying what I'd just thought out loud would have made me sound like an idiot.

'Like real estate,' Mank said, sounding depleted. It really bothered him when he had to admit that his fellow officers weren't all boy scouts. (Or just scouts, these days.) 'It seems like Detective Brooker owns a twenty-percent stake in a company called Urban Investments, which has a number of interests, including apartment buildings, bodegas, a parking garage and two small hotels around the city.'

That sounded expensive. Twenty percent? 'Where'd he get the money for that?' I asked.

'It's a good question,' Mank admitted. 'But the real problem is that one of the investments Urban made was a particular real-estate purchase, made only six months ago.'

Ken actually sat up, which was more than I would have expected. 'What?' He couldn't say that lying down?

'They own the Bronx apartment building where Damien Van Dorn was murdered,' Mank said.

We sat there for a moment. Just sat.

'Wow.' Ken exhaled. 'That's a pretty big coincidence.'

'Worse,' I said. 'There's not a chance in the world Brooker didn't know that.'

More sitting and staring. I don't know about the others but I was trying to absorb what Mank had just told us.

Ken seemed to come to consciousness first. He stood up, which for him can be a time-consuming process. 'Well, we have to go there,' he said.

I'm not that quick on the uptake. 'To the Bronx?' I said.

Mank nodded at Ken. 'He's right. That's the most likely place

Brooker would have taken Eliza. Julio's operation is based there; that's why Damien went to that building. Brooker clearly knows the place. He's one of the owners. He'd never expect anyone to show up there looking for Eliza. If she's still alive, I'm willing to bet that's where she is.'

I didn't want them to be right, but they were. I got up, too. 'Do you have your gun, Ken?' I asked.

He gave me a look that indicated he did. He's licensed to carry it but he doesn't have it on him all the time. I never carry a weapon because I really don't like them.

'So do I,' Mank chimed in.

I turned to face him and shook my head. 'You're not going, Detective Mankiewicz. You are a member of the New York Police Department and you have not been called to the scene. There's not even any evidence that a crime has been committed there. You need to let us do the legwork on this one and wait until you hear from me. But just in case Brooker still has me on his radar, I'm turning my phone off until we see what's going on up there.'

'I've been with you all night,' Mank said. 'I'm going as a private citizen, not an officer.'

Ken folded his arms across his chest. 'You don't want to have to get past me, Rich,' he said.

Mank looked my brother up and down. 'No, I don't. I guess I'm not going.'

Ken and I started toward the door. Mank cleared his throat and we looked at him.

'I'll drive,' he said.

My brother and I exchanged a look and waved him toward us. 'Where will you park?' I asked.

'Anywhere I want. I'm a cop.'

THIRTY-FIVE

At night the building looked worse, and it hadn't looked all that great to begin with. Luckily there was no game at the Stadium that night or the foot traffic would have been impossible. I guessed the Yankees were still out of town.

'How do we approach it?' I'd asked from the passenger seat of Mank's car. 'Do we go in together or do I go in and you follow if I need you?' I was still operating on the unlikely theory that Mank would just sit quietly outside in his car and not do anything about the possible abduction and presence of murder suspects inside the building. It's lonely in my reality.

'We're all going in together,' Ken answered. 'There's strength in numbers and no advantage to sitting outside and wondering what's going on.' My brother has the capacity to think logically and it's really annoying.

Mank, driving with his usual casual intensity (if that's even possible), did not comment on my leaving him out of the scenario. He would just ignore my arguments and do what he thought was right. Men are infuriating.

I decided to show my displeasure by putting my chin on my chest and not speaking again while we were in motion because that's exactly how mature I am. Luckily, by then we were close to our destination.

We did not linger at the entrance to the building. Just suffice it to say we got inside the lobby. Don't ask me how. There's no sense in you being privy to something that could get you in trouble.

Mank had done some research before we left the apartment as to the lessees in each of the spaces here. The three most likely residences for Jules's *pals* were upstairs, on the second and fourth floors. We weren't sure of their names, so checking the mail boxes wasn't going to help. It would be trial and error. Hopefully not too much error. Our 'informant' from our previous visit had mentioned the fourth floor but he'd also been drinking something that smelled like embalming fluid.

Ken started moving around without speaking as if he were the lead officer in a war movie. He pointed at his eyes, then up the staircase, then at me. I looked at Mank but he appeared to be as baffled as I was. 'What?' I asked.

My brother looked royally irritated. 'I'm going to go up first,' he said in a hiss, 'and then you follow me and we'll hit the door.'

I gave him a light shove at the base of the staircase and passed him on the way up. 'We're going to knock on the door and wait,' I instructed. 'What if the first one isn't the apartment we're looking for?'

'Their problem, not ours,' he mumbled, but he followed me dutifully up the stairs, and I heard Mank's footsteps behind him. I could picture the amused expression on the detective's face. Dammit, he was cute.

Our informant from our first visit was nowhere to be seen, and given that he'd thought Julio was one of the people living here when I had seen the drug dealer's considerably-more-upscale apartment in Manhattan, I wasn't in a hurry to seek out more information from that gentleman. He'd tried, probably against his sense of self-preservation, but all we'd found had been in the basement we'd come to see anyway. And, unfortunately, more.

We reached the door to 2D and I practically had to restrain Ken from throwing his considerable shoulder into it. I held up a palm and showed it to him, he looked disgruntled and then I turned and knocked on the door, three times, sharply.

The woman who opened the door was not Jules, not Brooker, not Eliza and not anybody else I'd ever seen. She spoke in Spanish, and I know a few words. They weren't enough. There was no one behind her as far as I could tell, so I thanked her because I didn't know the words for 'I apologize,' and we backed away from her door, which she closed, looking puzzled as to why the Jehovah's Witnesses were so big this year.

The second door yielded nothing. No one answered, and between my hearing and Ken's it was fairly obvious that there weren't any people inside, although we did hear a dog snoring a little. There was no reason to break down the door, although Ken seemed eager to try if just for fun. He was outvoted.

Based on the records Mank had scanned, there was only one other likely apartment to search, with no small children listed as residents and no people over the age of seventy-five. It was two more flights up.

Despite what Ken might have wanted us to believe, we were not in military gear and we were not carrying automatic weapons on our persons, so climbing up another couple of flights wasn't really much of a concern. But my brother, who had adored GI Joe as a child, was playing it up to the hilt, turning each corner as if an assailant might be around the bend and taking the stairs two at a time. It was doing nothing more than playing soldier but Ken felt like he was making a contribution and I guessed there was some value in that. I'd devote some time to determining what that value might be at a later date.

After much macho posturing we finally ended up at the door to 4B, our last likely place to search. Ken plastered himself against the wall next to the door, facing Mank and me. Mank managed not to laugh out loud and gestured toward the door, inviting me to make the first move. I felt like this was an invitation to knock on an apartment door, so I did.

Unlike the last try, there was considerable sound from inside as soon as I knocked. Voices were in conversation, maybe heated conversation, although I couldn't make out the words. I think Ken could because he looked even more grim if such a thing were possible. His expression indicated to me that things inside the apartment weren't going well. I knocked again, louder.

Then I heard a voice that sounded much like Eliza's with decent volume say, 'Let me . . .' something, and that was enough. I wanted to kick the door in but some strange, un-New-York instinct in me said to turn the doorknob, and the door just . . . opened.

No, it didn't. This was New York. Nobody leaves their door unlocked. I considered my options and listened again. Then I heard someone say the word *gun* and that did it for me.

I threw my left shoulder hard into the door near the lock and it gave a little but didn't break. So I gave it another shot and it broke through, which was lucky. My brother would no doubt have insisted on knocking down the door and then lording over me how much stronger he was for the rest of my life. The door swung open.

I pushed into the apartment with Mank and Ken (in that order)

behind me. I noticed Ken had drawn the gun he'd brought with
him and Mank had not. The scene that I'd interrupted was – and
there is no other word for it – chaotic.

Standing in a fairly large main room was Brooker, along with
Jules, a man with a birthmark next to his right eye, another
moody-looking man I didn't recognize (who did not have a
birthmark next to his right eye), and Eliza. What I wasn't
expecting was that the only person holding a weapon (in this
case, the handgun Anton Chekhov had no doubt given her at
Rainbow's apartment) was Eliza. She was pointing the gun at
Brooker, who looked downright incensed but had his hands in
the air. I could still see the bulge of his service weapon under
his right arm, though. Eric/Jules/Julio did not appear to be armed
and seemed to be mostly baffled, which in my experience was
his default expression.

Oh yeah, and standing to the side, shoulders hunched like a
defeated athlete, was Brian Hennessey.

'Different,' Ken said.

THIRTY-SIX

'Eliza,' I said in the friendliest voice I could muster, 'what's going on?'

'That man grabbed me off the street and took me here because I'm trans,' she said, pushing the gun even more toward the new guy without the birthmark. 'I think he killed Damien and if he tries anything, I'm going to shoot him.'

'That's pretty straightforward,' I said. I wasn't sure if Eliza had gone off the deep end or if Brooker had, or (and this seemed a slightly more unlikely possibility) I had. In any event, at least one person in the room wasn't acting with terrific judgment and I wanted to make sure things didn't escalate further. I especially didn't want Eliza shooting anybody. 'But maybe we should put the guns away for now and try to figure this out, huh?'

'That is the best choice, Fran.' Mank had not pulled out his service weapon but he was inching his way carefully toward Brooker. No doubt he'd seen the gun under Brooker's armpit too and wanted to defuse the situation as quickly as possible. 'Why don't we start by finding out who everyone here might be?'

'Don't talk to us like we're children,' Eliza said. 'This isn't *Sesame Street.*'

Mank made it to Brooker's side and pulled a handkerchief out of his own pocket. Of course Brooker's fingerprints would be on his own gun but there was no sense in getting Mank's on them, too. He pulled Brooker's gun out of the holster carefully and deposited it into his own pocket. Brooker, staring at Eliza, didn't look at all pleased. That was probably good.

'You're right, Eliza,' Ken said. 'We're talking down to you and we shouldn't. But I don't know who that man is, the one that you're pointing the gun at, or this one.' He looked at Jules for clarification, since we knew they were in some way connected.

'That's Andrew, man,' Jules said of the man with the birthmark. 'I don't know nothing about him snatching this guy, or girl, or whatever, off the street. I just got here.' Jules had an instinct

toward self-preservation and very few others. When he referred
to her that way I thought I saw Eliza move the gun toward Jules
but she stopped herself and kept it trained on Brooker. 'The other
guy came with Neil. I don't know him.'

'That's my associate, Mr Martin,' Brooker said. A shudder
went through my neck.

'That ain't my name,' Mr Martin said. Enlightening.

Mank showed Brooker his shield and took two steps away
from him, keeping Brooker's gun out of his reach. 'What's going
on, Detective?' he asked. 'Were you just checking in on your
investment property? On the night your partner was killed?'

To his credit, Brooker did not pretend he didn't know what
Mank was talking about. 'I'm here because someone in the room
is an informant, and you know I'm not going to tell you who
that is,' he lied. 'I thought I could get something on Merchant's
shooting.'

'How come Eliza says you took her off the street when she
was with Fran?' Ken wasn't pointing his handgun at anyone yet
but you knew he wanted to. If I hadn't been there he probably
would have done so already.

'I honestly don't know,' Brooker answered. 'Can I put my
hands down now?'

'No!' Eliza shouted. 'You sent that guy and he put his hand
over my mouth and dragged me away. You know you did it!'
Eliza indicated she was talking about Mr Martin.

'You're crazy,' Mr Martin said. 'That guy must have done it.'
He pointed at Andrew.

'I just live here, man,' Andrew said. 'All of a sudden everybody's in my house.'

Mank, still walking backward, stepped toward me and stopped.
He looked serious and baffled. I couldn't blame him. The last
thing I'd expected when I walked in was to see Eliza holding
everybody – even her father, who was still looking like a scared
puppy – at gunpoint.

'What are you doing here, Brian?' I asked him, being the only
one of the latest arrivals to have met the man before.

'I don't want to say,' he mumbled.

'You don't have to say anything,' Brooker advised him.

'Shut up!' Eliza was feeling her power in the room but her

face said that she was at a loss for what to do next. 'You don't get to tell him what to do!'

Mr Martin looked annoyed. 'She's disrespecting you, Detective,' he said to Brooker.

'Let it go.'

'Please, Brian,' I went on. Maybe if I ignored the drama I could get toward an understanding of the situation. 'Tell me how you got here.'

Brian Hennessey turned his body so he was facing me and, more importantly from his perspective, away from Brooker. 'He called me and said he had Eliza and I needed to come here or she'd get killed,' he said. He looked at his daughter. 'I can't let that happen, not ever.'

'That's not true,' Brooker tried.

'Yeah, it is,' Mr Martin said. 'Don't you remember?'

'I *said* shut up!' Eliza shouted. It was a minor miracle nobody had called the police about the noise, but this wasn't that kind of neighborhood. 'He took me to blackmail my dad, but it's because I'm trans!'

Brian shook his head slowly. 'No, honey. It's not. Brooker didn't say anything about you being trans. I have something he wants and it was the only way he thought he could get me to give it to him. He was right.'

The timeline was confusing me, but then so was everything else. 'What did he want from you?' Mank asked Brian while I was trying to determine how long Eliza had been here, and how she'd managed to conceal that gun until just before we had arrived.

I saw Ken inching his way toward Eliza and hoped he wasn't going to be stupid enough to try and wrestle the gun out of her hands. He could easily accomplish that, of course, but he might hurt her and in the process send the room into even more chaos.

Brian looked sad. Of course, he had every right to be concerned, but sadness seemed to be stemming from Mank's question. 'I had it for a freelance article. I was going to sell it to a big news organization, maybe on TV.' That certainly didn't help at all.

'Sell what?' Mank asked. Ken was now at Eliza's side and speaking quietly into her ear. He had to lean over quite a way to do that. I don't read lips and he wasn't speaking loudly enough even for me to hear him. Whatever it was, I hoped it would convince her to give him or Mank the gun so we could sort this all out. If such a thing was possible.

'Brian,' Brooker said. It sounded like a warning. But if he was threatening Eliza, I felt like that tactic was a little hollow at this point.

On the other hand, Brian looked stricken, as if he'd done something awful. 'I don't want to say.' I didn't see how that was relevant.

'It was a computer thing,' Andrew said. 'I heard the call.' Maybe he thought he was being helpful, but Brooker looked positively murderous and Brian was on the verge of panic. Whatever that 'computer thing' was, it clearly had a lot of value in this room.

Jules, standing next to his associate, gave Andrew a very hard push, sending the bigger man to the floor. 'You know you're supposed to keep your mouth shut!' he yelled.

'I'm sorry.' It was pretty obvious Andrew wasn't seriously injured.

'Yeah, shut up, man,' Mr Martin told him. Mr Martin was clearly a couple of steps slower than everyone else.

Ken, having finished delivering whatever message he had to Eliza, walked slowly back toward me. He leaned over (not nearly as far as with Eliza) and whispered in my right ear, 'The gun isn't loaded. She says she doesn't want to hurt anyone.'

'You can't shoot everyone here,' Mank said to Eliza. 'The only sane way to work all this out it to put down the gun and talk this thing through. Then maybe we can figure out what happened and where this is going to go.'

Eliza looked at Ken, who gave her a small nod. He seemed to be vouching for Mank in general. Eliza took a deep breath and handed the gun . . . to Ken, who put it in his pocket immediately.

And that was when Brooker produced another handgun from his ankle. You might think that would be a gasp-inducing moment of panic but that's because you don't know my brother the way I do. Ken reached over and grabbed the gun before Brooker really had a hold on it, then lifted the detective off the floor by holding the lapels of his suit jacket and pulling up.

'Hey,' Mr Martin said. It wasn't a friendly word.

Brooker, as you might expect, looked amazed, eyes wide and mouth open. Not the way Damien Van Dorn looked when we found his body. 'Put him down, Ken,' I said. 'It's time we all sat down and answered a few questions, don't you think?'

THIRTY-SEVEN

'I didn't kill Damien Van Dorn,' Brooker said. 'I didn't kill anybody. I've never fired my weapon in fourteen years on the job.'

We were all gathered in the living room of what I now understood was Andrew's apartment: Jules, Andrew, Mr Martin, Brooker, Eliza, Mank, Ken and me. Everyone but Ken and Eliza was seated on various broken-down easy chairs and two sofas. It was, by New York standards, a huge room.

Brooker, to be fair, had been subdued physically by Ken and placed, almost gently, on one of the sofas, facing me, Mank and Eliza. That hadn't sat well with Mr Martin, but even so he'd taken a look at Ken and done nothing about it. Next to Brooker was Jules, who had been carefully checked for any residual weapons, and Andrew, who had surrendered a small handgun and a retractable knife voluntarily. Andrew seemed to be somewhat stumped by all that was going on, and while it was for different reasons, I could relate. Mr Martin was just still, like he was waiting for a cue.

'OK,' Mank said. 'You didn't kill Damien, who wasn't shot, anyway. Let's even say you didn't kill your partner, Merchant. We have witnesses who name you as the supplier of certain pharmaceuticals to Damien and some of his friends. Did you not do that, either?'

'Damien told me it was a guy named Neil,' Eliza volunteered.

'A lot of men are named Neil,' said Brooker.

'Did they all kidnap Eliza off the street and call her father with a ransom demand?' I asked. Enough of letting Mank conduct *my* interviews. 'What was it you told him to bring in exchange for his daughter, while you weren't killing anybody?'

'I don't know what he's talking about,' Brooker said. It was possibly the dumbest answer he could have offered, because immediately all eyes in the room turned toward Brian, who looked warily at Brooker but then at Eliza. He straightened his spine and put his head, which had been leaning forward, back.

'It was a small plastic bag,' he said. 'Inside there would have been a drug called Xylazine, an animal tranquilizer that's called tranq on the street. Except this particular bag, I'm guessing, would have been empty. I didn't have that one, but I knew about tranq and I had spoken to Neil about it.'

My mouth got a little dry all of a sudden. 'What would this stuff do if it was given to a person?' I asked Brian. He'd written on pharmaceuticals for a trade magazine for years and had insight into more substances than I even knew existed.

'If it was a large enough dose, and it would have to be pretty large, it would make the victim stop breathing,' Brian said. He stared at Brooker with an expression of unexpected defiance. 'Give them enough, and they'll suffocate.'

'Why a small bag?' I asked Brian.

'Because it would have had an evidence tag on it, I'm guessing. The cops are aware of tranq and they can generally get access to things that are confiscated in drug raids, with a little effort.'

There is, it should be noted, no such thing as a deafening silence. If you don't hear anything during a silence, it's because there's no sound. But I'll admit the silence sounded more silent in this moment that almost any other I'd ever not heard.

Everyone looked at Brooker.

His expression changed more dramatically than I would have thought possible. From a man being falsely accused of a tragic crime, he became an aggressive angry entity, still human but acting upon his basest animal instincts. He wanted out and he didn't care what he had to do to achieve that.

'Get out of the way!' he screamed and everyone just stood there and stared at him. Ken took up a position between Brooker and the door because he would clearly be the hardest one to get by physically. Mank reached into his jacket. He didn't want to draw his gun in a crowd like this but he couldn't be caught without it if force became necessary, which certainly seemed likely.

I am the negotiator in the family; I always seek a peaceful solution. Maybe I could talk Brooker down. 'Why did you do it?' I asked. 'Was it just because Damien couldn't pay his debt to Jules, here?'

'You have nothing!' Talking Brooker down was going to be somewhat more difficult than I might have anticipated. 'You can't prove a thing!'

Mank, the police detective, was now in his element, right hand still in his jacket pocket. 'If Brian knew about the bag of tranq, others did too,' he said. 'Like Merchant. He knew you were supplying Julio, didn't he? Was he in on the action, Brooker?'

'Don't call me Julio,' Jules said.

'No!' Then Brooker realized what he'd just said and his eyes widened. 'There was no action! I wasn't supplying anybody with anything!'

Eliza laughed, of all things. 'Everybody on campus knew it was you,' she said. 'I didn't know your name, but I saw you almost every day. And you had to know that Julio was sending Andrew after Damien, or did you send the two of them yourself?'

'I didn't go after no Damien,' Andrew said, and he looked at Mr Martin. 'I don't work for that guy, Brooker.'

'You trying to get me in jail?' Mr Martin asked. He was just catching up.

'How did you find out about the tranq?' I asked Brian.

'I knew the detective here from my time with a trade magazine about the uniform business,' he said.

'There's a trade magazine for the uniform business?' I asked. That just seemed so specific.

'There's a trade magazine for everything, although most of them are all online now,' Brian answered. 'But I met Detective Brooker doing a story about the NYPD's uniform standards a number of years ago when he was Officer Brooker and we kept in touch.'

'Shut up, Brian.' That was the best Brooker could do.

But Brian, having warmed to the topic, didn't take the hint. 'So when I heard someone was supplying pharmaceuticals to the New Amsterdam campus I got curious and I called the detective here. And without him telling me much of anything, I could figure out he was the supplier, in some small part through confiscated drugs. I'd been researching it for a story I'm trying to sell to *The New York Times*. They're interested and this will probably make them even more interested.' Brian made the mistake of chuckling lightly.

'Son of a *bitch*!' Brooker lurched forward, presumably to confront Brian, who backed away reflexively, putting up his hands as if to push Brooker away.

Mr Martin also made a quick move, but then he looked at Ken, who had barely lifted a hand. Mr Martin was just smart enough to stop.

Brooker caught himself, trying not to look even more guilty, but Brian was still in info-dump mode. 'When I found out Damien was dead and how he had died, I wondered if it could be tranq,' he said. 'And there was a story in the *Daily News* two weeks ago about a seizure of the drug in the Bronx. My friend Neil here was listed as the detective on the case.'

This time Brooker couldn't control himself and tried to dive across the room toward Brian. But he didn't get the chance because my brother took a step to his left and blocked Brooker's path. 'Don't be stupid, Brooker,' Ken said. 'You're done.' He stepped closer to the cop.

Brooker might have been done, but he was also quick. He was close enough now to stick his hand into Ken's pocket and remove the gun that was there. And given that Ken was standing right in front of the detective, he pointed the gun at my brother.

Ken, for his part, looked less terrified than bemused. He was probably asking himself (as I would later, if we were still around) how he could have let himself be disarmed so easily. There was a gasp from Brian, Jules and Andrew seemed mostly confused, and Eliza looked angry. I was rooted to the spot because a gun was pointed at my brother's chest.

'There are too many guns in this room,' Ken said.

'There are too many guns everywhere,' I answered. I'm not sure where that came from.

Mank was inching around, not toward Ken but in Brian's direction, possibly because Brooker seemed most angry with Eliza's father.

'Brooker,' I said, to get his attention away from my brother.

The man with the gun wasn't really paying attention to me, which was his mistake because I could literally toss him out the window if I wanted to, but he did start to back away from Ken and toward the rest of the group, who were in a semicircle deeper into the living room. Nobody was sitting anymore.

'I'm a good cop,' Brooker said, apparently gearing up to deliver a bad-guy-says-why speech from an action movie. I would have welcomed that, but then he stopped talking and continued backing away from Ken, whom he seemed most wary of in this group. Savvy analysis on Brooker's part.

'You are,' Mr Martin said. He had obviously graduated at the top of his yes-man class.

'Killing a college kid doesn't make you a good cop,' Brian told Brooker. Brian's instinct for self-preservation appeared to have taken a vacation. 'That makes you a murderer.' (Just as an aside, 'murderer' is not a profession. We should watch the use of the word. OK. Commercial message done.)

Brooker was, luckily for Brian, paying even less attention to what he said than he had to me. I couldn't tell what his intent was now, but I could see that Jules and Andrew looked especially afraid. I was certain they had weapons somewhere in this apartment but only when I watched them for a full minute did I notice they kept glancing to a desk too far away to reach without being noticed, right on the wall outside the kitchen.

I tried to catch Jules's eye to warn him off the plan, but he was alternating between the desk and Brooker. Andrew was more staring straight ahead in a dazed sort of aura.

'The kid wanted out of the business and that would have been fine, but he was in for almost twenty grand and he said he couldn't pay,' Brooker went on, as if nothing else had been said. So he was intent on that villain speech after all. 'I offered him a discount on what he had to pay Julio, but he didn't want to take it, said he couldn't afford anything at all. God knows where his money was going. Then he said if I didn't let him off the hook he'd go to the cops. The *real* cops, he said. Little bastard.' It felt like Brooker was starting to see his future, it wasn't pleasant, and he was unraveling. If he thought he could get out of this apartment alive and not in custody, he didn't realize the people he was up against or he had completely jumped the rails and was out of touch with reality.

Either way, it wasn't great for Brooker and I wasn't sure the rest of us were doing that much better.

'So you sent Mr Martin to see him,' I said, thinking aloud. 'He tied Damien up and forced the tranq down his throat. That's why there was a stain on Damien's shirt. Did you give him water to make it go down easier, Mr Martin?'

'I just do what I'm told,' Mr Martin said. He was destined for a speaking tour, clearly.

'What about Merchant?' Mank said loudly. I could tell he was trying to attract Brooker's attention and keep the danger away from everyone else. 'Why did you have to fake his suicide?'

That seemed to have the desired effect, although I questioned whether it was the best tactic for Mank to take because Brooker had the gun and wasn't exactly presenting the very picture of rationality. He turned away from Ken instead of backing up and faced Mank, meaning the gun was facing Mank, too.

'Merchant wasn't squeaky clean,' he said. I didn't think anyone had brought up his former partner's ethos, but Brooker was certainly taking it that way. 'He wanted a piece of the action and if he didn't get it he said he'd turn me in to internal affairs.'

'You killed Merchant?' That was the first time anything said in this room had registered with Jules. 'I liked Merchant.' Taste is specific to each human being.

Brooker didn't acknowledge Jules's comment. 'Everything would have been fine if people had just accepted their roles. And you!' He lurched ahead at Mank but I saw his target was Eliza.

He pointed the gun directly at her. 'This isn't because I have anything against you,' he told her, his left eye tearing a bit. 'This is because I told your father I'd kill you if he said anything about that evidence bag. I have to keep my word.'

There was a deep end, and Brooker had gone off it. He was hysterical, and not in a funny way.

'So the evidence bag itself was what you were saving,' I said. 'You didn't put anything in it, you just saved it and probably substituted another one when you filed your report.'

I moved toward him but he pivoted and pointed the pistol at me. He was sweating. 'Don't,' he said, voice much colder. Mank shook his head. He was behind Eliza so I stopped.

Then I looked over at my brother, and Ken was hiding a little grin. I wanted to hit him over the head with something nearby, like the sofa, but there was no time. I decided I'd do so later.

Brian took the moment to step directly in front of his daughter.

'If you need to kill someone, Neil, it's not going to be my daughter. Understand? She's done you no wrong.'

'But I *promised*,' Brooker said. Clearly the stress of knowing he was going to be caught, booked, indicted, tried, convicted and jailed – as he'd seen happen to so many people based on his own actions – had broken him, at least in this moment. I thought for a moment that Brooker wanted Mank to draw his weapon and shoot him, but I knew Mank wouldn't do that unless he absolutely had to. Brooker had turned a very bad corner. It would take a *lot* of treatment from mental health professionals to get him functional again.

'I absolve you of the promise,' Brian said. 'You don't have to deliver on it.' That was a clever tactic. I didn't think it would work, but it was worth a try.

As I expected, Brooker shook his head. 'You don't get to make the rules, Brian. You took the chance and put your kid in danger. Now you pay the price.'

Out of the corner of my eye I saw Jules trying to be inconspicuous as he inched toward the desk, where I suspected any weapon he owned might be. Andrew was next to him, but standing absolutely still.

Mr Martin just seemed to be wondering what he should do and if he might have to kill someone. That was probably what he was hoping for.

Brooker didn't look in that direction, but he said, 'Freeze, Julio. I'm still a cop and I know you don't want to have some firearms charges added to the list of things you're going to jail for.' How long Brooker would remain a cop was a topic for another time.

Jules stopped in his tracks and put his hands behind his back, as if he were a soldier in the 'at ease' position.

Eliza, barely visible from behind the human shield that was her father, called over, 'I wasn't helping Damien with his business. I didn't do anything.' She was missing the point, from Brooker's perspective. 'My father only came here because you threatened me. He would have stayed quiet if you didn't, right, Dad?'

Some people are great liars; they can make you believe even the most outrageous fabrication. Some people are good liars, and they can create plausible explanations that sound like they could be true.

Brian Hennessey was a terrible liar. Sweat pouring from his forehead, lips trembling, his arms spreading to provide the most possible protection for Eliza, he said, 'That's right, honey. I wouldn't have said anything.'

He would totally have blown the whistle on Brooker anyway and everybody in the room knew it. Even Mr Martin.

But especially Brooker, who probably didn't care if it was true or not. 'Stand aside, Brian.' He raised the gun to aim more specifically at Eliza. 'I wouldn't want to miss and hit you.'

Mank took a rapid step to the left from behind Eliza. 'You're not going to shoot anybody, Brooker.' And that's when he reached into his jacket, a move that was clearly going to take too long. Mr Martin was already in motion toward Ken.

I was too far away even to jump at Brooker. The only (pathetic) thing I could think to say was, 'I forgive you, Mank!' But it was too late. Brooker's finger was already tightening on the trigger.

I wanted to shut my eyes, but I didn't. And that's why when I heard the gun click, I also saw it not fire.

'It's Eliza's gun,' I said to myself.

Brooker stared at the weapon and then threw it at Brian, who suffered a glancing blow to the left temple. That gave me enough time to dive over an overstuffed, tattered ottoman and take Brooker down with a flying tackle. Ken had already stopped Mr Martin with a quick jab to the head. Mr Martin was down.

From behind me I heard Mank say quietly, 'Thanks.'

THIRTY-EIGHT

'I pulled the gun because I figured someone else would first. If I said a lot of crazy stuff and had a gun in my hand, they'd be afraid of me and maybe I could stall until I thought of something.' Eliza was slumped, tired, in the armchair we have in our living area. And she was being attended to by her father, Aunt Margie, Ken and me. Mank was looking on but not participating at the moment. Julio, Andrew and Mr Martin were also facing charges, especially Mr Martin (whose real name was William Bailey), who would be charged with giving Damien a lethal dose of tranq on Brooker's orders. My bet was he'd make a plea deal in exchange for testifying against Brooker.

'What was going on before we got there?' I asked her. We'd been fully debriefed by some uniform cops and yet another detective from Brooker's precinct, plus an internal affairs representative who clearly wished that none of this had ever happened. Frankly, I think everyone there would have signed on for that. But we'd been questioned separately, in locations around Andrew's apartment, and I hadn't been privy to what Eliza had told the cops. Even I couldn't hear clearly from that far away amid all those conversations. It starts to hurt my head after a while.

'You already know Mr Martin grabbed me from behind you at New Amsterdam,' she answered. 'Just put that big hand over my mouth and made it look like we were walking together when he was really dragging me away. I got the impression it wasn't the first time he'd done something like that.'

'And he brought you to Andrew's apartment in the Bronx,' Ken said. Eliza was still more open to Ken than to me. You can't question people's taste. 'So Brooker wouldn't be directly connected?'

'Yeah, and he said that I'd be fine if I didn't try to get away.' She shrugged, the most Eliza thing I could imagine she'd do. 'I figured I needed a place to crash and I wasn't going back to the

construction site, so if I wasn't going to get hurt I'd stick around
and see if I could find out who killed Damien.'

Mank leaned forward because any information he could get
on the murder was helpful. Forget that it wasn't his case or that
she'd already been questioned by at least six cops in the Bronx.
A detective never just lets something go. 'Did they say anything
that led to Brooker?' he asked.

'Well, Andrew didn't show up for a while. I guess he'd called
Julio because Andrew came maybe a couple of hours later and
he brought Chinese takeout. There wasn't much I could eat
because it all had meat, but then they felt bad so they ordered a
veggie lo mein and had it delivered.'

A drug dealer and his paid enforcer were proving to be the
most thoughtful characters in this story and that was weird, but
not if you'd met Andrew. 'What did they say about Brooker?'
Mank said, pushing it a little bit more.

'Not much, but they were definitely getting nervous when he
called and said he was coming over. I didn't know he'd threatened
my father then,' Eliza said.

Instinctively, everyone looked in Brian's direction. He seemed
embarrassed. 'Once I heard about Damien, I had a feeling Neil
was involved because he was on the case, and it was being treated
as a strangulation when it clearly wasn't, based on the public
report from the medical examiner,' he began. 'I called him and
said I was researching an article and wanted to know if he'd had
any cases that involved xylazine, which they call tranq on the
street. I could pretty much hear him tense up on the phone and
he said he'd confiscated it once or twice but that was it and then
he had to go and hung up. I'm not normally a suspicious man
but that said something to me.'

Aunt Margie, the crime reporter, rubbed her chin. 'But then
he threatened your daughter.'

'Yes. He called me this afternoon and said he'd taken Eliza
hostage, and if I didn't give him all of my data on the evidence
bag, which I didn't have, he'd . . .'

'Kill me,' Eliza said for him.

Brian blotted at his face with a cloth handkerchief. It wasn't
that hot in the apartment and he was paying particular attention
to his eyes. 'Yes. He gave me four hours to get him what he

wanted. I didn't have much, just a couple of cops in his precinct who'd said there was a small stash of tranq that had gone missing from their evidence room. But his name was never mentioned.'

Eliza looked slightly puzzled and turned toward her father. 'You went there knowing he'd killed someone and he was mad at you. You could have vanished without a trace or turned him in to the cops, but you came to that apartment to face him. Why did you do that?'

Brian searched her face as if looking for the part of his thinking that had been lost. 'My daughter was in danger,' he said.

Eliza looked at her father for a very long moment. I don't know about the rest of the people in the room, but I felt like I was intruding. Finally they both sat back on the sofa and looked shaken. Eliza kept stealing glances at Brian as if to confirm that he really was the same father she'd had all her life.

We sat and talked for another hour or so, then Mank confirmed online that Eliza was no longer a suspect in Damien's murder, I was no longer a suspect in Merchant's murder, and all was, at least locally, right with the world. Brian and Eliza said their goodbyes and headed back to their home, where Eliza said she'd stay for a while, until she was done with New Amsterdam for the year, anyway.

We never did find out why Laura had signed her cat's name to her lease, but it was pretty clear she'd just found out it was possible and thought it was funny. There was no strong evidence she was involved in Damien's business and she was never arrested. Neither was Rainbow.

I felt like I'd just hosted the weirdest party of the year. After a few minutes Aunt Margie went back down to her apartment and Ken, with what he thought was a whimsical glint in his eye, said he was going to his room to sleep. That left me alone with Mank.

He stood and dusted off his pants, which didn't need dusting off but it was a way to avoid looking me in the eye. 'So you forgive me, huh?'

'It was a moment of stress,' I said. 'I wasn't thinking.'

'Oh, no. You don't get to take it back now.' He took a step in my direction and raised his eyes to my level, which for him was up. 'You forgave me. You were right to be mad, but then you forgave me and I'm forgiven and you can't go back.'

I took a deep breath and let it out to simulate a sigh. 'OK, fine. You're forgiven. But we're not back where we were. Not yet, anyway. Right?'

'Right.' Then he gestured that I should lean over so he could say something quietly, and when I did, he kissed me.

Damn. The man was still a really good kisser.

THIRTY-NINE

Three days later I got an email from an address I didn't recognize and I almost deleted it because the subject line said something about a rebate. Then I saw the first line.

My dear daughter.

That was how Mom always started her letters. It was like getting an email from a Jane Austen character.

I'm sorry it's been so long since you've heard from me. You know there are people out there who are not pleased with your father and myself, and they have been making our lives interesting, but not unpleasant. We've just been moving around a lot.

I hope things are going well for you and Ken. I still haven't told Dad that I'm in touch with you, but I think he suspects. He's been acting especially alert lately, a sign that he thinks our level of danger could go up soon, and one of the things he worries about is that any communication with the two of you or Margie could lead to a breach of security. Personally I think it's worth the risk. Once we reconnected I realized how much it had hurt to stay away. I won't do that again.

The first thing you need to know is that your father and I are just fine. We're not in immediate danger and we're not ailing at all physically or mentally. But our lifestyle for all these years is getting a little tiresome. I'm hoping we can do something about that in the not-terribly-distant future.

Another thing that's pretty important for you to be aware of is that there's a man who calls himself Malcolm Mitchell. (He sometimes uses Malcolm X. Mitchell, which is both silly and offensive.) He might approach you in one way or another, but you should stay away from him at all costs. He's trying to use your efforts to find Dad and me to trace us, and his interests are not in line with ours. You probably know about our ongoing work. He's one of the people – or works for them – who want us very badly to fail. Don't make contact with him.

I'm sorry it's taken me so long to find you again and I promise it won't again. Once more, if you feel it's best to tell Ken that we've been in touch, I will trust your judgment, but the last time we corresponded you indicated that wasn't your intention and you had your reasons. Again, what you decide is what you should do.

Know that your parents love you both and wish we'd been a family together for all these years. I hope someday we can try to mend the damage we've done. Just know it was for your protection and we want you to have happy lives.

All my love,
Mom

OK, so I teared up a bit when I was reading it, especially that last part, and there are sections I haven't included here because frankly, they're none of your business. But it was bothering me that Malcolm X. Mitchell had almost convinced both Ken and me that he was trying to help. We shouldn't have been that gullible.

With Eliza safe once more and Brooker and crew in cells awaiting trial (no bail for Brooker or Mr Martin), Ken and I could get back to what we laughingly called our normal lives. Take on new clients, help families reconnect when they wanted to, all the things I'd envisioned when I had talked my brother into joining me in a detective agency that would specialize in adopted people and all their families.

But given our own family circumstances and our, let's say, *unusual* origins and existence, there was never a time we could completely let down our guard. I'd probably made a mistake opening up to Mank, although I knew he'd never betray my secrets. But I'd have to resist the temptation to do the same again.

I was stewing about all this when there was a knock on my

bedroom door and Ken opened it, looking tired. He probably needed a charge. I looked in my bag for the portable battery-operated charger he'd sent me, but he waved a hand. 'I'll go plug in right after I go to bed,' he said. 'I just wanted to see how you were doing.'

I extended the hand with the portable charger. 'Use this for a while,' I said. 'I have something I need to tell you.'

He sat down.